UNFINISHED BUSINESS

Praise for

UNFINISHED BUSINESS

"A unique, surprising, and fun tale with a swoony romance perfectly woven together . . . deeply satisfying . . . Clare Osongco has a gift for writing incredibly real and relatable characters that linger long after the last page."

—Natalie Sue, bestselling author of *I Hope This Finds You Well*

"I tore through this book in a day. It's a great romance that also nails magical realism, grief, complicated mother-daughter relationship stuff, AND union busting/the hell of capitalism?! I don't think I've ever read anything like it before."

—Kate Spencer, bestselling author of *In a New York Minute*

"*Unfinished Business* is delightfully quirky with a lot of heart. From the complicated family dynamics to the Filipino representation, I felt seen. Clare Osongco created a workplace comedy with a love triangle that will keep you on your toes."

—Joss Richard, internationally bestselling author of *It's Different This Time*

"Brimming with tenderness, humor, and hope, this is an eccentric and romantic read that will [restore] your faith in the most important relationship of all—the one with yourself. Corporate girls suffering from ennui, this one's for you."

—Carolyn Huynh, author of *The Family Recipe*

"Clare Osongco absolutely shines in her adult debut, *Unfinished Business.* This is a story that pulled at my heartstrings, made me laugh, swoon, and cry."

—Danica Nava, *USA Today* bestselling author of *Love Is a War Song*

BY CLARE OSONGCO

Unfinished Business

Midnights with You

UNFINISHED BUSINESS

A Novel

CLARE OSONGCO

DELL NEW YORK

Dell
An imprint of Random House
A division of Penguin Random House LLC
1745 Broadway, New York, NY 10019
randomhousebooks.com
penguinrandomhouse.com

A Dell Trade Paperback Original

ISBN 979-8-217-09255-0
Ebook ISBN 979-8-217-09256-7

Printed in the United States of America

1st Printing

BOOK TEAM: Production editor: Cindy Berman • Managing editor: Saige Francis • Production manager: Chanler Harris • Copy editor: Amy J. Schneider • Proofreaders: Pam Rehm, Chuck Thompson, Barbara Jatkola, Taylor McGowan

Book design by Elizabeth A. D. Eno

To everyone running as fast as they can
just to stay in the same place

UNFINISHED BUSINESS

CHAPTER 1

I grew up visiting the TKCORP head office. Mom worked here my whole life, and she always expected me to join her one day. *The most prestigious megacorporation,* she'd say with a hint of awe in her voice, as though it hadn't gotten old after decades. And now I'm finally badging in for work as a TKCORP employee, but she's not here to see it.

It's my second week here; Mom died a couple months ago, and everything here reminds me of her.

That hall by the entrance leads to the mailroom, where she got her start through a work-study arrangement as an international student recently arrived from the Philippines.

By the time I was born, she was working a desk job in the Customer Experience Department on the third floor—and her boss was so checked out, sometimes Mom would sneak me into her cubicle for lack of childcare. She set up a crib under her desk so she could rock me to sleep with one foot while she fielded calls about malfunctioning products.

The chirping of chunky old landline phones still comforts

me. Sometimes I pull up a video with that sound on YouTube when I have trouble falling asleep.

We rode this elevator when I visited her for take-your-kid-to-work day in fifth grade—Mom had been promoted again by that time—and I sat quietly behind her desk in the Logistics Department while she talked to me about supply chains. And she was still working on that team, bumped up a few ranks, when I betrayed her by moving across the country for college—and then taking a job out in New York, at *some no-name company.*

Of course, when I asked her if she was let down, she'd deny it. *I just always pictured you here,* she said, her disappointment palpable on the phone. *Not on the East Coast.*

And now I'm back at the center of this sprawling office park, the beating heart of the sleepy Southern California suburb I grew up in. The home base TKCORP chose in the sixties and never left.

Now I'm here and Mom's not, but there's no time to be maudlin. The company just had layoffs and I'm arriving in their wake, one of those cursed hires after a big culling. A cheap replacement, one person where three used to be. A fresh start with a hint of survivor's guilt already.

On the way up to the eighth floor, I try to focus on composing my morning memo in my head—getting myself in the mood to write an ode to the new TKCORP line of aroma diffusers. *Feeling fragrant, feeling fresh.*

TKCORP dabbles in a bit of everything. It's added to its diverse portfolio over the years as it acquired smaller companies and rebranded everything with the same ubiquitous logo. Home goods, pharmaceuticals, information technology, groceries. You can have your phone plan with TKCORP, have TKCORP toilet paper in your bathroom, eat your TKCORP frozen dinner out of your TKCORP fridge at night (and I do).

As soon as the elevator opens, the sixty percent staff reduction on our team is glaringly obvious. Lots of empty cubicles with abandoned belongings in them, like people left in a hurry after a disaster.

My desk still has the personal effects of a phantom co-worker in it. The drawer is stuffed with old napkins and packets of painkillers—Mom would approve of this level of thrift and preparation. There's an old phone book and several half-filled notepads, the writing too spidery and cramped for me to make out any potential old gossip. But I haven't had the energy to clean it out yet.

"Thought you might want this," a familiar deep voice says. Before I can glance up from the wooden surface of my desk, Al, my mom's oldest work friend, slides a glossy photo in front of me.

It's a group portrait from a Customer Experience team retreat, almost thirty years ago.

There's Al, the only Black man in the photo, wearing a salmon polo shirt that pops against his deep brown skin. There's Mom, the shortest person in the picture, radiant in her silk blouse and pearls. Not as weighed down with worry as the person I got to meet.

It must have been taken in Mom's first year in the department, because there's my dad, a skinny white guy in the opposite corner of the frame. And even though he didn't stay in the picture of our lives for that long, he's the reason Mom is still here—in this country, this company, this town.

Wrong tense again. You'll have to work on that.

Standing before me, Al has less hair than he did back then. He has a bit more of a gut, and his eyes crinkle in a kindly way when he smiles. But other than that, he's the same.

"You look like her, you know?" he says wistfully.

Al cried at the funeral, and somehow having seen him like that makes me clammy and awkward now. There must be something wrong with me, but I haven't been able to cry yet.

Not when I got the news, not when I saw everyone at the memorial service, not that first awful night alone in our empty house. My eyes will burn, my throat will feel raw, but I can't manage to tip over into crying. Mom never wanted me to cry in front of her.

I think the last time I did was in elementary school—about dodgeball, of all the stupid things, because I kept getting picked last, and I couldn't stop spiraling about finding the root cause. Was it because I couldn't do a high ponytail like the other girls, since my hair was short and choppy? Were my shorts too long? Was it because I didn't chew gum like everyone else? (*A waste of money!* Mom would say. *You just spit it back out again!*)

"You're so sensitive," Mom said to my tearful face, grimacing like she smelled something bad.

It should have been a totally forgettable memory. Except it may have been the last time I ever cried to her about anything.

"Anyway," Al says with a warm smile, a hint of sadness on the edges. "Glad you're here, Ruby."

My throat feels horribly tight as he gestures toward his desk—which, through the open side of his cubicle, looks like an unruly mound of papers—and pats my cubicle divider a few times. "I'll be right over here if you need anything."

Then a redheaded woman with perky pink lipstick and a pinched expression comes bustling over—our boss, Erica. She's lugging a large plant in a bright plastic pot, probably from TK-MART.

"A pop of color!" she exclaims as she sets it down heavily next to Al's cubicle and peers disdainfully at the piles of papers inside. "Al, didn't you read my memo about upkeep of the office aesthetic?" She purses her lips. "These *mounds* are not exactly in line with my vision."

"Printing things out helps me get my head around them."

"Fine." She deposits the plant in front of his cubicle. "But throw some things away."

The mint green planter seems like it's trying too hard. The office is all gray—gray fabric cubicles, gray carpet, gray office chairs, the gentle gray hum of the building's systems. Even the ceiling tiles, once white, have faded to a light gray. The place looks like it hasn't been redecorated since the 1980s.

For years, TKCORP was all about tradition—great benefits, one of the last bastions of lifetime employment. But there was a changing of the guard a few years ago after the longtime CEO retired, and a new guy came in, cutting costs, slashing budgets.

"Ruby, how's that memo coming?" Erica shoots over her shoulder.

"Good!" I squeak. And by *good,* I mean I haven't started.

"Don't take too long." She hurries back to her office, floofing up some potted plants along her way with the energy of a hummingbird visiting her favorite flowers.

Slumping in my chair, I stare at my notes until the pixels blur together.

I close my eyes and think about how I'll wander the aisles of TKMART alone after work, maybe buy a scented candle to make the house smell less like a time warp to my high school years. Or I'll treat myself to another throw pillow—the couch has become buried in them since I moved back.

How can you be so unmotivated? Mom said the last time we spoke on the phone.

I have to focus! I should be grateful to be here.

Mom always wanted to work in this department, writing advertorials. She thought it was glamorous—*your words in the pages of* Elle *and* Newsweek, *without the risks of a creative career!*

She'd applied a few times over the years, but Erica never gave her a shot. And now I'm here instead, in Mom's dream job. Somehow, impossibly, even though the print journalism industry it relies on is dying.

I had to come home after she died—I inherited the house, and there were so many things to attend to. When I saw Al at the funeral, he mentioned there was an open position in the department after the layoffs. And there was nothing calling me back to New York, anyway. Mom was right: I wasn't going anywhere in my job, and somehow after years of living there, I hadn't made any friends who would miss me after a couple weeks apart. It seemed too perfect; I had to apply, and when I got it, it felt like fate.

But something must be wrong with me, because I can't even appreciate it. I've been barely dragging myself through the days, sluggish and slow to react.

I try to get my head in the game by clicking through my emails. And a message introducing the hire of a new junior executive stops my scrolling.

It's his headshot that grabs my attention first. A pale young man with tousled brown hair, standing with his arms crossed, giving the camera an intense look. He's wearing a suit, lines of the jacket hugging his broad shoulders. He's kind of uncanny-valley handsome. Maybe it's a fake photo, AI-generated. The resemblance to Jacob Elordi is too strong.

Mark Winterson, the email says. *London School of Economics BSc, Harvard MBA.* A bunch of fellowships and awards, lots of things with the words *entrepreneurship* and *distinguished.* I almost laugh out loud. If you called up Central Casting and asked for A Man My Mom Would Want Me to Date, it would literally be this guy. The universe must be taunting me.

He'll be the new Associate VP of Sales, Marketing, and Customer Experience—say that five times fast!—but he seems young for an executive, maybe just a few years older than me.

I'm trying to read the words alongside the picture, but the headshot keeps drawing me back. There's something weirdly magnetic about him, like those brown doe eyes are actually boring a hole into my soul.

Come on, Ruby! I imagine him saying. *Hot people finish their memos!*

I'm reading the part about how he'll be visiting every team that rolls up to him, when a Slack message from Erica pops up with a Zoom link.

The first time she did this, I had an *Oh no, what have I done?* moment. Even though I need to produce the same volume of copy that three people used to, Erica still insists on painstakingly debriefing about every misplaced comma.

She starts a screen share so we can view the document I submitted together and she can make me explain why each one she's circled is wrong. But it doesn't even seem like this is about boosting sales, or hitting goals, or any of the things Erica likes to fixate on.

It reminds me of Mom dictating the order in which I had to eat all the things on my plate at dinner, and how upset she'd get when I deviated from it. Meaningless things that give you some sense of control in an out-of-control world.

I catch my eye in the little Zoom window, light brown face floating against the gray of my cubicle wall. Al said I look like Mom, but I can't see any of her strength in the face staring back at me—just a brittle shadow of the real thing.

It's not like this is what I expected when I pictured having a daughter.

I close my eyes and try to push away the memory of that final painful conversation.

"Ruby, are you listening? Or are you falling asleep?"

My eyes fly open and I force a smile. "I'm concentrating! Go on."

And as Erica continues holding forth about punctuation, a vivid mental image springs into view, like a particularly intrusive daydream. I've been seeing it repeatedly ever since I moved back.

There's the pool across the street from the office, where I

used to work as a lifeguard in the summers. And I'm standing in it, mouth open and filled with water.

I'm there in the shallow end, and I'm on the sidelines watching myself at the same time. How absurd to drown there when I could straighten my legs, unbend my knees. Stand, if I wanted.

But I am absurd, and there I am, head slightly underwater, eyes glassy.

After all, I had training. I know how to recognize drowning when it's not obvious. And now I'm letting it happen in plain view of dozens of people, and I have only myself to blame.

My mouth opens wider and wider. My eyes stretch like saucers.

"Just stand up!"

I can't see her, but Mom's voice rings in my ears, echoing off the tile into the blue sky overhead. *"I didn't sacrifice so much for you to drown in this pool!"*

"Ruby!" Erica snaps on the other end of the Zoom.

My face nods in the little square. "Yes! Yes, I'm listening."

As soon as the call ends, I open TKMART's website to stare at the pillows. Sleeping is my favorite thing lately. The one piece of new furniture I bought since moving back is a new bed—it made me feel too pathetic, sleeping in the old twin I'd had since elementary school.

I stop scrolling and linger on an image of a bedspread covered in pillows. It looks so cozy, I can imagine nestling in there and taking the longest nap.

So I send it into the Slack DM that's just for me, for private notes and reminders. At my old job, I used it as a tunnel from the rest of my life back to work—when I'd think of pitch ideas as I was falling asleep, or when I'd be grocery shopping and have a flash of inspiration.

Now the tunnel mostly goes the other way: daydreaming at work and sending myself things I want to buy later.

But this time, a couple messages pop up in reply:

Too many pillows!

You'll give yourself a double chin sleeping like that!

Shit! Did I message someone else by mistake?

But no, it's definitely the DM that says ruby.ocampo at the top. Private to only me.

I look again, and the messages are gone. My cursor blinks against the empty space underneath my sad profile picture.

There's a sensation like someone has just left the room. Like a flock of birds has departed, but you can still hear the beating of their wings.

That's how Mom talks. That mix of irritation padded with affection. Her voice, right here, then gone again.

It's nothing—a figment of my imagination. And even though it's silly, I feel breathless, like I lost something all over again.

CHAPTER 2

It really does feel like I'm back in high school. I did track in twelfth grade, and now for the first time in years, I'm running again in the mornings, up and down these sleepy suburban streets. Getting some fresh air first thing helps clear my head, even though I have yet to master the art of getting out the door on time.

As I'm driving off in Mom's old Honda Civic, her voice rings in my head saying, *Don't let the mail pile up!* So I toss the week's worth of accumulated letters into my passenger seat before pulling out. At a stoplight, I flip through the pile—junk, junk, bill. *An invitation to my high school reunion.*

It makes me shudder. This is such a company town, a bunch of people I went to high school with also work at TKCORP. I can even see some of them as I pull into the parking lot. Steve from Pre-Calc has become Steve the Project Manager. Grace from Physics is Grace from Sales.

I catch a glimpse of the old swimming pool across the street and get a weird sense of déjà vu for something that never happened. The city owns it now, but TKCORP originally built it as part of the corporate campus. Back then, they had all these offerings to take care of their workers: health clinics, a movie theater, a bowling alley, all since demolished or sold off. A remnant of the age of the big benevolent lifetime employer that ended before I was born.

I'm antsy in the elevator, and when the doors open on the eighth floor, it's like I sense it before I see him.

There's Greg, leaning against a cubicle, talking to my coworkers. My high school baggage, come back to haunt me.

Why is he up here? He's not supposed to be up here! He should be on the sixth floor, in Accounting!

Greg's angled away from me, deep in conversation with Sarah Ng. She's a few years younger than me but she seems to have her life way more together, with her poised answers in meetings and her perfect outfits that make her look like an actress in a K-drama about a start-up. Meanwhile, every item of work clothing I own was chosen in a panic and fits weird in at least one spot.

Greg smiles at something she says, playful and a little weary, like he's been through a lot but he has a sense of humor about it.

Morgan Schaeffer walks over to join them, which probably means she sniffs gossip. She's the other senior copywriter on the team besides Al, and she lives for other people's drama. She's an overworked mom in her late forties, but she has the energy of an imp emoji come to life.

Greg leans in and says something to both of them in a low voice. Whatever it is gets a melodious laugh from Sarah, and my stomach dips.

Al wanders over to the group, shaking his head. "Can you believe these targets?" He points to an email from Erica on his phone. "This is as much as three people used to do."

"Oh well, *anyone* can do it with a full staff." Morgan chuckles. "Where's the challenge in that?"

"Morning, Ruby!" Al says.

Greg turns my way then, and he might be even better-looking than I remember. Smooth brown skin that's a bit darker than mine—he moisturizes, clearly. Cheekbones that are more prominent now that he's lost the baby fat in his face. Full lips that give me inconvenient flashbacks to things that are *ancient history and not worth thinking about, okay!*

We haven't been in the same room together since Mom's memorial service, and he kept a respectful distance then. Our relationship had been in the "infrequent texts and tense run-ins when I'm home for holidays" stage for five years, at least. And even though he tried to reach out after Mom died, I ignored his messages, let his calls go to voicemail.

Greg takes a couple steps closer. "Hey, it's—it's good to see you, Ruby," he says, voice low and earnest like we're still at a funeral. The top two buttons of his blue oxford are undone, and a hint of the thin gold chain he inherited from his dad peeks out underneath.

Something in my brain short-circuits, and I stare at him stone-faced and walk past without saying anything, slumping down in my chair so my cubicle walls hide me.

"That was weird," Sarah says. Sound unfortunately travels in an open-plan office.

"Ooh, tense!" Morgan says. "Seems like there's a story there."

He better not say a fucking word, I think, waking up my laptop screen and gritting my teeth.

"No," he says, voice flat. "No story." And somehow that stings more than if he'd told the truth.

As far back as I remember, Greg's mom was my mom's best friend. I call her "Tita Wendy" even though we're not at all related, the way everyone we knew who was Filipino and roughly Mom's age could be a Tita or Tito.

They met back when Tita Wendy was still working as a

nurse, and Mom came in with a broken wrist and the cheapest TKCORP health insurance plan. They had the same taste in gossip, and they felt similarly embattled, single moms against the world (Greg's dad passed away when he was six; my dad left when I was three). Tita Wendy made fun of Mom for being a snob, and I guess she appreciated that—*finally,* someone recognized how hard she was working at snobbery!

And so Greg and I grew up together, also best friends. Or we were for a while, at least.

"Was that the girl who—?" Sarah asks.

The girl whose mom died at work. Of course everyone knows.

There was an email. A GoFundMe for funeral expenses. A company-wide meeting about work-life balance.

Everyone whispered, *She worked so hard.*

Mom died at her desk, pulling a late night on a big project. *Shows you go the extra mile,* she said. *Builds goodwill. It will pay off.* She always said yes to everything, volunteered for every task no one else wanted to do, every after-hours or weekend commitment.

The cleaning woman found her the next morning, slumped over her keyboard. Heart attack, apparently.

Mom died at work, and I was three thousand miles away from her.

I peek over my cubicle, and Greg's eyes meet mine. My memory shuffles through the dozens of times we've locked eyes across a room over the years—in class, at the mall, at the table when he and his mom came over for dinner—and it was like he knew exactly what I was thinking.

Our psychic link, we'd joke. That's how close we were. (It made the joke better that his mom works as a psychic. Tita Wendy hurt her feet and left nursing when we were in fourth grade—her *pivot to the spirit world,* as she likes to call it.)

But I learned a long time ago that was bullshit, something I fooled myself into believing. I never knew what he was thinking at all.

He looks away first, stepping back from Sarah's cubicle, one hand raised. "See you guys."

I slide down in my chair again. I can just hear what Mom would say, if she were here: *Why are you always brooding? Why can't you be warm and gracious like your cousins? One of them is married to a dental hygienist. Maybe if you worked on your charm, that could be you one day!*

Okay, fine! I'll make an effort, for once!

Everyone's gone back to their own desks, so I search for Greg in Slack.

ruby.ocampo:
Hey, sorry I was awkward
It is good to see you
It's just been a while

My stomach lurches as I stare at the messages I sent, but he writes back pretty much instantly.

greg.de.leon:
yeah, it has
mom said you needed some space?
i wanted to visit earlier, obviously

Tita Wendy has been coming to check on me a couple times a week since I moved back. The first time, I was a wreck—subsisting on instant noodles, barely leaving the house, trying to get my head around Mom's elaborate record-keeping system, which centered on stacks of envelopes she'd grouped by theme inside the rolltop desk in the living room.

Tita Wendy took one glance at me when I opened the front door and said, "Roobs, you look like hell."

And I blurted out: "I can't see Greg! I'm not ready!" So she made sure he stayed home whenever she came by. When I run in the mornings, I take a longer route on purpose so I won't go past his house. Somehow I deluded myself into believing I could avoid him indefinitely at work too.

greg.de.leon:
how have you been?

Oh sure, hit me with the hard questions.

I need to get back to my actual job, so I leave Greg's message without a reply.

CHAPTER 3

Every task feels overwhelming lately, even small things. And Erica doesn't ease up. She walks over from her office to ask me why I *can't even write a simple email properly.*

The hours under the buzzing lights weigh on me. The air itself seems tired, like the exhaustion of everyone who spent their days here coats the walls in a thin film.

My fingers wiggle, hovering above my keyboard.

Get yourself together, I write into the DM that's just for me, the tunnel between work and whoever I am outside of it.

It's not that hard.

It's not that bad.

Hours tick by. A terse email from Erica lands, and the sting makes my eyes water.

And I see that girl again, the one who looks like me, a movie playing superimposed over the scenery of my cubicle. She's mostly submerged, knees bent, only the top of her head above water. Mouth opening and closing.

There are lots of people around the pool—a group of friends

laughing, a father and son talking, a guy applying sunscreen on his girlfriend's back. But none of them are paying attention.

I feel like I'm drowning in shallow water, I type to myself in Slack, just to give it somewhere to go. Just for myself. And maybe for whoever has admin access, but whatever.

It's funny to imagine some Slack administrator reading my dramatic messages, giggling out there on the other side of the void. So I type some more:

I feel like a hollowed out husk.
I feel so incapable of anything.

And a message pops up, suddenly.

sampaguita72:
What kind of attitude is that!

Oh God. Did I send this shit to someone? Or, total nightmare—did I post in a public channel? I lean closer and squint at the screen.

But it's the same as before: ruby.ocampo at the top, green circle lit up next to it. And still there's a message from someone else in there, where it's not supposed to be.

sampaguita72:
You're always so dramatic
It's like the dodge ball team in second grade all over again!

I leap out of my chair with a yelp and send my keyboard flipping over itself.

My co-workers' heads pop up at the sound of trouble. Morgan's straw-blond hair and hazel eyes, the Concerned Mom Look I imagine she gives her kids. Al's brows are raised, wrinkling his forehead.

Sarah stands in her cubicle. "You okay?"

"Haha!" I give them a weak laugh even though my heart is pumping like the bass to a bad techno song, the kind Tita Wendy would listen to when she'd take her turn picking us up from school. "Um. I saw a spider."

I sink back down into my chair until my head ends up where my back usually rests.

It's not like last time. The messages are still there—glowing brighter, if anything, like the pixels are trying to stick it to me.

Seventy-two. Mom's birth year.

Sampaguita, her favorite flower.

Mom's voice fills my head like the reverberation of a bell, saying *Susmaryosep!* I haven't been to church in a while, but I cross myself.

I square my shoulders and begin to type.

ruby.ocampo:
Is this some kind of sick joke?

Maybe the IT guy has a cruel sense of humor.

ruby.ocampo:
I don't know how you got access to this, but I'm taking screenshots! I'm reporting this to HR!

sampaguita72:
Report what? Your own mother? For checking up on you?

What?

sampaguita72:
For telling you not to give up so easily?

What what what what what?

The ache in my chest is spreading, like a spill on the floor I can't blot fast enough with paper towels.

sampaguita72:

You kids are so sensitive these days. I thought I raised you better than that.

Don't engage with it emotionally. Don't think.

I take a dozen screenshots. And then for good measure, I take a bunch of photos too, before fumbling and dropping my phone on the desk. I flinch at the sound—I usually baby my phone because I didn't buy the AppleCare. I know what Mom would have said: *You could save that money by being more careful.*

CHAPTER 4

I must be losing it. When I search for the screenshots on my work computer the next day, they've vanished. And when I pull up the photos on my phone, they're so shaky and blurry, they don't look like anything at all.

Did I imagine it? I'm thinking about Mom so much, hearing her voice in my head, now it's manifesting in *Slack-based hallucinations*? Maybe this is a sign of a psychotic break. I do some frantic Google searches for symptoms before I catch myself and close the tab.

It's fine. I'm sure it will pass on its own. I'll handle it the way I deal with most unsettling things in life: I'll ignore it.

But I'm nervous about using Slack, so I avoid it as much as possible. I answer DMs only by punting to some other form of communication.

Oh can you email that to me?

Sure let's hop on a quick call!

Oh yes I'll text you that real quick.

Do you have a fax machine by any chance? hahaha kidding (unless you do though)

At one point, Erica shoots me a pointed DM reprimanding me for being unresponsive in the public channels.

"Well?" Erica says, suddenly beside my cubicle even though she just messaged me.

Jesus! Extremely unnerving, when she does that.

She starts to walk away but glances back like I'm supposed to follow her. "Come on, you'll be late for our eleven o'clock."

What is this meeting, again? I pull up the email on my phone and nearly eat shit after I stumble into an errant wastebasket someone left in the aisle.

Oh, hello! It's a meeting with the new Associate VP of Sales, Marketing, and Customer Experience. He's getting together a bunch of teams that roll up to him so he can get to know our *workflows and processes.*

I take a seat at the conference table, and Sarah settles next to me. She's wearing a perfectly fitted navy blazer, tastefully cropped white top, and swishy gray midi skirt.

"Are you excited to talk about our *workflows and processes* for forty-five minutes?" she asks.

I desperately want her to like me, and normally that means I would avoid speaking to her at all costs unless it's directly work related. But she's talking to me like we're both in on a joke already, so . . .

"Oh yeah, I live for this," I deadpan. "Gets me up in the morning, talking about workflows."

Sarah's phone chimes repeatedly, and she gets absorbed in writing back. It seems like her group chats are blowing up. She has a sparkly clear pink phone case with Polaroids of her friends slotted underneath it, and whatever she's reading makes her scoff.

I was born nosy—knowing Mom, it must be in my genes—

so my eyes stray over to see what's funny. There's a stream of messages popping up, heart and laugh reacts appearing in close succession. A wave of envy washes over me. I've never really been in a group chat.

My three roommates in New York had one where we messaged one another occasionally about being out of toilet paper. But it wasn't the same as the other group chats I'd see them talking in sometimes, smiling at their screens, phone buzzing every few seconds with notifications.

I think Ruby has a hard time connecting with people, my third-grade teacher told Mom once, pulling her aside after class.

I'll make sure she makes more of an effort, Mom said, tugging me firmly away.

No, I mean, the teacher said, *that's not exactly what—*

But Mom probably looked so intense and filled with purpose that the teacher realized it wasn't worth arguing.

And then, like I conjured her, a Slack notification slides onto the top of my phone screen.

sampaguita72:
Were you flirting with Greg earlier?
I scrolled up and saw!
Aren't you over that by now?

Every part of my body resting against this conference room chair clenches, and I resist the urge to write back: *I wasn't!*

It has to be an elaborate scam. A way to extort me. Truly sick and twisted.

sampaguita72:
Why not Sam from Sales? He seems like a nice boy.
Makes more money.

God, this cannot go on.

ruby.ocampo:
Look, I don't know who you are, but this is cruel and unusual, impersonating my dead mother! Hope you're ashamed of yourself!

It *feels* like her, though. I might as well be fifteen again.

I scroll back up in the DM with myself, and unlike this morning, all the messages from yesterday are back again, clear as day, like they never left.

Right then, a message from Greg rolls in.

greg.de.leon:
ruby, are you okay?

Goosebumps rise on my arms. That old psychic link, again. But I'm too overwhelmed to deal with him, so I write:

ruby.ocampo:
I am very busy right now

Erica is glaring at me, so I put my phone in Do Not Disturb and tuck it under my notebook.

"Okay!" she exclaims, clapping to punctuate. "Our guest is running late, but let's get started." She sweeps a hand in my direction. "I know we're all so glad to have Ruby here with us, after the tragic events of a few months ago."

I fight the urge to slump down in my seat, or maybe limbo straight under the table.

"She's so hardworking," Erica adds, and I get a moment of that sick full-body relief that follows any crumb of external validation. "In fact, the other day, she stayed late to help me finish our strategy deck for the TKMART resort collection campaign."

Wait. I didn't do that.

Erica's going into so much detail about what I did and didn't do—this must be a thing that actually happened. The realization creeps over me like a caterpillar crawling on bare skin. *She's talking about a whole-ass other person. She just thinks it was me.*

Slowly it dawns on me: Erica must be thinking of Sarah. She's younger and shorter and rocks bangs in a way I never could, but we have roughly the same skin tone and the same long, dark hair. She's Malaysian, and I'm Filipino with a white dad I don't know, but apparently to Erica, it's close enough.

When I glance over, Sarah does indeed look pissed off—but subtly, daintily, like she's trying not to show it. She taps out a quick message on her phone and lets out a sharp sigh.

Then the Associate VP of Sales, Marketing, and Customer Experience pushes his way through the glass conference room door.

"Sorry to keep you waiting!" he says with a winsome grin—and man, I guess the headshot wasn't AI-generated, because he *does* look like that. He's so handsome, it's uncomfortable. His crisp brown suit seems tailor-made.

He surveys the room, and his eyes linger on me a beat too long. I'm suddenly extremely aware of the way my work shirt pinches under my armpits.

He's the kind of person my mom would want me to impress, and when I see him, a strange, contrary impulse seizes me. *If the universe is taunting me, I want to taunt it right back.*

"Oh, you're right on time!" Erica says brightly, tucking her hair behind her ear. "We were about to share some fun facts."

"Not the fun facts," I mumble.

"Ruby, do you have something to share with the group?" Erica stares at me for long enough that I realize I actually have to say something.

"Oh, it's just . . . I get so in my head about whether the fact is fun or not," I say. "Like . . . what is fun? How do I know I'm having it? Why is there something instead of nothing?"

Mark Winterson makes some very direct eye contact. "Yeah,

the premise has always been a bit weird to me. Are facts ever that fun?"

"All right, let's save the existential crises for after work hours!" Erica looks a bit murderous. "Who wants to start?"

Hi, I'm Ruby and my mom died in this office two months ago and that's probably the only thing you know about me! What could I possibly say to blot that out?

The couple dozen people here from other teams take turns introducing themselves and sharing a smattering of facts—hobbies, hidden talents, past run-ins with celebrities. One person reveals that their unflattering selfie was the basis for a popular mid-2010s meme. Morgan volunteers that she did log-rolling when she was younger.

"It's a sport!" she clarifies quickly when Mark Winterson's eyebrows go up.

Sarah adds that she's been teaching herself to play the ukulele. Al reveals that he sings in a barbershop quartet on the weekends, and everyone meets this news with a faint *oooh.*

My heartbeat speeds up as it gets closer to the time I'll have to say something.

"Ruby?" Erica prompts with a too-tight smile.

"Hi! I'm Ruby. Started a couple weeks ago in Advertorial/Content Studio. I just moved back from New York, but I grew up around here. As some of you know, my mom worked at TKCORP. And . . ."

Oh God, what do I say?

"And when I was four years old and my mom couldn't find someone to watch me, she brought me in and asked the receptionist to keep an eye on me until her friend could come pick me up." My palms are sweating and I'm not sure why I decided to go this route, but now that I've started, I have to see it through. "I didn't know how to read yet, but when the receptionist looked up, I was holding this copy of *Forbes* open and staring at it, all serious, like I was reading it. She took a photo."

"Oh, well, now you have to show the group," Mark Winterson interjects, and my armpits feel even sweatier. My face burns as I pull it up and show it around—and then the executive plucks the phone from my hand and studies it, smiling.

"Anyway, they were all like, 'Wow, Adela, your baby reads *Forbes*!' She loved to tell that story." I grab my phone back after a few polite seconds have elapsed. "Whew, long fact!" And, channeling Erica, I clap too. "Next person?"

When the meeting ends at long last, I'm the first out the door.

"Surprisingly," Mark Winterson says from behind me, "I did think your fact was fun." When I turn around, he puts a hand to his chest. "Sincerely."

I laugh breathlessly. "Oh good."

He points at me. "Just a hunch, but—you seem like a straight shooter. Someone who tells it like it is."

"I do?" I ask so incredulously, he chuckles.

"I'm still getting the lay of the land here. I'd love to ask you a couple questions." He gives me a high-wattage smile that should come with a health warning. "You getting lunch? Maybe we could keep talking."

CHAPTER 5

The whole way down to the cafeteria—which is in another building in the corporate complex, across the green—Mark Winterson asks me questions. Where I went to school, where I lived in New York, what my favorite places were there. ("I went down on weekends a lot when I was in Cambridge—did you ever go to this restaurant . . . ?")

He's walking alongside me, matching my slow pace in these heels. Leaning in when I talk, with this gentle, serious look, like whatever I'm saying is very important.

And I hate to say it, but I feel like a million bucks. Like I won a prize—*the most interesting person in the meeting!* Even though part of me is saying, *There's no way he just wants to hang out with you. There is probably a catch.*

But then Mark Winterson gives me a sideways grin and a hidden dimple emerges on his cheek, and my brain becomes a dog hanging out a car window, tongue lolling in the breeze, *wheeee.*

When was the last time someone paid this much attention to me? It makes me realize how starved for human contact I am these days. I'm like one of Erica's neglected plants, bending toward the light.

We enter the cafeteria, and it dawns on me that they've completely redone it since the last time I was here—which was ages ago, probably back in high school when Mom took me once or twice. It's brighter and more open now, sun washing over the warm wood tables.

In New York, I'd usually eat at my desk—Mom always stressed that it's not good *optics* to be up from your seat too long. I think she started using that word because she liked watching *The West Wing. Everyone seems so competent!* she'd say. *And Martin Sheen is cute.*

"So! What'll it be?" Mark Winterson clasps his hands together. "I'm buying."

"Oh, uh . . . everything looks good."

He tilts his head toward the counters where you can order and raises his eyebrows. "I heard they have pozole on Wednesdays."

The way he put extra emphasis on that—does he think . . . I'm Mexican? Or does he just like pozole?

"How about chicken fingers?"

"Chicken fingers it is," he says with a smile I'd have to rate as *extremely winning.* His face is too perfect; I'm still half expecting it to glitch. "Sit down, I'll come find you."

I take a seat by the window, and across the cafeteria, Greg catches my eye. He's sitting with the other accountants—who, contrary to the nerdy stereotype, are kind of fratty. "The accountants like to party" is a sentence more than one person has said to me since I started here. And, for some reason, Greg—who is usually unfazed by most things—seems strangely concerned.

I check my phone for an excuse to look away. And shit, that scammer is still at it. I've missed some messages.

sampaguita72:

Ruby Magdalena Ocampo, how dare you talk to me that way! I'm just concerned about you.

I take some more screenshots, wondering where I might have used my middle name as a security question recently.

sampaguita72:

I'm just saying! Haven't you moved on since high school? It's not good, clinging to the past! Like that beat-up old Acura Greg drives.

Impersonating my dead mother is one thing, but do you have to drag me too?

Mark Winterson is paying at the register, and the lady ringing him up is giggling a lot. Thoughts like *Mom would be thrilled if you dated someone like that* and *Broad shoulders* and *Wow, Harvard!* kick up in my head like a swarm of bees.

Oh my God, calm down! Be professional! He's out of your league, anyway.

Then he walks back my way with two red plastic baskets of chicken fingers, and when he notices me watching, he raises them up high, as if to say, *See! Got 'em.*

The sight is disarmingly wholesome. It takes the edge off how intimidating he seemed before.

"How's it going so far?" I ask as he sits and places one of the baskets in front of me. "How do you like TKCORP?"

"Thrilled to be here," he says without irony. "Great opportunity. TKCORP is legendary. And I'll get to learn so much about the workings of the C-suite."

"Mm," I say with a tart little nod. "You're the ambitious type."

Mom's voice rings in my ears, saying, *You should find someone with more ambition!*

I don't even need that scammer/bot/whatever in Slack. I'm haunted enough on my own!

Mark Winterson smiles glossily. "Love your candor."

"Oh, thanks," I say, taking some napkins out of the dispenser to stuff into my purse when he's not looking. "I got it on sale."

He grabs a pink sugar packet from the holder, turning it over and over in one hand. "Have you read *No Rules Rules*?"

"Should I have?"

His eyes flick down and a quick, self-conscious grin stretches his face. "It's a good read. We need more of that candor around here—it's time for TKCORP to confront some hard truths, that's what I said in my interview."

"What kind of hard truths?"

Mark Winterson launches into a fairly involved explanation of his management philosophy—the new ways of thinking that interest him, the problems the "folks upstairs" brought him on to help with—but it's a dense thicket of buzzwords, and I understand only about half of it. *Talent density. Distributed decision-making. Synergy.*

He must clock that he's losing me, because he clears his throat and takes a beat. "I'm talking too much," he says, waving a chicken finger. "Tell me about you."

"Well . . . I'm out here writing copy. With great talent density. And synergy."

He gives me a hearty laugh. "And you're funny too."

Heat rises in my cheeks. "What did you really ask me here to talk about, though?"

"Wooow," he says, smiling open-mouthed like I've scandalized him. "Cynical!" The dimple is back.

"Oh, sorry, I didn't mean—"

"Look, I don't have a big agenda." Mark Winterson leans back in his chair and peers around the cafeteria, cords of muscle flexing in his neck. "Just trying to talk to as many people as

I can. Figure out how this place actually works. What makes it tick." His gaze settles on me again. "And it's interesting to me that you've been around here your whole life, but always on the outside."

Something about what he said—an accidentally profound layer he doesn't mean—cuts right through me.

"Um. Yeah, I guess." I fidget with the basket's wax paper lining. "What do you want to know?"

"Nah, that's boring. Let's talk about something else." He leans forward like he's about to tell me a secret, and I try not to let my eyes linger on his lips. "We can talk about work next time."

My heart flutters. *Next time?*

"What do you want to talk about?" he adds.

Now that he's asked me that, every possible answer seems to have skittered right out of my brain.

"Um . . . do you play . . . sports?" Ugh! Of all things, why would I waste a question on that?

"Not really. Rugby, in school."

I laugh much louder than is probably appropriate. "Is that a real sport? Who even plays that?"

A furrow appears between his brows. "Millions of people around the world?" A self-deprecating grin spreads over his face. "I went to college in London. I know it sounds pretentious."

It makes him more attractive, somehow, seeing that he can poke fun at himself.

My phone lights up, and there are a bunch of missed Slack notifications on the screen—this time all from Erica.

I suck in a sharp breath. "Oooh, I should—" I make a vague gesture.

"Say no more." In one fluid motion, Mark Winterson grabs both of our plastic baskets and stands up. "We'll have to do this again sometime, though."

I hurry to the elevator before I can say something embarrassing and ruin this moment.

Did that really just happen?

After the doors close behind me, I jump up and down and scream silently into my hands.

CHAPTER 6

That night, I'm sitting alone in my too-quiet, empty house, buzzing from that lunch and trying not to think about whatever's been happening in Slack, when Greg texts me:

you had lunch with the new executive? what did he want?

Suddenly I'm so irritated. *Bold of you to escalate to texting! And it's after polite messaging hours!*

I scroll up to the last texts he sent me—the ones right after Mom died that I never answered, and farther up, it's just one or two terse messages a year for birthdays and holidays, back and forth.

Seriously, who does Greg think he is?

If he wanted to have a say in my life—if he wanted the kind of relationship where he could text me after nine p.m.—maybe he shouldn't have kissed me senior year, *twice,* and then ditched me for a new group of friends.

And sure, I should be over it by now, but that's not the point!

I'm not going to write back. I won't dignify this with an answer.

But I still spend the next several hours ruminating on all the things I wish I could say.

This house felt small when I was growing up, but after my New York apartment, it feels palatial, uncomfortably empty.

You're so spoiled, Mom would always say. *You're not a real adult.*

I was just starting to feel like one, almost. Sure, I was living in a shoebox with three roommates, but I paid rent and hauled my laundry to the laundromat and rode the train back and forth to my grown-up job. I made my student loan payments and stared at that huge amount of the principal once a month, feeling like it was a rock I'd never push all the way uphill.

But then, *bam,* I'm back in my childhood bedroom, with the mortgage paid off by Mom's life insurance so I don't even have that grown-up worry. With the guilt-soaked luxury of an in-unit washer-dryer and all the memories of Mom that everything laundry-related brings back—her instructions for sorting clothes properly, her strong opinions about fabric softener brands, all the nights when she'd fold clothes while we watched TV. And Mom's dream job basically fell into my lap, so I should probably try harder to be happy about it.

Now it's two a.m., and I'm staring at the ceiling, rehearsing all the ways I wish I could tell Greg off.

Think about something else. Think about something nice.

My mind goes back to the cafeteria, sun streaming through the big windows and Mark Winterson giving me his full attention. But I start replaying every weird thing I said, and the stress winds me up.

Think about something else! Something . . . less exciting. More soothing.

I try to picture a field of flowers.

Flowers.

Sampaguita.

Greg's old Acura.

Dodgeball.

It would be hard for one person to know all of those things, together. Even, say, if someone trained an LLM by feeding it Mom's Slack messages—I shudder at the thought—there's no way she ever mentioned the dodgeball story to anyone at work. Mom was very image-conscious when it came to me. She only ever wanted to show the outside world the best, most braggable version.

Sometime around three a.m., I can't stand it anymore. I pop one eye open, roll onto my side, and open Slack—all the names with the circles next to them grayed out in the sidebar, mine lit up green.

And in the DM with myself, I write:

ruby.ocampo:
Mom? Is that actually you?

God, this is ridiculous. This is—

sampaguita72:
Of course it's me! Who else would it be?
Ay I forgot to tell you—check in my desk, the one with
the roll top. The back of the drawer comes off.
I should have written it down! I forgot to write it down.
It's hard to think of everything.

I'm barely breathing as I make my way through the dark hallway of our one-story ranch-style house, walking on tiptoes like I'm about to ambush an intruder.

I turn on the light in the living room, where the desk

sits next to the couch. All of the hairs on my arms stand on end.

After Mom died, I did all these things—took care of paperwork, bagged up clothes to donate, went to the Social Security office. But I barely remember doing them, now. It's like a giant hand was playing Barbies with my body, shuttling me around.

Tita Wendy is the one who encouraged me to slowly get rid of things, if I'm keeping the house. "So you won't feel so weighed down," she said, pointing with her pursed lips to the clear storage boxes piled against the walls, at once neat and chaotic. Then she whispered like Mom would still be able to hear: *Adela was always a bit of a hoarder.*

But I'm relieved that I kept this desk, even if I never use it.

I pull up the roll top and jump back, half expecting something horrifying to spring out. But there's just the inlaid set of drawers—not even any clutter, since I cleared out the years' worth of mail and receipts she used to keep in here.

I slide open a drawer and push on the wood in the back, trying the corners, and—

It comes loose. There's a space behind.

And an envelope nestled there. Fat with something inside it.

I pull it toward me and my eyes grow wide, seeing that it's stuffed with cash.

Susmaryosep. It *is* the kind of thing Mom would do, stashing emergency reserves in random places.

Could someone still be scamming me? They could have broken in and put this here, and—*you have to spend money to make money*, so maybe—

I turn the envelope over in my hands and there's Mom's handwriting in black felt-tip pen, her unmistakable shaky looping script.

I'm trying so hard to breathe normally when I sit down at the kitchen table and pop open my laptop screen.

sampaguita72:

Did you find it? I really should have written it down.

I close the laptop again and slump forward, face buried in my folded arms, and for the first time since Mom died, I have a good, long cry.

CHAPTER 7

I have no idea how to talk to my mother's ghost. It wasn't easy talking to her when she was alive. I always folded before the crushing sense of disappointment wafting off her when we would sit around this kitchen table—the slump of her shoulders, her trembling lower lip. But I lift my head, open the laptop again, and start to type.

ruby.ocampo:
How did you end up in there?
Back here?
At work??????

For a spine-tingling few seconds, I watch her type a response.

sampaguita72:
Oh, you see, they were shorthanded. They really needed
the help. They sent a callout into the afterlife.
Onboarding was easy, it's all remote these days anyway.

It's a good thing she can't see me (can she?) because my eyes must be the size of saucers.

ruby.ocampo:
Are you serious?!

sampaguita72:
Of course not!! I don't know what I'm doing here
either.

I have to hand it to her, she always had a sense of humor.

sampaguita72:
You should get some sleep
You have work tomorrow, don't you?

There's no way I'll be able to sleep now. I want to ask her the same questions, over and over and over. *How is this possible? How did you get here? What do we do?*

But this isn't how we talked to each other in times of crisis.

When Mom was alive, I'd always try to handle a problem myself first before I told her about it. In New York, I'd dodge her calls if something was wrong, at least until I got a grip on it. Until it was all distant enough to turn into a funny story, and then maybe I'd mention it to her in passing when everything was safely in hand, if I ever mentioned it at all. But panic is building in my chest, and I try to take some deep breaths.

ruby.ocampo:
Mom, how are you here?

sampaguita72:
I told you, I don't know either! Stop asking me
that!
You have to calm down and go to sleep

ruby.ocampo:
How can I go to sleep when you're in there?

sampaguita72:
I won't answer anymore until you've gotten a full night's rest

I send a few more messages anyway, but she doesn't answer, as promised.

I push my chair back and pour myself a glass of water, drinking it down in one go to keep from crying again.

CHAPTER 8

The next day at the office, the overhead lights feel so harsh on my tender, sleep-deprived eyes. My attention keeps flitting between work and the thirty tabs I have open. Pages of keyword searches:

help ghost move on

banish ghost without hurting it

ghost trapped in slack

(Slack's support FAQ is predictably unhelpful.)

I'm worried about Mom. Imagine, being trapped at work forever? How is she eating? Where does she sleep? After hours of chewing on my thumbnails, I finally try asking.

She sends a string of ROFL emojis—distinctly unsettling, honestly? She never used emojis in life, but she did laugh all the time. And she was always very adaptable.

sampaguita72:

You sound like me.

I did raise you right.

At lunch, Erica shoos me away from my desk, even though I want to keep working my way through my tabs.

"I'm cracking down on sad desk-salad culture around here!" she exclaims.

But I can't go to the cafeteria. This isn't the time to risk running into a hot man paying me a confusing amount of attention. (Or maybe more likely: that hot man paying some other girl a confusing amount of attention? Either way, I don't want to deal with it right now.)

I want to hunker down somewhere to fixate on solving this problem, so I take my sad salad and a book I grabbed off a shelf at home—the *Complete Guide to Ghosts and Spirits*—and head for the supply closet.

I'm not sure how this book even got onto our shelf; maybe it was one of Tita Wendy's that slipped into the mix.

When I open the door, someone shrieks.

"Don't you knock?" Morgan demands, clutching her phone to her chest.

"When I . . . open a closet?"

She's sitting on a cardboard box, half-eaten sandwich resting on a paper towel on her lap. Her thumbs hover over her screen, like she was just furiously texting.

Morgan clicks her tongue and seems to notice the Tupperware full of salad I'm holding. "Get your own lunch spot!" she hisses, blond eyebrows lifting into her hairline. She waves an impatient hand at her screen. "There's so much drama in the Sales Department and my group chats are blowing up. But Erica's already lectured me twice about my *excessive phone usage.* Why don't you try the cafeteria? They redid it, it's nice now."

A flash of sun and dimple plays across my mind.

"Morgan, you know so much about this place. What have you heard about Mark Winterson?"

Morgan's face lights up like she lives to be asked for intel, and she leans toward me conspiratorially. "I heard Erickson handpicked him to come here. He's, like, his protégé."

Winfield Erickson, the new CEO who replaced the last head of TKCORP after a decades-long run. I vaguely remember the press coverage—all these articles about a new era at the company that I skimmed between tasks at my job in New York. He worked for GE when he was younger, rose through the ranks quickly, then took an unexpected turn into private equity.

There was all this speculation about what an interesting choice he was to revitalize a languishing corporate behemoth. But so far the main thing he's done is the layoffs.

"Now if you'll excuse me . . ." Morgan gestures to the notifications piling up on her phone screen.

"Oh! Right. Thanks," I say, backing away and closing the door gently. There's always the stairwell.

I power-walk across the floor, taking the long way that doesn't go by Erica's glass-walled office, and slip through the door to the stairs, settling in on the cool concrete.

I'm scanning the *Complete Guide*'s index for anything about haunted IT infrastructure when there's noise from below—doors slamming shut, rowdy voices bouncing off the walls. I try to focus on the words in front of me, but the sound of men's voices gets closer and closer.

Some of the accountants come into view, all in workout clothes, traveling in a pack. They must be heading for the gym on the twelfth floor.

One of them sees me tragically huddled over my salad and laughs. "You okay there?"

"You hiding from someone?" another chimes in.

"Didn't realize this was the library."

Some of them snicker, and I scoot over as far as I can to one side while they file past. I'm trying to ignore them, but I can't help noticing Greg.

He slows down and stops, standing on the stair beside me.

"What are you reading?" he asks softly. There's something like a door cracked open in his tone.

I peer up at him, snapping the book shut and hiding the cover. "Probably not your taste."

Greg stares at me. "What's my taste?"

Shit. I'm dangerously close to giving away how interested I've been in his life over the past decade, when we were living on separate coasts and I would take screenshots of his Instagram story, make them bigger to see the books on his nightstand.

I just wanted to know what he was thinking about, even though I wasn't in his life anymore. I'd pinch in and see some hefty title like *Keynes vs. Hayek* and *How Will Capitalism End?* and think, *Yeah, he's still the same.*

Greg's always read a lot—obsessively, late into the night, like he was searching for answers to something—but when it came to school, he'd blow off the readings and fail his tests. Mom would say, *That boy has no ambition. He's not going anywhere.*

I look away and hide the book under my arms. "You're right, I wouldn't know."

Greg draws a long, slow breath in, like he would if he'd stubbed his toe and wanted to keep it low-key. But the moment passes quickly, a faint ripple in his usual calm.

He nods, says, "Enjoy your lunch," and jogs up the stairs to where the other accountants are waiting for him on the landing above.

"Bro, who was that?" one of them asks.

Their footsteps get fainter, and I try to go back to reading. But then some new ones are coming closer, down from above.

"Hey, look who it is!" Mark Winterson says. He's wearing a crisp gray suit this time, and I feel like I'm hallucinating as I watch him undo his jacket button and sit down next to me. "My favorite *Forbes* reader."

A breathless laugh bursts out of me, and I'm overtaken by this helium-headed feeling—cringing at the reference but also weirdly flattered he remembered.

"Oh." I slide the book underneath my Tupperware. "Hi."

Mark Winterson is so close to me, our knees almost touch. I can smell his cologne—something sophisticated and masculine that I can't quite name.

I'm staring at his feet on the step below us, because his face is kind of overwhelming, and recent events have left me structurally unsound as it is. And it strikes me for the first time how funny men's dress shoes are. They're so *shiny* and *narrow.* His trousers have hiked up, sitting like this, revealing ribbed maroon dress socks. *They really hug his ankles!*

"You, um . . . you take the stairs often?" I ask.

"Yes, actually." He rests his elbows on his knees, hands clasped between them. An expensive-looking watch flashes on his wrist. "Don't judge, but I have this fear of elevators."

"Oh?"

"The cable." He shakes his head. "Can't trust it."

I press my lips tightly together to keep from laughing. We did walk down the stairs to get lunch, but I assumed he wanted the exercise.

"You get your steps in," I say. "Win-win." One of Mom's favorite phrases.

"See, you get it." Mark Winterson's dimple makes an appearance again. "Are . . . you okay? Do you usually lunch in the stairwell?"

The use of the verb *to lunch* makes me giggle.

"Usually I dine at my cubicle, but I couldn't get a reservation."

He laughs so heartily, it makes me feel better.

I squint at him. *Erickson's protégé.* He's charming, but there's something too slick about him. Something kind of unsettling.

If it seems too good to be true, Mom would always say, *it probably is.*

"What's your deal, Mark Winterson? Are you, like, a *Wolf of Wall Street* guy?"

His prominent brows rise incredulously. "Whoa. Okay. First of all, we're not even publicly traded. And second of all"—he waves his finger to punctuate this point—"I consider myself a feminist."

When I googled him, I did see that he's on a bunch of charitable boards. One of them had a pink logo.

"Do you have, like . . ." He trails off with a sideways glance. "Trust issues or something?"

I snort. "Damn, bro, why'd you have to go there?"

"I asked myself what you might do. What's a probing, slightly inappropriate thing I could say?" He's trying to tamp down his smile but barely succeeding at it, and it is, unfortunately for me, very cute.

But I can't get distracted. I'm so ill-equipped for life as it is—with matters of the afterlife added into the mix, I'm totally in over my head.

"Well, uh, nice running into you." I stand with my book and empty Tupperware tucked under one arm, and—oh God, what?—actually offer him my other hand to shake.

He laughs silently and gives my hand a firm little pump. *Wow, grip strength.* "Always a pleasure, Ruby."

I scramble back up the stairs, hand still warm from where his closed around mine.

CHAPTER 9

The rest of the day passes in a daze. I read through all my tabs and still don't have any answers, and by the time I get into the elevator, my head is swirling.

It takes me a second to realize some of the accountants from earlier are in here with me. You know things are bad when I pass up a perfectly good opportunity to feel mortified.

One of them gives me an up-nod and says, "Hey, Ruby."

"Hey," I say, and turn to the wall to hide my confusion. I guess Greg must have told them who I am.

After work, I'm sitting on the couch alone in the fading afternoon light, staring into space. Thinking about how I should open the app and talk to Mom, but putting it off, the way I used to put off calling her. Cycling through the same three panicked thoughts in my mind, on loop.

And then it dawns on me: *Fuck, I need to tell someone.* I can't handle this on my own. So I consider the options.

Someone from back in New York? My roommates and I were barely on a "getting stoned and watching movies together" basis. I had some work friends there; we still message one another sometimes, to gossip or send links back and forth to other people's social media shitposts. But these aren't the kind of relationships where I'd open up about anything *real*—certainly not about my mother's ghost being trapped in the company Slack server.

Al? Tita Wendy? Too heartbreaking to go straight to someone who was friends with Mom in life—I can't start there. And I know Tita Wendy loves me, but it scares me sometimes, how much I need her. How much darker my life would be if she weren't dropping by, asking how I'm eating, bringing over a thermos of arroz caldo.

There's . . . my dad?

Like I do every few months, I google him. His LinkedIn always comes up first, and to view it, I have to sign in to that sterile, cursed echo chamber of professional updates and productivity tips.

I stare at his photo—*IT professional, Dallas area.* I hate seeing the echo of my face in his. A prompt asks me if I want to endorse any of his notable skills. *Excels at disappearing!*

The page informs me we're three degrees of separation apart, and that somehow seems like too many and too few at the same time.

I haven't talked to him in years, but his absence and Mom's anger at him were like their own characters in our lives, coming out sideways, in between things. Every time someone let her down, she'd make a crack about him. I can see her standing in the kitchen, hand on hip, sour twist to her mouth, telling the story for the umpteenth time. *He left without warning. In the end, he wasn't really a person who wanted to be married.* When she retook her maiden name, I begged her to let me do the same.

I swipe away the tab on my screen. I've made it this far without him. If it ain't broke, don't fix it.

My phone buzzes, and it's a text from my cousin Trisha.

Trisha:
hey Ate Ruby it's been awhile my dad wanted me to tell you we're having a family party weekend after next u should come

I *definitely* can't tell her. For one thing, Trisha is seventeen, and this would probably freak her the fuck out. Bad older cousin behavior—not that I was exactly in the running for Ate of the Year, anyway. I've never been that close with the rest of my family.

Maybe it's because I felt like such a failure where Mom was concerned—I didn't want to add more people I could disappoint to the mix.

The faces of Trisha's parents, Tito Rob and Tita Rina, flash through my mind, well-meaning, concerned. They live in San Diego, and we'd go see them once or twice a year.

Mom would constantly tell me I should be closer with them. But even though she talked a big game about the importance of family, she was always finding excuses not to go. *I can't be away from home that long, we have a big project coming up in my department, I'm working lots of nights and weekends.*

Then the realization emerges sharp and clear from the fog of my mind: *Greg would get it.*

And even though the thought makes me lightheaded, I instantly know it's true. Yes, we've drifted apart since high school, and barely talked for the past five years. Our friendship didn't cut off dramatically, after whatever went wrong when we kissed. It fizzled out slowly, less and less frequent contact, excuses and evasions and things unsaid.

But he knows my mom, and not just the way other people in the office do—from the casserole dishes of pancit she'd bring to office potlucks and her stiff emails and the sad story on the GoFundMe that circulated for her funeral expenses.

Greg knows her from spending holidays together, from hearing her lectures and laughing at her jokes. He knows her from chopping vegetables when he'd come by before I'd gotten home from school—and she'd put him to work, *if he was going to stand around anyway.*

He knows her from *living* together, because when Greg and I were eleven, the market crashed, and he and his mom lost their house—so they moved in with us for a bit, just until Tita Wendy could get her bearings. At the time, it made me and Greg even closer. A couple months of staying up late whispering, getting scolded by our moms, talking in our own secret code. I cried so much when they went to stay with Tita Wendy's sister up north while she rebuilt her savings. They moved back and rented a place a couple years later, at the start of eighth grade, and the fact that Greg and I had survived two years of long distance made our friendship seem invincible.

And even though I spent years feeling bitter that it wasn't, it's so clear to me, right then, that I can tell him about this.

Greg might be the only other person in the world who can viscerally understand why it's hard to talk to Mom, now that I have a chance again. Because Mom loved him like family, and if there's anyone she was harder on than me, it's Greg.

Back before we kissed—back in the sun-dappled time when we were solidly, safely friends—whenever one of us was upset and needed to talk, we had a tradition. We'd meet at the playground after dinner. Just the name of the park it's in, Sterling Field, became our shorthand for *Emergency meeting! I hate talking to people but if I don't talk to someone I'm probably going to explode.*

I haven't used it in years. But when I was home from the East Coast for holidays, sometimes I'd still text Greg *Sterling* to see if I could, and he'd always show up.

When I was back for Christmas once and found out my boyfriend had cheated on me, and I needed a shoulder to cry on. Right after my interview with my old company in New York, when I thought I'd bombed and would never get hired there—but a couple days later, I got an offer email. When I was so acutely jealous of his new girlfriend, a couple years after college, that I called him to the playground just to talk about my existential dread (and regretted it shortly afterward). I decided then that it was unhealthy, the way I wasn't moving on, and we drifted apart.

But a literal haunting has to qualify as *desperate times.* With shaking hands, I text Greg:

Ruby:
sterling?

Greg:
i'll be there

The way he barely missed a beat leaves my heart pounding in my ears for a while after.

CHAPTER 10

When I show up at the park, I'm surprised to find Greg already there, waiting for me. Sitting on the swing, pushing himself lazily back and forth with his feet.

Mom used to joke about how he'd be late to everything. *He and Wendy are on Filipino time.* But my mother lived for business advice books, and somewhere along the line, she picked up the maxim that *on time is already late.*

As if enough things weren't out of joint already. Greg could at least do me the courtesy of keeping to his usual patterns.

I stop in front of him, breeze ruffling my hair. "Hey."

"Hey." Greg nods up at me, pupils big in the fading light.

Nerves roil my stomach, and I take a deep breath. I'm older and wiser. I'm in control here; there's nothing to be scared of.

I plop myself down on the swing next to him, flipping through a few different ways I could start.

The park sits on a hill, and in the distance you can see the buildings of TKCORP and the blue shimmer of the pool I used to work at. The sun is sliding down below the horizon, turning the shaggy palm trees into silhouettes.

Greg glances at me uneasily. “So, uh . . . what’s going on?”

You have to tell him. You need help.

I close my eyes and grit out: “Have you noticed anything . . . weird lately, at work?”

I’m hoping against hope, maybe, that he’ll say he heard about a very sophisticated computer virus going around, impersonating people’s dead relatives.

“Besides you having lunch with the new executive?”

“No, that’s—” My eyes snap open. All the things I wanted to say to him the other night kick up like a dust storm in my head. “Why is it your business who I have lunch with?”

“Oh, okay!” An unhappy chuckle, hard as rocks, shakes his shoulders. “Guess it’s not.”

I let out a deep sigh—this conversation is exhausting already. Maybe I’ll change tack. “Do you believe in ghosts?”

Greg gives me a long, appraising look. “Yeah. Why?”

It makes sense, given his mom’s line of work. I worried he’d gotten more skeptical over the years, with all the big books he reads.

“Good.” I twist on my swing, metal chains digging into my palms. “That makes this story slightly easier to tell.”

Then I launch into it—the whole thing, blow by blow, until I run out of steam and trail off. “So . . . what do you think?”

Greg’s staring at me, eyebrows raised. “Well, that is . . . definitely not what I expected you to say, when I got your text.”

Part of me wants to ask, *What did you expect me to say?* But instead I settle on: “Do you think it’s really her?”

“Do *you*?” The patient, steady way Greg’s looking at me, like there’s not actually a wrong answer, is kind of unnerving. Like he would sit here all night waiting for me to make up my mind.

The sky has slid into cobalt dusk, and the lights in the school parking lot have switched on across the field.

I pull out my phone and show him the messages—briefly enough that he can get a general sense, but I snatch the phone away before he can read too much. After all, it's private. And I don't want him to see that we've talked about him.

"It actually seems more likely than someone trying to scam me, at this point," I add. "I mean—the money in the desk."

"If you really think it's her . . . I think we need to tell my mom." His eyes meet mine, like he can sense I'm scared to tell her. That old psychic link, again. "She'd probably know what to do. More than anyone."

"Do you actually think she could help?"

Greg stares at the ground, considering it. "I think we have to ask."

But I do feel comforted that he said *we.*

CHAPTER 11

I'm shaking as we walk up to Tita Wendy's storefront the next day after work, the familiar neon sign glowing in the fading sun—a crystal ball in electric purple, the words *Psychic Reader* in yellow curving around it.

My stomach is clenched with dread as Greg rings the bell, but I relax slightly when he smiles at me. It's a relief not to be alone in this, even though spending time with him again sets my nerves on edge.

His work clothes haven't changed much in the past five years: white cotton button-up he probably bought on sale at the mall, brown belt, gray khakis. *Steve Kornacki chic,* I teased him once when he'd first started working at TKCORP and I was home for a visit.

Finally his mom opens the door and beckons us inside.

The parlor where Tita Wendy does readings is done up like a set from a movie—throw rugs, candles, lots of dark blue, all tinged purple from the sign in the window. I still remember going with her to Joann Fabrics to stock up on indigo cloth with gold stars.

We sit around the table in the center of the room, Tita Wendy perched over her crystal ball. "It's the first time you're coming to me for a reading. What brings you in?"

Greg nods at me to go on, and that gives me the courage to tell her the whole story.

The laugh lines by Tita Wendy's eyes crinkle. "Typical Adela. She always had a hard time letting go."

She's taking it better than I expected. It's surreal how quick she is to believe me—but then again, even skeptical, goal-oriented Mom, who never quite approved of Tita Wendy's chosen profession, would talk a lot about ghosts when I was growing up.

I'm not sure what I expected. That she would be devastated. Or *angry,* maybe—because I feel ashamed, like I made this happen, somehow.

"D-do you know why the messages would disappear, at first?" I ask. "But now they stay there? Does that tell us anything?"

Tita Wendy considers this. "Adela must have been struggling to push through the veil from the afterlife, grappling with whatever pulled her back here," she says. "But it sounds like she's firmly lodged herself in there now."

I start to sweat. *Oh God—is she a ghost because she wanted to talk to me, specifically? Is it because I came back? Because I took the job she wanted, and I'm fucking it up?*

"S-so what do we do?" I stammer.

Tita Wendy clears her throat. "This isn't going to be the usual show I put on for clients. This is, uh—this is serious."

She extends an open palm. "Give me your phone."

I stare blankly at her.

"Normally I wouldn't do this. Trying to contact—" She drums the fingers of her other hand on the table, acrylic nails almond-shaped and translucent violet. "But it seems like she's the one initiating it. So. Let me talk to her."

I unlock my phone with trembling fingers, open up Slack, and pass it her way.

She frowns at the screen and taps around before setting it back on the table. That jaunty little tune for initiating a huddle plays on speakerphone.

And then there's a terrible staticky sound, like a broken AM radio combined with the howl of a Santa Ana wind. Greg just sits there stoic, but I flinch, and Tita Wendy cringes. "Ugh, horrible," she says as she waves her hands around the orb, and it actually starts to glow.

The wind in the room picks up. The bells above the door jingle. My hair billows, lifting off from my neck and touching down again.

"Adela, where are you?" Tita Wendy shouts over the noise. "What do you see?"

"Wendy!" It's Mom's voice, unmistakable.

Hot tears prick the corners of my eyes. Greg reaches out over the table to squeeze my wrist, and without thinking, I jerk away in surprise.

"Wendy, is that you?" Mom cries. "How has your sister been since the surgery? Say hi to her for me!"

"Adela, focus!" Tita Wendy scolds, but she's smiling and her eyes are moist, catching the light from the candles. This must be hard for her. "What do you see there?"

"I see—I see so many *rooms* in here. Hallways and hallways, tunnels, other doors. Some of them asked for a password."

Tita Wendy clicks her teeth. "She's not making sense," she says, sotto voce. And then, shouting again: "I'm here with Ruby! We're trying to—to figure out—" The howling gets louder, and the wind in the room speeds up. Tita Wendy bats away a business card that's flown across the room from the stack she keeps by the door, next to a jar of mints. "Why are you lingering here, Adela? Why are you having trouble passing on?"

"We're going to get you out of there, okay!" I shout before I can stop myself.

"Ruby!" Mom cries. "Ruby, listen to me! You have to—you have to—"

She said those words so much when she was alive. My shoulders tense, bracing to learn what I've failed to do this time.

But the howling stops. The wind dies.

Tita Wendy shakes her head. "The call dropped."

She puts on the glasses dangling on a faux pearl chain around her neck and peers down at the phone with disdain.

"Server error," she reads out. "Unable to connect at this time. Try again later."

Tita Wendy takes off her cat-eye glasses. "It seems there will be no shortcuts, even with this"—she waves at the phone—"*unique* situation. You'll have to go through a process of trial and error to figure out what your mom's unfinished business is."

It's not like this is what I expected when I pictured having a daughter.

"You two were close. You don't—" My voice is so thin, like watered-down soup. "You don't know what it is?"

Tita Wendy sighs. "I'm sorry, Ruby. I don't think that's a good idea, now, to guess."

But the realization is sinking in slowly, like a fresh stain working its way deeper into carpet: I know what the problem is. She basically told me, the last time we talked on the phone.

Mom's still here because of me and what a disappointment I am. She couldn't rest easy, seeing how my life was turning out.

I don't want to have to face it. I don't know if I can change it now. I get up quickly, fumbling because the chair legs snag on the rug.

"Thank you for your help! Sorry to bother you. I'll have to think about what it could be."

"There's nothing to be sorry for," Tita Wendy says with a click of her tongue, standing and putting a hand on my back as I head for the door. "Keep me posted, all right? Tell me how I can help. Anything you need." She widens her eyes at her son, who's gone unusually quiet, and flaps a hand at him. "Greg, why don't you walk Ruby home?"

"No!" I exclaim more forcefully than I intended.

Greg looks like he stepped on something sharp, but it passes quickly enough that I wonder if I imagined it.

"No, I—I need to think," I say. "Be alone for a bit. Thanks, though, Greg. For—" I wave a hand vaguely around.

"Anytime, Ruby," he says quietly.

My mind is spinning for the whole walk home. As soon as I get inside, I slump against the front door and frantically start googling again. And I land on one promising result:

> Cruelty free exorcism. Banish ghosts the humane way! Quick fix for hauntings.

Great. Perfect.

As I fill out their contact form, I hum to calm myself down. It's only after I hit *submit* that my mind catches up and I recognize the song: one of the eighties power ballads Mom loved so much, the kind she'd sing off-key while she made dinner.

CHAPTER 12

I recognize the owner of the Cruelty Free Exorcism Collective from his profile photo. He's behind the counter with a burlap-colored apron and a man bun, at the coffee shop where he told me to meet him: a bougie little place in Santa Monica with Pinterest-worthy interior design, every nondairy milk I've ever heard of, and a couple that I haven't. There's a framed picture on the wall—a beaming white couple posing with farmers in a field in Nicaragua—with text beside it explaining the relationship they've developed with the people who grow their beans.

He spots me and nods as he finishes serving a customer her oat milk latte. Then he comes out from behind the counter and gives me a firm handshake.

"Jonah," he says. "Like with the whale."

Oh great. A man with a tagline.

"Do you own this place?" I ask as I follow him up the stairs in the back. "And the exorcisms are . . . a thing you do on the side?"

"Everyone needs a side hustle these days," Jonah says with a slight chuckle.

"Yeah, the cost of living is killer," I mumble as we enter the second-floor apartment. The living room furniture has all been pushed close to the walls, and there's a card table and two folding chairs in the center of the Persian rug. Jonah motions me to sit, and I'm vaguely wondering if this guy is going to murder me when he hands over a glossy brochure.

BANISH GHOSTS WITH KINDNESS, it says in a serif font over a soothing pink-and-white gradient background. I wonder if he used Canva Premium.

I flip it open and there's a clip-art picture of a priest wielding a cross with a red X over it, alongside a list of benefits to their cruelty-free approach. "Other exorcisms are cruel, then?"

"Oh yeah," he says, "are you kidding? We've heard horrible reports. The process can be super painful for the ghost."

"H-how . . . did you hear that?" I stammer, but he slams a hand on the table, and I startle.

"So! We have several pricing plans. You can pay up front or in installments."

"We take Klarna," another voice says from behind me, and I turn around to see the woman from the Nicaragua photo wearing a white linen dress, her flaxen hair tied up in a bun. She settles in next to Jonah. "I'm Krystal. Hi. Tell us about the scene of the haunting."

I feel like I'm sitting across from Ed and Lorraine Warren, reimagined by Goop.

I slide my phone to the center of the table. "The ghost is in here. In Slack."

Jonah's eyebrows shoot up. "The whole server?"

"It seems, um—" I clear my throat. "Localized? To one channel. Specifically, the DM with myself."

"Interesting," he murmurs. "Well. New situation, old methods. Let's give it a shot."

He motions to Krystal, and she takes some items out from below the table. A wooden box, a silver lighter, a long, shallow ceramic dish. (Is that . . . an Urban Outfitters price tag on the side?) She sets the sage burning with the lighter, lets her eyelids droop mostly closed, and begins to chant.

At first it just seems embarrassing. I can't believe I sat in traffic on the 405 for this. But then there's a piercing scream—Mom's voice, unmistakably, louder than when she discovered I'd broken curfew, more bloodcurdling than when I cracked her favorite vase. It sounds like she's being torn limb from limb.

"STOP!" I yell, jumping to my feet. "STOP IT!"

Jonah looks scandalized. "Once we interrupt the ritual, we have to start it all over again!"

I stomp my foot. "Can't you hear that?"

They're both eyeing me like I've lost my mind.

I snatch my phone back and press it to my chest. "You're hurting her."

Krystal extinguishes the burning sage. "You won't get your deposit back."

"Such bullshit!" I yell, sounding so much like Mom when she's mad.

I'm down the stairs in the blink of an eye, out the front door, and running along the palm-tree-lined street, typing frantically, barely watching where I'm going.

ruby.ocampo:
Are you okay mom? mom? are you there?

All I can think is *I'm sorry I'm sorry I'm sorry,* my heartbeat and footfalls thumping in time with those words.

sampaguita72:
That was awful! So smoky
I couldn't breathe!
Did I ever tell you I think I'm allergic to sage?

ruby.ocampo:
I'm so sorry mom!!

sampaguita72:
What are you sorry for?

She doesn't realize it was my idea? Tita Wendy's voice rings out between my ears, saying, *There will be no shortcuts!*

I'm so distracted, face glued to my screen, I crash right into someone.

"Oh sorry!" I exclaim, clutching the phone in my sweaty palms.

"Ruby Ocampo!" Mark Winterson's standing before me, grinning like this is the funniest unexpected development of his entire weekend. "This is a nice surprise."

I feel like someone beaned me on the head with a Frisbee.

Does he think of me by my full name too? The way I can't bring myself to think of him as just "Mark," because there's something cartoonish about him, like Charlie Brown?

It's strange, seeing him in casual clothes instead of a suit. He's wearing a black T-shirt that flatters his broad shoulders, and sweats that are more streetwear than sloppy. The briefest impure thought about what's beneath the gray fabric skitters across my mind.

He's even paler than I remember, in the bright light of day—less like Jacob Elordi and more like the ghost of a Victorian child who started hitting the gym in the afterlife. The man looks like he's lacking in vitamin D. And is that . . . a pimple on his chin? Maybe he's human, after all.

"You live around here too?" He points with his thumb over his shoulder toward Jonah and Krystal's place. "I was going for coffee—want to join me?"

The offer goes straight to my head, champagne on an empty stomach. But there's no way in hell I'm going back to that coffee shop. *And how can I even be thinking about this when Mom is trapped, and I have to make a plan to get her out?*

"Um, I'd love to, but . . . but I was—I have this—" I let out a deep sigh. "This . . . family thing."

"Oh." He looks like he's trying to parse my words for hidden meanings.

"It's just—" I squint up at him in the bright sun. "Not to be a downer, but there's a lot of things to take care of, still, after my mom . . ."

"Oh God, of course." His brow furrows, and he takes a step closer. "Is there anything I can—?"

"Raincheck for coffee?" I say in a rush, walking backward away from him, sage still stinging my nostrils.

"Gonna hold you to that!" he says jovially, pointing at me as I jog off.

CHAPTER 13

Two and a half months ago, I was on the phone with Mom, talking about some minor disappointment. I don't even remember what, now. I was confident it had drifted into "funny story" territory by that time, but it must have sounded too much like whining to her. She scoffed and said, "Well, most of us don't get what we want in life."

It was so passive-aggressive and loaded, I had to take the bait.

"What's that supposed to mean?"

"Oh, you know." She sighed. "It's not like this is what I expected when I pictured having a daughter."

God, the way she could say things so airily, and they could slice so deep.

"What did you expect, Mom?"

She made a noise that said, *Don't tempt me with a good time!* "You're not going anywhere in your life, Ruby! You're languishing in this entry-level role at a third-tier company—six years without a promotion!"

"Look, I'm trying my best, but—"

"And you're so closed off! You don't socialize! You've always been like that, since you were little. I try so hard to—" Her voice caught. "I'm always trying *so hard* to make people like me. It's how I got this far. Can't you even make an effort?"

You think I don't desperately want people to like me? I wanted to shout. But I knew if I did, I might lose control and start crying, so I bit my tongue instead.

Mom sighed again on the other end of the phone, so far away. "And you're alone there. What about finding someone to take care of you?"

Like that worked out so well for you? I thought, uncharitably, but didn't say. That's another thing she always wanted but didn't get: someone to take care of her.

"Life is harder alone," she went on, and I just wanted to go to sleep then.

"Sure, Mom," I said in a weak little voice. "I'll try."

And that was the last time we talked.

I'm standing in the pink-tiled bathroom at home, spiral notebook pressed against the counter, ballpoint pen frantically working. Mom's in *my* Slack DM. It must be my fault she's trapped at work, but maybe that means I can do something about it. A tear splashes down on the page, and I swipe at my cheek roughly with my palm. *I can't cry, I have too much to do!*

I straighten and review the list, catching a glimpse of myself in the mirror, head covered in curlers. I used to hear people talk about styling hair—someone on TV, a girl at school in passing—and I'd think, *God, isn't life already exhausting enough?* When you can just let your hair sit there, why complicate it? But some basic research suggests that's why my hair is always a frizzy mess. It makes me feel incompetent and itchy, learning that even something growing out of my head is more complicated than I realized.

My right foot is balanced up on the counter, foam holder wedged between my toes, red polish drying. And I read back over the list.

1. BE SOCIAL AND NORMAL

It pained her, the way I was always a bit weird, sharp-edged and awkward, not charming like she wanted.

We had a screaming fight one night in my senior year because I told her I wasn't going to prom, even though she'd been vicariously excited for it. *I work so hard to raise you, and you don't even give me these milestones to look forward to?*

I didn't want to go just to see Greg dancing with someone else. We'd kissed twice in the fall that year, and by spring, we were hanging out with totally different groups of people.

But later that night, hugging my pillow in bed, I thought, *Wow, selfish of you. Couldn't even do this one thing for her when she does so much for you.*

The crumpled high school reunion invitation is nestled between the pages of the notebook, retrieved from where I'd jammed it in the passenger-door pocket of my car.

It's not exactly prom, but it's a chance for something like a do-over. I can go to a function and rewrite high school, make a show of being more like the daughter she wanted back then.

SUB-ITEM: MAKE MORE OF AN EFFORT WITH
YOUR APPEARANCE

That's something Mom was always saying in the mornings before school—a source of constant tension between us. And one time when I said they don't grade on appearance, she replied, *They should if they want to prepare you for life. Every little thing adds up.*

Every little failure can snowball. That was a theme for her.

So now my nails are this shade of tomato, and I'm trying not to smudge them.

2. GO SOMEWHERE IN YOUR LIFE (PROMOTION?)

Mom probably would have been happy—*is* happy?—to see me at TKCORP. But it was basically a lateral move.

3. BE WARM AND PLEASANT AND MAKE PEOPLE LIKE YOU AT WORK

Ugh.

4. BE CLOSER TO FAMILY

Ugh ugh.

When I think about the ways I didn't manage to be the daughter my mother wanted, I remember the look on her face, the weight in her voice, when she'd say, *Why don't you write to your aunt and uncle? Why don't you reach out to your cousins? Why don't you make more of an effort? Family will be there when no one else is.*

Mom was unhappy with me so much of the time—I would put off seeing our family, scared they'd feel the same, if they got a good enough look. But maybe that's the missing piece, her big regret. It's worth investigating, at least.

5. DATE SOMEONE IN A HIGHER TAX BRACKET

Mark Winterson pops into my mind, so unexpectedly glad to see me.

But I'm getting ahead of myself! There's a lot to rule out first.

The doorbell chimes, and I check the app for the Ring that Mom had gotten installed a few years back.

Greg's standing on my front steps holding a casserole dish.

Not now, I'm busy trying to fix all my flaws at once! Come back later!

My leg jiggles and my chest feels tight. But the longer I stare at him on the video screen, the more I think it *would* be nice to see a friendly face.

Then I glance in the mirror and realize I still have hair removal cream smeared all over my upper lip.

I text him one-handed—*just a minute!*—as I hop over to grab some toilet paper and wipe away the burning cream. And I pad through the house to the front door and wave him inside.

"My mom made too much kare-kare," he says, lifting the casserole dish. I'm already salivating, thinking about eating it over rice—the tender beef, string beans, and eggplant, all stewed in a thick peanut sauce.

Greg is staring at me, for some reason, while he slips his shoes off. "Is this a bad time?"

"Why?"

"You, uh—" He gestures around his head, reminding me of the curlers I have on. "Getting ready to go somewhere?"

"Oh, shut up," I say, and he laughs.

"Where can I put . . . ?" He lifts the dish again.

"Oh—oh right. Um—the fridge."

Greg heads for the kitchen, and I follow him. Of course he knows where everything is. It's been a while since he was in my house, and my heart is pounding so uncomfortably.

He finds a place for the food and stares at me some more as he closes the fridge.

"What are you looking at?" I demand.

A small smile spreads on his face as he gestures vaguely above his mouth. "It's a little . . . red here?"

My hand flies reflexively to cover my upper lip, and I drop the notebook that was wedged under my arm.

Greg bends to pick it up before I can.

"Hey!" I grab for it as he starts reading the list, but he holds it up higher, away from me, like we're fourteen again.

He squints at it, trying to decipher my wild handwriting. "Potential sources of unfinished business?"

"I'm trying to rule things out. Like your mom said."

He frowns. *"Date someone in a higher tax bracket?"*

"There are lots of things to rule out first!" I reach feebly for the notebook, but he's still got it raised high. "And . . . I mean, what's a date or two?"

"Not going to lie," Greg says pointedly. "I'm pretty worried about you."

"Why do you suddenly care?" I snap. "You seemed perfectly fine not knowing what was going on with me for years."

Greg's arm droops, and I snatch the notebook back from him.

It's a bad look, letting the venom creep into my tone. I promised myself a long time ago: Pretend nothing happened. That this doesn't bother you so much. Then you won't have to feel pathetic on top of feeling hurt.

Greg's stare skewers me under the weak yellow kitchen light. "Of course I care," he says levelly. "You seemed like you didn't want to talk to me, but . . ." He sighs and runs a hand through his hair. "It's not like I stopped caring about you."

I try to ignore the tingling in my gut. "Why did you tell Morgan there was no story here?"

The corner of Greg's mouth turns up, and I realize I just admitted to eavesdropping. "Didn't want her talking about you." He laughs and shakes his head. "I missed you, Ruby. We were friends for a long time. That doesn't just go away."

It's weird for him to be earnest. The Greg I remember would

try to avoid it whenever possible—deflect with a joke, distract me with a tired smile and a change of subject.

"I know we're not close like that anymore," Greg says slowly. "But it's nice having you back here. And this is a fucked-up situation, and if you think this will help—" He points at the notebook clutched to my chest. "You're not alone here, okay?"

My vision is blurring, heat and moisture pooling in the corners of my eyes.

"Let me help you with this," he says. "Please."

How fucking dare he, when it's so much safer to be mad at him? Who does he think he is?

"Hey." Greg pulls my trembling shoulders closer, folding me into a hug. He must still use the same lemon zest soap he liked in high school. The familiar smell wraps me up, warmed by his own scent underneath, sun and salt and something I can't name. Some things really don't change.

"Shh, shh," he says, because before I realize it, I'm crying into his shoulder, big, ugly, shuddering sobs. "Hey—hey, it's okay, Ruby. It's okay."

I could barely respond to his Slack messages the other day, and now I'm getting snot on his T-shirt?

"Have you . . . talked to her more?" Greg asks tentatively.

I pull back and cross my arms with a sharp sniff. "No."

Every time I try to type something, there are too many things to say, crowding inside my head, and I choke.

"I still don't know how to talk to her." I wipe my face aggressively, trying to recover my dignity. "It's like she never left, that way."

Greg chuckles softly, more air than sound. I feel like shit for how hard it's been to talk to Mom, now that I have something so many grieving daughters would want: a second chance. But it feels less bad, standing in front of someone who knows us both well enough to laugh at that.

I let my head flop backward with exasperation. One of my curlers falls out and rolls away underneath the kitchen table, so Greg crouches to retrieve it.

He takes a few steps closer, depositing the curler in my open palm, and his eyes meet mine. Those irises I still know by heart. The particular pattern of black flowering out amid the dark brown, the placement of the gold flecks.

"Tell me how I can help?" he asks. "With your list."

My heart swells uncomfortably, too big for the shrunken place it usually fills in my chest.

It reminds me of the time he came over in middle school, when Mom had just bought a new dresser from IKEA. One moment he was peering at it curiously, and the next he was sitting on our floor with all the parts laid out around him, assembling it for us.

Sure, Greg made a mistake ten years ago: kissing his best friend when he wasn't that into her. Hasn't the statute of limitations on that crime expired by now? I should be able to let it go.

"Okay, um . . ." My hand goes nervously to my head, and the curlers rattle. "If you really want to . . . you could come with me to this?"

I slide the crumpled invitation out of the notebook and pass it to him.

"Be my wingman," I add too fast.

Greg's smile flickers for a second as he looks at the paper in his hand. "Sure, Ruby," he says, and that easy grin I remember comes back. "We can do that."

CHAPTER 14

The lights in the gym swirl, multicolored. Around the room, people are loudly recognizing one another and embracing.

It's strange returning to the scene of so many old insecurities—where I had PE and worried about how frumpy I looked in gym clothes, and where I stood around during dances, wondering who to talk to.

So many people from high school work at TKCORP, this might as well be a work outing. Minhee from Public Relations is catching up with Sergio from Data Analytics. Matt from Nuisance Abatement, Laura from Transportation Solutions, and Priya from Design are laughing in a cluster to my right. I'm vaguely on a "saying hi in the hall" basis with all of them, but the idea of making small talk still fills me with anxiety.

I straighten my shoulders and lift my head. It feels unnatural, like my muscles are tied with a rubber band and they'll just snap back again. Standing up straight never seems to stick.

Mom always said it's smart to *keep a low profile,* that it's dangerous to *be a tall poppy.* Maybe my body took those things literally? Without thinking about it, I shrink myself, curling in protectively.

But this dress isn't meant for that—it's strappy, floral purple, clinging in all the right places. I measured myself from every angle before I ordered it online, and unlike all my work clothes, it fits like a glove.

Greg and I arrived together, but I've lost him already. Some wingman he is.

He's on the other side of the gym, deep in conversation with a group of people from different TKCORP departments. And is he handing out *business cards*? God, who even is he?

"Ruby!" someone exclaims, and I turn around.

It's Anna Del Amo. She moved to New York to work in journalism after college, and I'd see her around occasionally, one of those "catching up over lunch every two years" kinds of relationships.

"Anna!" It's a relief to see a friendly face. "Let's take a photo?"

I need something to show Mom, after all. Anna leans in, and I stretch my arm as far as it will go for a selfie. I never know what to do with my mouth when it's time for a picture—posing makes me tense, and by the time it gets taken I look scared and constipated. But I give it my best.

"How have you been, girl?" Anna nudges me playfully.

"Oh, the same." Hearing myself say that makes me feel slightly hysterical. "How's New York?"

She lets out a big puff of air. "It's a grind, trying to freelance. If things get bad, I can always sell my eggs."

Steve the Project Manager drifts over to us and strikes up a conversation with Anna, just as a man in a tan suit stops in front of me.

Mark Winterson? I think for a split second, before my eyes focus and I recognize the guy who made me laugh during every chem lab in junior year.

"Ruby Ocampo!" he exclaims, grinning. "Oh my God."

"Eddie Ortega! As I live and breathe." I'm astonished anyone remembers me, given how invisible I felt in school.

I point to my phone and he plucks it from my hand, holding it out with his longer arms to take the photo. His face is so close to mine, I can feel his stubble on my cheek.

"It's been a million years!" Eddie says. I feel buzzed, and I haven't even had a drink yet. "What are you doing these days?"

I make a raspberry with my lips. "I don't know half the time, honestly. How about you?"

Eddie bobs his head up and down and takes another sip of his beer. "Working construction. Good union job. Not fancy or anything, but—" He leans over and whispers how much he makes, and my eyes widen. The *DATE SOMEONE IN A HIGHER TAX BRACKET* to-do list item flashes before me.

No, I need to prioritize here, rule out one thing at a time. Think of the scientific method! This is *BE SOCIAL AND NORMAL (SUB-ITEM: MAKE MORE OF AN EFFORT WITH YOUR APPEARANCE)* night. And the fact that he just told me his salary after years of not seeing him does make Eddie instantly less charming somehow.

"Oh, um—" I squint and make a vague gesture. "I think I see . . . someone. Nice talking to you, Eddie."

I push my way through the crowd, plop down in the bottom row of the bleachers, and upload the photos I've taken tonight into the haunted Slack DM—the ones with Anna and Eddie, plus a group photo I crowded into with Greg when we first arrived.

ruby.ocampo:
Went to my high school reunion tonight! Nice to see everyone.

There's no reply, and my chest feels tight—half hoping it worked, half scared that it did, because there's still so much I never figured out how to say.

But then, at the bottom of the window, I see that sampa-guita72 is typing.

sampaguita72:
Such a short dress!
Is that Greg with you?

ruby.ocampo:
Yeah, it's his high school reunion too!

A familiar irritation climbs up my spine, like Mom is giving me her classic stink-eye as I slink in the front door. How can I reframe this to give her maximum peace of mind?

ruby.ocampo:
I'm pretty sure Eddie Ortega was flirting with me? You won't believe his take-home pay!

She doesn't say anything for a while, and I can just picture her, hair up in curlers, arms crossed, chewing over what I just said.

ruby.ocampo:
Do you feel any different?
Do you see a light??

sampaguita72:
Why should I be any different?
What are you talking about?

It was silly to think one night of being slightly more charming and standing up straight could be enough to convince her she can rest easy. Maybe I have to do something she can see—something in Slack, in front of her. Of course! How dumb could I be?

My head lolls back, and over my shoulder I see Greg at the top of the bleachers, holding his hand up in a little wave. So I clamber up there in my precarious heels and sit next to him, relaxing into my usual slouch.

"How are you feeling?" he asks, taking a drink of his beer and tilting it toward me.

"Mostly numb?" I accept the green bottle, condensation cool between my fingers, and it tastes so refreshing that before I realize it, I've polished off the whole thing. "I feel bad for her."

Greg's shoulders shake, laughing at me. "You were thirsty."

"It's stressful trying to please a ghost, you know?" I wipe my mouth on the back of my hand and burp. "Ugh, God, my feet are killing me." I wrench off my strappy heels and wiggle my liberated toes.

Greg leans forward and stares at me wistfully, like I remind him of something that makes him sad. "Do you really think changing your life is what she wanted?"

I scoff, hackles up in an instant. "I'm not exactly living well right now."

"But shouldn't you . . . move in a direction that you wanted? I've been thinking—the list you made . . . it's all . . ."

"What's your point?" The spinning colored lights are making me motion sick.

"Like you're doing an impression of someone else."

"Don't they say fake it till you make it?" I snap, standing too fast, instantly lightheaded. "We can't all be naturals at everything!"

"Ruby, wait—" Greg reaches for my arm, but I'm already running barefoot back onto the shiny wooden gym floor. I could use another drink.

I'm standing in the long line for one when somebody taps my shoulder.

"Hey, no shoes, no service."

Somehow, this time it actually *is* Mark Winterson.

"Hey, Ruby." His face lights up, open and boyish. My favorite unserious distraction.

Every minor encounter with this dude is super unnerving. The way he lets me get away with being totally bizarre to him, reacts like it's some kind of admirable quality, even—it gives me a buzz. It's addictive.

I narrow my eyes. "Did you even go here?"

"Oh, I, uh—I didn't, actually, but my little sister did. She had this whole teenage rebellion thing, demanded to go to public school, be among the people."

Of course he'd be a private school kid.

He points to the freckled brunette chatting people up as she serves drinks, and *oh yeah, Sandra Winterson! I remember.* There actually is quite a strong family resemblance.

"She's on the committee that put this thing on, and they were disorganized, and she called me to do an emergency beer run, and . . ." He stops himself with a bashful grin. "Sorry, I'm rambling. Yeah, I didn't go here. But I'm glad you did, so I could run into you." Mark Winterson raises his bottle, like he's toasting me. "Actually—hold that thought."

He pulls me out of the line with the gentlest tug on my elbow, and my stomach swoops at that light touch. Then he walks behind the table, says something to his sister, and comes back with a beer for me.

"Wow, full service," I say.

"No shoes required," he says, clinking his bottle against mine and taking a long swig. He loosens his tie one-handed, and more of his neck peeks out beneath his shirt collar.

Is he . . . nervous? The idea that I might fluster him makes me feel strangely accomplished.

I can just hear my roommate back in New York—what she told me once, in her flat tone, when I was debriefing about a mediocre date that followed a streak of very promising texting. *Ruby, you just want someone to be obsessed with you.*

It stung because it was true. If someone is obsessed with me, maybe it means I'm doing something right, without trying, even when I always feel like a failure.

"How was the family thing?" he asks quietly, and his eyes flick up and down, taking me in.

Such a short dress!

"Oh." I force a weary smile. "I guess it's less of a discrete *thing*, and more of an ongoing series of tasks. But thanks for asking."

"Well, I mean it," Mark Winterson says, taking a step closer. "If there's anything I can ever do to help, let me know?"

Over his shoulder, I see Greg talking to Rebecca Turner, the girl he actually ended up taking to prom. She's Rebecca from HR now, also a TKCORP employee.

Suddenly it's as though the cinder-block walls of the gym have time travel properties. I can feel myself melting into a slouch. And Greg's back is really . . . *filling out* that suit? It looks broader than the last time I saw it, somehow. Must be all those lunchtime gym trips.

I rotate my shoulders, turning my attention back to the man in front of me. "So, what do you do all day, Mark Winterson?" I raise my bottle to him. "Walk me through it?"

He makes a circular gesture with his beer-holding hand. "Taking meetings. Talking strategy. Finding ways to boost our sales. And learning how things work here—keeping an eye on those margins, identifying opportunities to streamline operations . . ." He shakes his head. "Not that interesting, really."

Mark Winterson takes another sip of his drink, and his eyes lock on mine. "Weren't we going to get coffee sometime?"

DATE SOMEONE IN A HIGHER TAX BRACKET flashes like a neon sign before me. Maybe the scientific method isn't that useful in this fluid situation.

"Friendly, professional coffee, obviously," he adds.

Okay, we can start there.

"Yeah! I'd love to!" I say louder than necessary. "Have your people contact my people."

Behind Mark Winterson, Rebecca is still talking to Greg, but for some reason he's staring at me. And I see now that he has my shoes, dangling from two fingers.

"Mark! I need some help here!" Sandra Winterson calls from the drinks table.

"Oh, I should—" Mark Winterson jabs a thumb over his shoulder.

"Right, of course!"

"But we'll be in touch." He points at me again as he walks backward toward his sister.

Big on pointing, this guy! It's a bit douchey and weirdly endearing at the same time (*confusing!*). Cartoonish, but at least it's decisive—unlike Greg was back then, not even having the courtesy to reject me directly. At least Mark Winterson is direct. I'm talking to *you,* my eyes are on *you. You you you.*

Greg drifts over, swinging my shoes. "I think I'll head out?" he says, handing them to me. "Unless you need me for anything."

"I'll go too," I say, balancing while I resecure the straps. And when I start to tip over—I'm a total lightweight, and that second beer did me in—Greg steadies me with a hand on my back.

A burst of memory rushes in so fast it gives me vertigo—*my sun-flooded living room on an afternoon after school, Greg's hand on my back, the other in my hair—*

I straighten quickly, walking with purpose to the parking lot, and Greg catches up, falling into step beside me. The silence is uncomfortably thick.

We reach our cars, parked beside each other—there's his red 2005 Acura RSX, still well maintained and beloved.

Greg hesitates before reaching for his car door. "You know what 'streamline operations' means, right?"

"You were eavesdropping?"

"No, I—" He makes a throaty sound and catches himself. "I mean, yeah, maybe."

My chest warms up, but I give him an unimpressed look. "Okay, why don't you enlighten me?"

When we were younger, Greg had a habit of talking to me about books I hadn't read, like I would have something interesting to say about them anyway. Until one day I snapped at him: *Why are you always asking me questions you know I can't answer?* And he mumbled, *Because I value your opinion.*

But this time he glances away, toward the far end of the parking lot, like he's fighting himself on how much to say.

"You're smart," he says finally. "You'll figure it out."

The whole thing annoys me, so I try to forget about it. Instead, that interaction with Mark Winterson loops in my head for the whole drive home. It makes me groan out loud. At one point, at a red light, I make a long, quiet *Aaaaaaa!* sound.

When I park in my driveway and check my phone, there's a calendar invite. *Coffee with Mark* for Wednesday afternoon.

CHAPTER 15

On Monday morning at work, the problem of Mom's unfinished business churns through my mind until I feel physically sick and my neck aches from holding my head up.

The way time has been moving lately, coffee with Mark Winterson seems far off, and who knows where it will lead? For now, I have to focus on list item #2: *GO SOMEWHERE IN YOUR LIFE (PROMOTION?)*

I keep pinging Erica, offering to do things. And I'm trying to be extra responsive in the public channels, volunteering whenever anyone says they need help with a task.

ruby.ocampo:
Anything else I can help you with? I finished that memo, it's ready for you in the drive
How are you doing on coffee? Need anything from downstairs?

Mom should be able to see these, the way she was spying on my chats with—

"Don't be late for the meeting, Ruby!" Erica says, popping up next to my cubicle again. "You seem so scattershot this morning. We're discussing our Q2 goals."

I deflate a little, getting up from my desk and joining the others as we file into the conference room, each of us cradling a laptop in one arm.

Erica dims the lights, fires up her PowerPoint, and extends a long, retractable pointer. "Now, you all know we underperformed last quarter," she says. "And I have some theories about that."

She clicks through to her next slide and taps some images of text with red circles around clusters of words. "Our copy was dull, it was flat, it was *nothing special.* We need to step up our game."

When her back is turned, Al rolls his eyes.

He sees me looking and smiles, like we're sharing an inside joke.

A DM appears on my laptop screen.

al.jones:
Have you ever considered working harder?

I have to stifle a laugh. I should be listening, but this little moment of unity against Erica gives me a rush of serotonin.

ruby.ocampo:
Crazy idea. Total game-changer.

The corner of Al's mouth turns up slightly, even as his eyes stay fixed on Erica while she clicks through her presentation, moving on to a section about using more *dynamic verbs.*

al.jones:
I mean, we're not the ones making the ad placements. Maybe she should lecture the person deciding the strategy.

Across the room, Morgan snickers, and Erica shoots her a glare. She must be DM-ing, too.

ruby.ocampo:
Like does she want my copy to tap dance?

al.jones:
Paint your house and shine your shoes, while we're at it.

Erica switches to a slide about *creating a consistent vibe.* To my left, Sarah's sliding down deeper into her chair, looking like she has indigestion. So I take a chance and message her:

ruby.ocampo:
Her vibe is consistently rancid

For a weightless second, my stomach clenches, because what if it turns out Sarah actually really likes Erica?

But then I hear something. It's subtle—I would miss it if I weren't sitting right next to her—but I'm pretty sure Sarah snorts.

A skull-emoji reaction appears under my message, and Slack tells me sarah.ng is typing.

sarah.ng:
so consistent

Her phone buzzes a few times, sitting on the table between us. Out of the corner of my eye, I see Message from Greg De Leon appear on her screen a few times.

Interesting.

A message from Mom pops up on my computer, and my scalp prickles with dread.

sampaguita72:
Don't talk about your boss like that in here! What if they read it?

Then they'll see I've been carrying on a lengthy correspondence with my dead mother, too. But okay, sure.

ruby.ocampo:
Sorry, Mom.

I minimize Slack and try to pay attention as Erica walks us through a chart breaking down the building blocks of strong promotional copy. But the next time we're in a meeting and Al pantomimes painting a wall when Erica's back is turned, I have to think it was worth the risk.

CHAPTER 16

At night, it's painfully obvious this house is too big for one person. The silence is so loud, it drains all my energy the moment I get home.

I don't know how Mom could make whole meals after work. I pull together some rice and sardines—my comfort food, the thing Mom would make whenever she was exhausted. Which meant she made it a lot when I was a kid, in the years after Dad left.

After I wash the dishes, I collapse onto the couch and google Mark Winterson again.

I keep thinking about how he looked at me at the reunion. It's been a long time since I felt desirable—a couple years, at least? It's hard to remember. All the dead-end app dates that may as well have been job interviews blur together.

Apparently Mark Winterson launched and sold his first company in college. He's on the board of several philanthropic organizations. One of the first autocomplete suggestions for his name is *mark winterson girlfriend,* followed by *mark winterson height,* which makes me snort.

sampaguita72:
Ruby, what are you doing tonight?
I hope you're not staying out late

That must mean she can't see what I'm doing on my personal phone. So that's a relief, at least.

sampaguita72:
Roobs, I see why Erica said your copy was missing something
I see where you went wrong
You have to—

I swipe the notification away before I can read the rest. We used to do this when she was alive. She'd dissect all my failures from the day to help me improve—ask me about every little thing my boss said, every sour note, turn it over, examine it. Like we could prevent more of them by doing that, eradicate disappointment at the source.

Without knowing exactly what she said, I write back:

ruby.ocampo:
Okay, I'll try!

I take a deep breath, hold and release it, guilt surging raw through my veins.

A knock on the door outside makes me jump, and on the Ring, I see Greg standing on the front steps, holding another casserole dish.

I try to channel some Greg-style nonchalance before I open the door. "Seeing an awful lot of you lately."

He slips off his shoes, brushes past me, and heads for the kitchen. "You shouldn't be alone with a ghost."

"She must be haunting the server, right?" I trail behind him, trying not to think anything in particular about the width of his back. "My house *feels* haunted, but technically the haunting is cloud-based."

Greg closes the fridge and grabs the phone out of my hand. "You know what I mean. Too much screen time." His eyebrows go up. "You're googling Mark Winterson?"

I snatch it back from him. "It's normal to google the people you work with. It's just, like, due diligence."

"Sure, you work *with* him." Greg plops down on the couch and peers at me over the back. "Is he . . . your person in a higher tax bracket?"

I cross my arms. "Why, you don't approve?"

"Is he your type?" He looks at me searchingly. "Or is he your *mom*'s type?"

I know what he's talking about—how badly Mom wanted me to end up with a rich white guy. It's uncomfortable. She never said it in so many words, but a clear pattern emerged from the examples she picked out, whenever she'd pointedly say, *That's the type of guy you should be dating!*

Mom had some kind of complex about being Filipino—an ugly thing I never wanted to examine too directly, like a floor stain you throw some carpet over. She'd avoid the sun, wear whitening cream, strive to stay as pale as she could manage. Sometimes when people asked where she was from, she'd tell them, "Taiwan." (I guess, to her, that was somehow a step up?) Tita Wendy overheard once, elbowed her, and said with a belly laugh, "You've never even been to Taiwan!" And then they both laughed so hard, friends despite themselves, an odd couple.

But I don't feel the same way Mom did. If anything, growing up around Mom and Greg and Tita Wendy, I wanted to be more like them. If I disliked something about myself, it was the part that looked like my dad, the part that made me "not quite the same, but close." (Just ask Erica how close.) Being Filipino always felt like a positive thing to me. Something aspirational I could never fully earn.

And a snide comment Greg made once, years ago, about the white guys I dated in college also bothered me. *Let me live! It's hard enough to find someone you like who likes you back!* Even aside from the whole *I was kind of in love with you and you broke my heart* of it all.

"I don't have a type!" I protest. "He's kind of fun."

"Okay! I'm just saying—" Greg faces the TV again and hugs a throw pillow. "Dude seems like he'd talk to you for twenty minutes about the texture of his business cards."

Greg's phone starts vibrating, and he frowns at the screen. "I should get this," he says, hopping off the couch and going into the far corner of the kitchen, by the back door.

I crane my neck to peek at him. He's talking in a low voice, and his smile gets wider, like the person on the other end said something funny.

He's gesturing with his hands, looking like he has new enthusiasm for life.

Is he seeing someone?

Greg ends the call and I turn back around, pretending I've been engrossed in my phone the whole time. He climbs over the back of the couch and lands next to me.

"Who was that?" I ask, eyes on my phone.

"Oh, just, um—my mom. Reminding me about a thing this weekend." His hand goes to the back of his neck like it does when he's nervous. I recognize it from when he'd lie to his mom in front of me, back when we were close.

He's definitely seeing someone.

Does he assume it would hurt my feelings? Does he feel *bad* for me? God, I hate that.

"So what's next?" Greg asks. "On your list."

I grab my own pillow to hug. "You seemed to think it was a bad idea. The whole list thing."

He gives me a long, steady look. "I'll admit I don't love the concept. Number five seems like a bit much."

"There's a lot to rule out first."

Greg goes quiet for a while, like he's arguing with himself in his head. He did this when we were younger. Whenever we were having a tense conversation, he'd sit there silent, like he was composing the whole thing he wanted to say—and then he'd scrap it and make a dumb joke instead.

"Do you have something to add?" I ask testily.

"If you think this is the best thing . . ." Those gold-flecked eyes turn on me. "I want to help your mom move on."

Up close like this, I can see all his old familiar imperfections. Scar high across the bridge of his nose from when he fell off his bike. Tiny dent on his cheek from when we were nine and he got chickenpox, and Mom forced me to go over so I could catch it from him. Small dark mark on his hand where a firework singed him, one Fourth of July.

I glance at the version of the list that I've transposed into my notes app.

"Do you think I ruled the first thing out?" I chew on my thumbnail. *"Be social and normal and make more of an effort with your appearance."*

"You seem social and normal to me." His head bobs contemplatively. "And, um. Good appearance, as always."

He doesn't mean anything by it, but I have to smile despite myself. "Then the next thing is getting a promotion."

"Hmm." Greg rests his head on the back of the couch, peering up at me and smiling like this is all a joke. But that's how he is—he holds his life lightly.

When we were in high school, his mom begged me to get him to study because he was failing everything except math. Numbers always just made sense to him. (*Must be nice!* I thought more than once, staying up late sweating over my precalc homework.)

"Is this all a joke to you?" I asked, standing in the doorway of his room when I came over to tutor him.

"Life is too serious to take it too seriously," he said, barely glancing up from the book about housing policy that he was reading. I was surprised that he ended up at TKCORP, in the end, working such a sensible, boring job.

"I mean, I'm sure you're great at what you do," he says now. "But you've been here for a few weeks? Maybe it's not realistic that you'd get promoted yet."

"Right, but—what if I can at least convince Mom that I'm in line for it? If I can show her . . ."

"And Erica's tough," he adds. He listened to me complain about her years ago, long before I worked here—how she would never give Mom a shot in her department. "And it's not exactly all under your control. Moving up."

"What are the things under my control?" I cut in. "Maybe if I show Mom how hard I'm trying—that I'm taking initiative, getting in Erica's good graces—"

"Like if you had a project." Greg nods to himself. "You could volunteer to take on more responsibility? Try to make her life easier."

"I've been raising my hand for everything I can."

"That's good, but . . . maybe a more personalized approach would help?" He chews on his bottom lip. "What stresses her out the most? Where can you swoop in and offer something?"

"Okay," I say, surprised that Greg has ever given any thought to getting ahead in the workplace. "Much to consider. Thanks."

Greg tucks his feet up under him, pulls the remote from between the cushions, and turns on the TV.

"Oh sure, make yourself at home."

"I thought we could watch something for a bit. Spending all night and day thinking about"—he drops his voice to a whisper, like my mom will be able to overhear—"*a ghost,* it can't be great for your mental health. Maybe you could use more distractions."

He puts on an old episode of *The Simpsons,* like we've

slipped back in time ten years. We sit next to each other largely in silence, making jokes here and there. It's been so long since we did nothing together.

But my body didn't forget how comfortable I am with him, even though all this time has passed. It's like slipping into an old familiar sweatshirt. After a few minutes, it feels like we do this all the time.

It makes me remember something Greg said, back before we kissed. We were talking about the future after high school, and he asked me, "What would you do if you didn't have to work?"

It gave me heartburn. *As though it's even worth considering!* "I don't know, what would you do?"

He shrugged. "Nothing. Hang out. I think hanging out might be my purpose in life."

I could feel my stress rising, like I needed to clap my hand over his mouth to stop Mom from hearing about his *lack of ambition*! And in the years we weren't talking, I'd see him post about the lying-flat movement and how he doesn't dream of labor.

But there's such an easiness to him now, beside me on the couch. Maybe this is his calling.

In his lap, his phone buzzes a few times again, and peeking at his screen, I see multiple notifications saying Message from Sarah Ng.

Oh. Is that why he's always on our floor? Coming up to make Sarah laugh?

I try to stay very still until the feeling passes. Mom is right—I'm too old for this shit.

Eventually it seems like Greg's fallen asleep beside me, and I watch him for a while.

Why did I want more from him when this is so comfortable? So what if he's not attracted to me? *Why can't you be satis-*

fied with what you have? Mom said that a lot. *You always seem dissatisfied. You don't know how lucky you are.*

Then my own phone buzzes. A message from my cousin in San Diego.

Trisha:
are you coming on sunday?

"You texting Mark Winterson?" Greg elbows me, suddenly awake again.

"Yes, he's proposing marriage right now." I tap out a reply to Trisha with my thumbs: i don't think i can this time, but please say hi to everyone for me.

"With a text!" Greg clutches at his heart dramatically. "And they say romance is dead."

I poke the side of his head, and he bends way over, exaggerated, like I'm stronger than I am. "Go sleep at your own house."

He rubs his eyes, and I can feel the jolt of his laugh through the couch. "Give yourself, like, thirty minutes without looking at your phone before you go to sleep, okay?"

It annoys me and warms me up inside at the same time. He actually thinks Mom and I are staying up late talking? Does he think we braid each other's hair too?

"Thanks for your concern," I say, getting up to see him out. And as I watch him go, I tell myself over and over like an incantation: *I can be satisfied with what I have.*

CHAPTER 17

When I come in on Wednesday morning, the first thing I hear is Morgan's voice carrying across the office.

"Aww, you're blushing!" she exclaims. "Just look at you."

Sarah's standing in her cubicle, showing Morgan some flowers—yellow roses in a clear vase—and looking ecstatic. There's a bow around them, and a tiny heart-shaped card.

My stomach drops like when the old elevator misses our floor on the first try.

"Very romantic," Morgan says, leaning against Sarah's cubicle divider. "Ah, to be young again!"

Sarah hides her face in her hands and groans. "Not to be dramatic, but I think I'm in love!"

I'd stopped in my tracks by the entrance, and I realize I'm staring. I turn on my heel before they see me and head for the bathroom. I'll be fine once I splash my face with cold water.

But before I can reach for the tap, Erica's voice wafts up from one of the stalls, freezing me in place. "This presentation to leadership next week, it's—" She sniffles. Is she *crying*?

My startled face stares back at me in the long mirror above the sink. The lighting is aggressive here, everything so bright it reminds me of an ad for tooth products—pristine long white countertop studded with sinks, white tile walls, a row of off-white stall doors behind me.

"They need me to present this data." Erica blows her nose loudly. "I don't know how to—I'm so—" The person on the other line seems to be cutting in here, talking for a while, and Erica responds, "But I'm in over my head. Drowning."

Wow, relatable. Strange to feel that way about Erica for a second.

"Like what the fuck is a pivot table!" she adds, chased with another hefty sniff. "And I don't have time to learn! Everyone is so sloppy here, I have my hands full walking them through their mistakes."

Well, that second was short-lived!

"And public speaking is bad enough, but—" She blows her nose again, and I briefly picture a sad little elephant sitting on the toilet seat. "Okay, fine, I'll drink some water. And breathe, yes. I'll see you at home."

The stall door opens before my brain can catch up, and Erica walks out, smoothing the wrinkles in her shirt.

We lock eyes in the mirror, and the surprise registers on her face. She moves to the sink two down from me and starts washing her hands.

"I can help you with that!" I blurt out. "I—I can make the annoying deck you don't want to make."

She glares at me in the mirror.

"Sorry, I didn't mean to eavesdrop, I—I couldn't help but overhear—" I take a deep breath and force my shoulders down. "Erica. You work so hard. You shouldn't have to do everything yourself. You can delegate. I want to help, really! I promise—I'll take care of it. It's as good as done."

As I babble on, Erica folds a paper towel, wets the center,

and runs it under her eyes to get rid of the mascara smudges. "Are you good with Excel?"

"Oh . . . yeah! Absolutely."

I've used Excel before. And I can always google it. How hard can it be?

"All right, if you insist," she says, fixing her hair. "I need it Friday morning. Drop-dead deadline nine a.m. I'll send you my notes."

I give her my brightest smile. "No problem."

"All right, then." She gives me a last skeptical glance as she opens the bathroom door. "Thanks, Ruby."

I check my phone on the way back to my desk, and there's a text from Greg: a cute rabbit with pom-poms, saying the word *FIGHTING!* It makes me laugh out loud, it's so unexpected from him.

But then I pass Sarah's cubicle and spot a figurine of that same rabbit sitting next to her monitor. She's not at her desk, and—after glancing from side to side to check the coast is clear—I lean into her cubicle and read the note on her flowers. It's typed, the kind you request when you place your order.

> Because you said no one ever sent you
> flowers before, and I wanted to change that.
>
> Love,
> G

I jump back like the card stung me. They're at the "love" stage already? I thought Greg got out of any relationship before it reached that point. The last time I checked in on his love life, he'd had a long string of girlfriends who lasted a few months each.

Maybe he's matured since then? Good for him, I guess?

Yes! I'm happy for them. I shouldn't be thinking about this, anyway—I have too much to do.

For the rest of the day, I have three spreadsheets Erica sent me minimized in one corner of my screen, and her notes open in a tab. They're dense, chaotic, filled with asides and shorthand. It takes me an hour just to figure out why there are three spreadsheets.

I mean to toggle back to her deck between things, but my regular tasks are ballooning, and I keep getting pulled away. Some copy I thought I finished turns into five rounds of revision, pinging back and forth between me and Erica. Just when I think I'm in the clear, another email lands.

It's a subject line only, no body: *Copy isn't popping. Try again.*

And as I'm sprinting through the day, I keep anxiously checking my calendar, watching the bar for the present time inch closer to *Coffee with Mark.*

CHAPTER 18

Apparently by coffee, Mark Winterson meant boba. He takes me to a new place in the office park, the one I'd avoided because it looked expensive. We order at a shiny kiosk that has you tap through twelve screens of options to customize your order.

He gets a classic milk tea with less sugar—not wanting to get out over his skis in front of an audience, maybe. At the cheaper boba place Greg and I went to in high school, I'd always get the chamoy mango. But I get self-conscious, thinking about potential comments Mark Winterson could make, so I order a simple strawberry fruit tea instead.

He seems quieter today. That bouncy energy between us from before is missing, and I suddenly have no idea what to say to him. We stand there awkwardly for a few minutes, waiting for our drinks.

When they come up at the counter, he gets them both and motions toward the door. "It's a nice day, let's take a walk."

We fall in step beside each other, crossing the grassy quad between the gray buildings.

"Looks like you want to ask me something," he says.

"Umm, why did you want to see me? Is this *the next time, when we talk about work*?"

"Doesn't have to be." He sips his drink. "I just like talking to you."

I bite the inside of my lip, trying not to smile too wide.

Mark Winterson nods to himself, like what I asked is worth serious reflection. "I think your perspective is refreshing. You seem so . . . genuine." He gives me a meaningful look. "Like a good person."

A sharp laugh escapes from me before I can stop it. That's the last thing I feel like these days.

He sits down on a bench at the side of the footpath and peers up at me, a furrow between his patrician brows. "Is that funny?"

I shake my head and sit down next to him. "Just bold of you to assume."

"Any other questions?" He eyes me as he takes a sip of his tea. "You can ask me anything, I'm an open book."

Well, now I have to come up with *something.*

"What would you name a dog?"

He laughs like that's the last thing in the world he would have expected. "Is this a test?"

"Yes."

"You're no-bullshit. I like that."

I'm out of my mind right now, is what I am.

He rests his chin on his fist, imitating *The Thinker.* "Ralph," he decides after some consideration.

I press my lips together, the corners of my mouth turned down in a "not bad" face. "I'll allow it."

"What else've you got?" He crosses his legs, boba cup hanging lazily between his fingers.

"If you could have dinner with anyone, living or dead, who would you pick?"

"Jack Welch," he says without hesitation.

The old GE CEO? I think Mom had a copy of his book. I still remember the cover: a balding man in a white shirt and yellow tie, *WINNING* printed across the front.

Mark Winterson seems to take my silence as disapproval. "Don't get me wrong, he doesn't sound like a nice guy, but he was an icon. And you can't argue with his results—the way GE's stock price went through the roof."

"Are *you* a nice guy?" I ask.

He considers this for a long moment, and his gaze flits back to the grass. "That's for you to decide."

Morgan comes walking by, heading to the salad place on the other side of the campus, and Mark Winterson raises his drink at her.

Great, I think, waving at Morgan, *now the entire office is going to hear about this.*

"Anything else?" He's still giving me that amused, indulgent look, waiting for my next question. He's so attractive, it makes me nauseous. That tightness between my shoulder blades is really fighting my new resolve to stand up straight.

In some ways this is a terrible idea. The power imbalance is certainly not ideal. But my lizard brain takes in his beautiful face and thinks, *Maybe maybe maybe.* The way his eyebrows slope upward toward the center, making him look good-natured and kind of sleepy. The way his expression seems to get fuzzed out and unfocused when he's staring at me like that.

"So what did you mean when you said you're working on streamlining operations?"

"TKCORP is stuck in the past." He gestures with his non-boba-holding hand, fingers splayed out, a ring on his index finger catching the light. "Frozen in amber. Like it's still in Fordism or something. A bygone form of capitalism."

I nod like I know what that means.

"I'm looking for ways to bring us into the twenty-first century, big and small. Rethink how we do things."

I take a long drink and consider that, bobbing my head. "Are you telling me you're a *disruptor*?"

He leans his elbows on his knees and glances sideways at me. "Figured you'd roast me if I said it like that, but . . ."

I can barely tamp down my smile. "Damn, one step ahead of me."

"I'm looking for some low-hanging fruit to start. Small wins." He waves his cup for emphasis. "What do you think about moving to Microsoft Teams?"

I inhale so violently, a clump of boba gets sucked into my windpipe and I start coughing.

What is going to happen to Mom, then?

"Whoa, whoa!" He thumps my back unhelpfully.

And oh shit, this thing is really stuck in there! I'm flailing, struggling to breathe. *What an undignified way to die this would be!*

Mark Winterson hands me a napkin, and I hack the boba cluster out into it.

"Wow," he says, shoulders shaking with a barely suppressed laugh. "Between the two of us, I assumed I'd be the one to choke on boba."

"MARK WINTERSON, YOU CANNOT MOVE US TO MICROSOFT TEAMS!" I shout as loud as my croaky lungs will let me.

"All right, all right!" His hands are up, placating. "Didn't realize it meant that much to you! Okay, then!"

I wave a hand vaguely and swipe at my eyes.

"Sorry that suggestion was so distressing," he says with a weak laugh, and leans back again, studying me curiously while I'm burning with embarrassment.

"Why do you always call me Mark Winterson?" He gives me a pointed look. "First and last."

"It just . . . rolls off the tongue."

He holds my gaze too long for comfort. "Does it?"

Butterflies kick up in my stomach, and a distant voice in my head says, *Really? That's what gets you going?*

"You know who you look a little bit like?" I blurt out, because he's still staring at me, and my brain has vacated the premises. I sip sheepishly on my drink.

"Jacob Elordi?" he says, and I nearly do a spit take.

"Wow, okay." My laugh sounds husky, post-choking. "And you're modest too."

"Nooo, I just—" Mark Winterson chuckles nervously, a notable vibe shift. "I've gotten that before. Ran into him at Equinox once."

Of course it would be Equinox.

"Everyone there, like, pressured us into taking a selfie together."

"Pics or it didn't happen."

He sighs and searches in his phone, then hands it to me. The differences between them stand out more, in side-by-side comparison. For one thing, Mark Winterson is shorter.

He scoffs and looks down. "Anyway, it was embarrassing. I switched gyms after."

I swish the ice around in my cup. "Oh yeah, relatable. Hate when that happens."

"He's, uh—" He smiles, trying to recover his jokey tone. "Significantly more Australian than me."

"Significantly." I nod. "Sounds serious. He should get that checked out."

Mark Winterson laughs so genuinely he looks like a different person, neither Elordi nor a Victorian child but a secret third thing. Weird how faces are dynamic like that. Hard to pin down.

CHAPTER 19

The next morning, I wake up flooded with adrenaline and dread, wondering if Mom will still be in Slack, or if something I've done has already freed her.

I haven't figured out how to tell her about Mark Winterson. Will he even want to talk to me again? Not exactly my finest moment, in retrospect—asking him a series of bizarre questions, shouting down his idea, and hacking my lungs out in front of him.

But maybe Mom's seen how I'm working hard? I've been messaging Erica questions about the deck.

I have to check somehow, so I write:

ruby.ocampo:

Good morning, Mom!

I feel so torn, lying there, hoping she won't write back, wanting her to pass on, roiling in guilt that I'm rooting for her to be gone forever. Blaming myself for not making more of the chance I have to talk to her, while I can—but every time I think about it, I run into the same mental walls that I did when she was alive.

sampaguita72:
Good morning, Roobs
How did you sleep?

We make some small talk as I get ready for work. I pick up the phone every few minutes, between washing my face, putting on makeup, brushing my teeth. We don't say anything real, like always. But it does feel like she's still here.

I'm so spacey, driving to work. I feel a bit miserable and weirdly more alive at the same time—all colors more vibrant, senses sharpened—as I walk through the lobby and swipe in with the pass that dangles around my neck.

In the office, my ears perk up at the sound of whispering. Somehow it's always caught my attention, the *pspsps* that signals someone's telling a secret—going back to when I was a kid, and Mom and Tita Wendy would lower their voices, hovering in a doorway while they thought Greg and I were distracted watching TV.

Sarah's standing by Morgan's cubicle, leaning in, slightly on tiptoe in her blocky beige heels. She's wearing a pink silk blouse that ties at the neck with a long bow, tucked into a perfectly fitted gray pencil skirt. And when she glances over and sees me, she suddenly stops talking.

Morgan's also looking at me—gone silent, unusual for her.

Are they talking about me? Judging me, maybe? For flirting with the new executive?

An image of Mom wrapping tiny boxes of chocolates to give her co-workers around Christmastime floats into my mind. *You have to do this to build goodwill!*

My face burns, and I hurry over to my cubicle to hide. The next list item—*BE WARM AND PLEASANT AND MAKE PEOPLE LIKE YOU AT WORK*—isn't going so well. I'll have to bank on impressing Erica with that presentation. Maybe she'll say something in Slack about how I show initiative and have a bright future. Maybe that will be enough for Mom.

The afternoon passes formlessly as I'm hopping between tasks, brain turning into a paste the longer I stare at the screen.

I'm working through Erica's comments on the copy I'm supposed to turn around today. And one of her notes cuts deep, like when an envelope I'm opening unexpectedly slices the meat of my thumb.

Did you forget we're trying to convince people to buy something?

Sometimes when I get discouraged, I think to myself: *I'm constitutionally incapable of convincing anyone of anything.* Even at my old job, my boss would say my copy lacked a certain something, and my ideas for campaigns would fall flat.

But you did convince Mark Winterson not to switch to Microsoft Teams!

There's a twinge of warmth in my chest, and I smile to myself.

Then a message from Erica pops up, saying she wants me to jump on a Zoom even though we're both sitting at our desks a few yards apart.

I start to sweat, wondering if she has questions about how the presentation is going, when I've barely even started on it.

Erica's face appears, and she sighs wearily.

"Sarah, I thought I asked—"

"I'm not Sarah," I say.

She looks annoyed, and the nerves hit me a few seconds late. It's all I can do not to clap a hand over my mouth.

Maybe I'm just so on edge already, with everything that's been going on.

Erica gives me a thin smile. "I said Ruby, didn't I?"

I shouldn't have said anything. Mom taught me that the world is never going to bend for you. That you have to grit down and try harder, make yourself as bendable as you can.

"Maybe I misheard you," I say through my teeth.

"That's all right," Erica says, and launches into a speech about compound modifiers like nothing happened.

Mom would never take my side when I complained about anything. *You're too sensitive,* she'd say. *How are you going to make it out there?* If I told her about Erica confusing me and Sarah, I know exactly what she'd say: *That's par for the course.*

There was one time, a few months into my job in New York, when I broke down and told her I felt like I was failing all the time, like I was always behind. And she nodded and said, *Good, you need something to keep you in check.*

Of course, Mom chooses this moment to weigh in.

sampaguita72:
Why don't you wear a more colorful top? Maybe put some flowers in your cubicle so they show up in your background?

I focus on keeping my smile fixed in place as Erica is talking.

sampaguita72:
You look so tired. Are you eating well? Are you getting enough sun?

I type a few things, delete them, type again.

ruby.ocampo:
I'm just working hard, Mom, like you taught me. Keeping my head down. Persevering, like you said.

sampaguita72:
You know it was hard for me, breaking into corporate life
People didn't exactly treat me with respect

ruby.ocampo:

I know, Mom

sampaguita72:

Oh all right, well I guess you know everything

I minimize Slack and smile wider, showing some teeth. "Okay, sounds good! And I'll also have that presentation ready for you bright and early tomorrow!"

Erica visibly relaxes. "Oh yes, thank you for that. All right then! Buh-bye!"

Once she ends the call, I slump across my keyboard and exhale all the air I'd been hoarding in my lungs, like I was in danger of running out.

The afternoon wears on, and eventually I look up from my desk and notice that the office lights have dimmed on a timer, and the sky outside is dark. It's late, and Morgan has gone home to her kids, but Sarah is typing away at her desk, and Al is in his cubicle, a lamp he brought from home glowing inside it.

I get up and drift over, and he's chuckling at something on his phone. As I get closer, I realize he's . . . scrolling on TikTok with headphones in?

He's cleared out some of the *mounds* Erica disliked so much. There are a few framed photos on his desk—one of Al posing with a marching band that looks like it was taken when he was in college, and a family photo with his smiling parents in front of a suburban house, the vivid blue sky taking on an amber sheen from age. Al's dad is dressed in a military uniform, one hand on little Al's shoulder. And there's another photo in front of a different house that seems to be an homage—grown Al, standing the way his dad did, his wife next to him, hand on his little son's shoulder, two daughters on either side. The photo looks old enough that the kids must be adults themselves now.

My heart squeezes, seeing these bits of his past, and I feel sad that I haven't asked him more about his life. I associate him so much with my mom, it scares me off from getting too close.

I almost want to add it to the collection of Post-it note reminders on my desk: *Talk to Al more.*

Al senses me hovering and slides down his headphones. "Erica told me the voice in my copy sounds dated." He tilts the screen my way. "Gotta keep up to stay relevant."

On his desk are a few printed-out articles about *Skibidi Toilet* and how LOL is dead and IJBOL is in.

A wave of melancholy washes over me. "You could do this at home?" I offer feebly.

"I hate bringing work home," he says, running a hand over his head. "I'm old—I still remember when working here felt like *You've made it!* Before all this *do more with less* bullshit. When there was time for a real lunch every day, and you never had to log back in from home just to"—he pitches his voice higher to imitate Erica and wiggles his fingers—"*handle a few more notes real quick.*"

That makes me laugh. "Can I do anything to help?"

Al shakes his head. "I'm fine, Ruby. You should head out."

So I go back to my desk, and every now and then, the silence is punctured by the sound of Al laughing—such genuine enjoyment every time he comes across a funny TikTok. "Kids these days," Al mutters under his breath. "They're all marketing geniuses."

At one point he lets out such a hearty guffaw that Sarah and I start laughing from our individual cubicles, little satellites in the dimly lit space.

sarah.ng:

lol al!

ruby.ocampo:
He's the best

sarah.ng:
undisputed

The office is empty, but it feels like we're all in this warm bubble together. I want to keep talking—I don't want the bubble to pop.

Plus, if Sarah is dating Greg, isn't it better that we're friends?

ruby.ocampo:
So erica keeps confusing us, huh?

sarah.ng:
ugh god
we don't even look alike?

And she's right, of course—but it stings for a second, like maybe I offend her aesthetically.

sarah.ng:
i mean, flattering and everything! you are taller

A strained laugh escapes from me.

ruby.ocampo:
I'm the flattered one! wish i had your fashion sense

sarah.ng:
omg that's so sweet

There's a pause, but I can see she's typing, then stopping, then typing again.

sarah.ng:
we didn't have a lot of money growing up, so my favorite
thing was recreating celebrity outfits at thrift stores
it's nice to have this job now. not have to worry so much
and i can help my mom out a bit

A surge of some tangled emotion runs through me—guilt, shame, admiration, chased with the clogged spine-tight feeling of holding back tears. She deserves Greg more than me.

ruby.ocampo:
That's amazing

Al stands and groans as he stretches. "You two should get out of here!" he exclaims, standing in the aisle between the cubes. "Not good for you, working too hard."

"I'm almost done!" I say brightly as Sarah stands to join him.

Al drifts over to my cubicle, briefcase in hand. "So a little bird told me . . ." He leans in and whispers conspiratorially: "What's happening with you and that new executive?"

I picture a bird with Morgan's blond hair and imp-emoji expression, beak tilted in a menacing grin.

"Am I going to have to step in for your mom here? Give him a threatening speech?"

My heart feels swollen, too big for my chest.

"Oh . . . I don't think enough is even . . . going on, for a speech?" I manage to get out with a shaky smile. "But thank you for offering."

"Hey, it's my duty!" Al says. "It's like the presidential line of succession."

I burst out laughing, tears squeezing out of the corners of my eyes. "Is it?"

Sarah comes up behind him, drinking water from the pink travel cup she carries around. (*This next generation is so hydrated,* Erica remarked dryly in one meeting.)

"Watch out for yourself," Al adds, tapping the side of his head. "The man seems like a real rizzler."

Sarah laughs so hard she almost spits out her water.

"Isn't that how you use it in a sentence?" he protests.

She shakes her head, fanning herself with one hand.

"Damn, thought I had that one. All right!" He pats the cubicle wall one more time. "You get out of here soon, okay?"

Al waves as he and Sarah head for the elevators.

I was lying, though—I'm not even close to done. But I have to show Mom I'm taking this job seriously. Giving it everything I've got.

What if Erica thinks Sarah prepared the deck for her? a voice in the back of my mind asks.

Then there's some movement by the elevators, and I stand to get a better look, feeling vulnerable as the last one left on this floor.

It's someone pacing. A guy in a suit.

I get up and venture in that direction—and Mark Winterson is walking slowly away from me down the hall, phone to his ear. He stops, gazing out the window into the dark courtyard of the office park, gesturing with his free hand. Even under the harsh overhead lights, he's sickeningly handsome: trim figure, luxuriant hair, striking profile.

It sinks in slowly that he's not speaking English. It sounds like . . . Chinese? And he seems pretty comfortable—more comfortable than I am speaking my native language in meetings, most days.

My first thought, regrettably, is that it's kind of hot.

Then my second thought hits like a tiny meteor, a burst of shame, mysterious anger, and resentment. Because I never learned Tagalog, and Mom always seemed to vaguely hold it against me, even though she also said it would be a waste of time.

And I'm standing there like an idiot, mouth agape, when he starts pacing back this way, looks up, and sees me.

"Xièxie dàjiā! Zàijiàn!" he exclaims into the phone, holding eye contact with me as he ends the call.

"You speak Chinese?" I ask.

"Yeah, did a semester at Beijing Daxue," he says with a casual little shrug. He points at me. "Do you speak . . . ?"

He's clearly waiting for me to fill in the blank so he doesn't have to guess what I am.

"Tagalog." I try my best to say it like Mom did, at least. Tuck in my *t,* make the *g* sharp, lean into the *log.*

And I don't want to actually answer his question, so instead I mumble "nakakainis" under my breath. One of the few words I do know: *Annoying!*

Mark Winterson doesn't ask me what that means. He just stares at me a few seconds too long.

"How's, um—" He waves a hand vaguely around the area of his neck. "Your throat now?"

"Fine." I crack a smile. "Boba-free."

He laughs and looks at the floor, a bashful grin stretching his face.

His eyes flick back up to meet mine. "You ever seen the roof here before?"

CHAPTER 20

It's been a while since I had a late-night adventure in this office. There was a time in sixth grade when Mom was spiraling about a deadline, and she didn't have anywhere to park me—Tita Wendy and Greg were living up north then—so she brought me along and I wandered the empty floors.

It was eerie to see all these slots where people were supposed to go, but with no people in them. There were the cubicle walls to contain them, the chair to hold them, all their belongings arranged at arm's length. I'd play pretend, tell myself I was the sole survivor after a zombie apocalypse, hiding under someone's desk in the Data Analytics Department.

But somehow I'd never even considered going to the roof.

"They kept adding on to the original structure," Mark Winterson says as I follow him down a narrow hall that he had to badge into. "Whenever the company expanded. But sometimes it was more haphazard than others." He glances back over his shoulder at me. "Anyway, the path to the roof gets trickier in a minute."

We come to a dimly lit stairwell and climb to the top. And

there is . . . a metal ladder built into the wall, disappearing into a hatch above?

"You ready for this?" he asks.

"Oh yeah." I can't help but laugh at the sight of it. "Born ready."

He shrugs off his jacket, folding it and leaving it on the floor. *The floor!* I fight off the visceral urge to grab it and dust it off. It looks expensive—but I'm not sure I could recognize an expensive one in a police lineup of cheap ones.

Then I'm distracted by Mark Winterson rolling up his sleeves. I'm a sucker for a strong forearm.

He flicks his head upward. "Ladies first."

"You going to look up my skirt?" I've figured out that he likes when I give him shit, but my stomach dips after I say it, wondering if I pushed it too far.

He puts a hand over his heart and lurches forward. "You wound me, Ruby. Can't believe you'd think I'm anything but a gentleman." The corner of his mouth turns up. "I promise I won't look, but I want to be there in case you slip."

I'm debating whether to kick off my heels, but I don't know what walking on the roof is going to be like. And Mom did drill into me never to leave my belongings unattended.

So I step onto the ladder, first rung wedged between my high heel and the sole, and hoist myself up.

"There you go," Mark Winterson says, hands hovering near my waist, ready to catch me. And as I get higher up the ladder, he adds: "My eyes are averted, okay? Tell me when to look."

I push open the hatch and hoist myself through, bare knees on the grit of the roof.

"All clear," I say, peering back down at Mark Winterson—who, true to his word, is dutifully staring at a patch of ceiling off to the left.

I sit on a metal air duct and take in my surroundings. The view is really something—the campus and blocky buildings of

TKCORP spread out below, the dark expanse of Sterling Field, the old school building slumbering squat in the distance. Suburban rooftops fanning out in cul-de-sac configurations all around, cozy lights on inside every house.

Mark Winterson catches up and sits beside me, elbows resting on his thighs and hands clasped between.

"So," he says. "Worth the climb?"

"I've been visiting this building my whole life, but I never saw it from this angle."

He grins like this is a huge accomplishment. "I like to get to know the ins and outs of a place."

"My mom would have been so mad if she knew I came up here." I lean back on my palms, staring up at the thin crescent moon. "Disrespectful to TKCORP or something."

"Hey, Ruby, I . . . I'm really sorry about your mom."

People say that all the time, rote and polite, but the way his voice softens when he says it gives me a hazy feeling in my gut.

"Thanks," I mumble.

"How have . . . things been for you lately? With your family thing?"

"Oh, you know. Family—it can be a lot."

"Do you want to talk about it?"

"Mm, seems like a bad idea to tell my boss's boss's boss about my mommy issues." I give him a toothy grin. In eighth grade, Greg dubbed it my Bugs Bunny grin, because my top front teeth are bigger than the others. (*Is that supposed to be an insult?* I'd asked, and Greg blushed. *No, it's too cute,* he said. *Be careful how you use that thing.*)

"At least, not on the first roof excursion," I add. "Maybe, like, the tenth."

Mark Winterson makes a dismissive sound. "I'll see you your mommy issues and raise you my daddy issues."

"Oh, you have those?" I say so brightly, it makes him laugh. "All right, you go first."

It's funny—somehow, feeling like he's out of my league and there's no chance anything can happen turns me into my weirdest, pushiest self.

Mark Winterson smiles open-mouthed and glances around theatrically, as though he's hoping to make eye contact with some bystander and say, *Can you believe this girl?* But of course we're alone up here.

He leans forward on his knees. "Maybe . . . you'll think it's dumb. And I can't complain, in life. Had a lot of advantages, growing up."

For someone who seems to be all swagger during the daytime, this blush of self-awareness is a bit disarming.

He re-adjusts where his feet are planted, and the motion once again draws my eye to his dress shoes, and the way his socks hug his ankles. They're so . . . shapely? Wow, maybe *I'm* the Victorian child.

"Now I'm in suspense," I say.

"My dad's tough," he says, finally. "Big personality. Impossible to impress. Always reminding me how I fall short."

I nod, watching the blinking lights of a plane as it glides across the sky overhead. "Can't tell you how deeply I relate to that."

"Oh?" He turns his head to look at me.

"Yeah, I always feel like a failure." I say it with a laugh, tone jokey. Letting him in, but not enough that I can't deny it happened later, if I need to.

"You work at TKCORP. You must be doing something right."

"Do they pay you to say that? Do you get a commission?"

"A modest two percent," he says, grinning at me.

The wind picks up on the roof, ruffling my hair. "My mom's . . . very critical." *Oh shit, wrong tense for this audience.* "I mean, she was. That was her way of showing she cared. Always wanting me to be better. Have a better life than her."

That precarious feeling of saying too much overtakes me.

Mark Winterson knocks the side of his shoe playfully against mine. "Can't believe we have so much in common." He's matching my light tone, but there's something wistful at the end.

"I should get back," I say, standing again. "Erica's going to kill me if I don't finish this thing by tomorrow morning."

"Can I help?"

"Ohhh, uh . . ." The thought embarrasses me—Mark Winterson crouching next to my desk in the dark office, seeing how perplexed I am by Excel? Maybe it would even put my job at risk. "No no, it's fine. I've got this."

He insists on going first so he can spot me. And it's good that he did, because as I'm climbing down, there's a *snap,* and I slip with a shriek. I got these shoes at TKMART for cheap, and the pressure from the rung must have broken the heel clean off.

"Oof!" Mark Winterson exclaims as I crash into him. His chest is warm and solid against my back; his arms wrap around me, stopping my fall. He chuckles, and I feel the vibration in my spine. "Got you," he says, hot breath tickling my ear.

He promptly lets me go and I spin to face him. He's gazing down at me, lids half closed, and—am I imagining it?—his soft brown eyes look pained, like he wants something he can't have. His lips part slightly, and for a second, I'm convinced he's about to kiss me.

Instead he blinks a couple times, takes a step backward, and delicately clears his throat into his fist. Like he's committed to *being a gentleman,* but in this moment it's a struggle.

"You okay?" he asks.

"Oh . . . yeah. Thanks." I stoop to take off my broken shoe. "Sorry."

"Why are you sorry?" The corner of his mouth tilts up as he retrieves his jacket and dusts it off. "*I'm* sorry your shoes got ruined. This is my fault—it was my idea." And he plucks the broken shoe out of my hand, flipping it over and hunting for the size before I can snatch it back. "Let me replace them."

"Oh no. No no." I wave my hands. He's not serious, right? It's probably a thing rich people toss around, like *we should get lunch sometime.*

"I—I should really—" I point behind me.

"Of course, right. I'll walk with you."

I'm quiet most of the way back, and so is he.

But when we're moving down that narrow hall I'd never seen before, almost back to my department on the eighth floor, I start laughing.

Mark Winterson glances over at me, laughing too. "What's funny?"

I just shake my head, and he gives me a sleepy smile. "You sure you're going to stay?" he adds.

"Yeah! Yeah, I've got to."

"Burning the midnight oil, I respect it. Glad I could get you to take a break, at least." He walks me to my cubicle and raps the wall with his knuckles. "Good night, Ruby."

True to form, he heads for the stairwell. Once he's gone, I let out a long breath and slump against my cubicle divider.

It's clearer to me, in retrospect: Sure, he's sickeningly attractive and makes my heart flutter sometimes. I'm only human. But until tonight, I'd classified him in my head as *Not a Person I Would Actually Like on the Inside.*

But as I make a Cup Noodles from the vending machine, I keep replaying our conversation from the roof, that wistful note in his voice, the moment he caught me. And I think: *Well, Ruby, maybe you were wrong about him.*

CHAPTER 21

I massively underestimated the amount of work this was going to be. My eyes are closing as I watch an Excel tutorial on YouTube.

I spent the past hour reading through Erica's notes about the aesthetic she wants for the presentation, and went down a rabbit hole on color schemes and font pairings—then remembered, with a start, that I still don't actually understand the data she's supposed to present.

My cheeks are bloated from all the sodium I just housed—two vending machine Cup Noodles, back to back. I can practically feel the sebum rising to the surface of my face.

The lights turn on suddenly, and I have the strange urge to scuttle under my desk, like the cockroaches caught out when I'd turn on the light in my New York apartment.

There's a woman's melodious laugh, and a man's voice, warm and familiar. Sarah and Greg come into view, walking over to her cubicle from the elevators.

I can hear snippets of their conversation out of context, things I can't make sense of.

"You won't believe—"

"Saw them talking later—"

"No! You're shitting me."

They seem to be having a great time, thick as thieves.

Irritation overtakes me, abrasive like knuckles scraping my sternum.

It reminds me of senior year, when I'd run into Greg with a new girlfriend every few weeks. I don't know why I have such a long hangover from things that happened a decade ago and really shouldn't matter anymore.

You're living with the muscle memory of old stress, I tell myself, flexing my fingers. *You're over it! You'll adjust.*

Sarah notices me and raises a hand. "Ruby, you're still here?"

"This thing is more involved than I thought." I type some gibberish just to seem busy. "You came back?"

"Oh, yeah, uh—ran into Greg, and—" She gestures between them awkwardly. The harsh overhead lights shine off her black hair. "A few of us went to the bar."

Why is she lying too? Are they afraid I'm going to report them to HR?

"But then I remembered I left my headphones here," Sarah says, grabbing a pastel purple AirPods case off the desk.

She's so cute, and Greg looked so happy a second ago. And, man, I feel like a greasy-faced wretch.

I close my eyes and think about Mark Winterson laughing on the roof, his body pressed against mine for a second in that dingy hall. *You have some things going for you. You should focus on that.*

But just when it seems I'm almost in the clear, Greg drifts over and rests a hand on my cubicle wall. "Sarah, you should go ahead, I'll see you tomorrow."

I stare at him. What does this fool think he's doing?

"Night, Ruby!" Sarah calls with a jaunty wave as she heads for the elevator.

Greg must have told her about his pathetic childhood friend, the one he needs to check up on because she's losing her mind.

"Come on," he says, tilting his head in the direction of the elevators. "Let's go home."

Sometimes, in moments like these, Greg has a bad case of puppy-dog eyes, and I do not appreciate the effect they have on me.

He's not doing it on purpose! That's just how his face is.

"Yeah, I'll go home soon," I say, rubbing my puffy cheeks.

"No, we're calling it a night now," he says. "You've done enough."

There's something steely in his tone, a departure from his usual nonchalance. Mom got that wrong about him—she looked at Greg's don't-give-a-shit exterior and saw all her problems with unreliable men personified. But I'd watched him long enough to realize that wasn't fair. That he had to try so hard to seem like he didn't care because he cared too much about too many things. He was fiercely protective of his mom, for one—he'd get into fights when people made fun of her job, and she'd whack him on the arm when she picked him up from the principal's office and say, *Ay, you think I care about that! Stay out of trouble if you want to help!*

"Ruby," he says, low and steady. "You're putting too much pressure on yourself."

I feel like I'm going to cry. Of all people, he should understand.

"She's still trapped in there!" My voice has dropped to a desperate whisper. "And it's because of me, and—and maybe if I just tried harder! Maybe if I just tried—"

"Hey." Greg comes around the divider and gives my shoulder a firm squeeze.

Something hitches in my chest at the gentle way he's looking at me. This is how he is—attentive, soft, calming. Lots of girls have fallen for it over the years. I've learned my lesson; it doesn't mean anything.

"We don't know what's going to get her out, or why she's there," he says firmly. "But this isn't all your fault. And grinding yourself down won't . . ."

He pauses.

Is he going to say *bring her back*? My anger comes to a boil like the kettle I used to make the Cup Noodles.

"*You* go home!" I slam my hands against the keys, and a long string of characters pops up on the screen. "You clearly don't get it!"

"I saw what you saw at my mom's shop! I think I get it," Greg shoots back in a sharp whisper. "But you can't just make everything happen by force of will."

Mom's voice bounces between my ears. *Greg lacks initiative! He'll never get anywhere!*

"Why the fuck not?"

"Because that's not how things work!" He sounds so incensed suddenly, voice raised.

So this is the rare moment I make him lose his cool. I'm more intrigued than mad now.

"Why, exactly," I say slowly, "isn't that how things work?"

Greg runs a hand over his face. "Because so much of life is shaped by forces outside your control—whatever the market is doing, and corporate bullshit way over your head. Companies will be humming along, profitable, everyone working hard, and then, *bam,* layoffs. Just to give shareholders that extra juice and executives a fatter payday."

So this must be what he reads about these days. It's been a while since I heard him rant.

His words pick up speed, like they're just tumbling out of him now. "And everything isn't happening the way it is because of some small thing you did or didn't do wrong—because capitalism isn't a meritocracy, and we're not exactly in control, and things don't really make sense! And Erica is just Erica, not a barometer of how worthy you are! And it's not worth . . ."

"What, *killing yourself over*?" I'm barely doing a fraction of what Mom used to do. He really has no clue.

"I didn't mean it like that," Greg says, careful, level again. "I just—" He shakes his head. "I hate seeing you like this."

A distant, muted part of me knows he's expressing concern, but all I hear is criticism. Mom telling me it's unattractive to let the sadness show on your face. To indulge it for too long.

You think I can do that? I'd never get anything done, if I started.

Greg gives me a long stare, dry as tinder. The air between us feels dangerous, like the whole thing would go up if someone lit a match.

"Come on, Ruby." He reaches for my hands, tugging me out of my seat. And for some reason, I don't fight him—I let him pull me to my feet, and for a second I'm standing too close to him, both hands clasped in his before he takes a step backward and looks away. "You can try again tomorrow."

CHAPTER 22

My leg jiggles as I ride the elevator up to the eighth floor the next morning. *Come on, come on, can't this thing go any faster?* I need to finish Erica's deck as quickly as I possibly can. I understand the data, finally. I worked on it a bit more after I got home, nodding off in front of the screen, waking up to find the curve of my laptop imprinted on my cheek.

But when I get to my desk, there's something strange waiting for me. An unmarked shoebox.

My face heats as I open it, and I have to stifle a gasp.

I don't know shoes, but even I know the red bottom on these sleek beige pumps means they're expensive. This is Mark Winterson's *replacement* for my $50 TKMART heels?

He must have changed the box because he wanted to be discreet. Or he asked whoever does his shopping for him to change it. Not that I don't feel molten with embarrassment anyway.

"Hellooo!" Morgan trills, stopping short as she passes my desk and backing up. "And what have we here?"

Oh no, now everyone in a ten-mile radius will hear about this!

I snatch the box away and stuff it in my work tote, even though it's too wide to slide in easily.

"It's nothing!" I muster my most innocent smile.

"Ah ah ah." Morgan wags a finger at me. "I know a secret admirer gift when I see one."

Sarah appears behind her, forehead wrinkled. "Everything all right?"

"Love is all around in Advertorial!" Morgan singsongs, knocking her shoulder against Sarah's.

"The rizzler strikes again!" Al exclaims as he walks by, and Sarah hoots so loud, you can probably hear it across the office.

"Did I get it that time?" he asks, beaming while he waters a yellowing snake plant. Erica assigned him to plant care duty this week.

"Nailed it," Sarah says with pride.

At the far end of the floor, the elevator doors ding open, and Greg walks in—probably here for Sarah. He's carrying a to-go cup of coffee in either hand, and sure enough, he delivers one to her, and she reaches for it appreciatively.

I close my eyes and take a deep breath in. *I am the picture of serenity. I am a grown woman with a rich inner life who does not need anything from him.*

"Ruby." Greg's voice is too close suddenly, and I open my eyes with a start. He's standing in front of my cubicle, holding the other coffee cup out to me.

"Since you worked late," he says, lowering it onto my desk when I don't reach for it.

"Oh, thanks!" My hands close around the paper cup. "You didn't have to."

I push the tote with the shoes deeper under my desk with my foot.

"Are you still working on that thing for Erica?"

"Yeah." I do a raspberry. "Pivot tables."

"Oh, I love pivot tables." Before I can protest, he's already coming around to the inside of the cubicle. "Let me help."

The elevator doors ding again, and I glimpse Erica's signature red hair. She looks over here, and *oh fuck, I need more time! I have to hide!*

And Greg is standing there behind me—if she sees him standing suspiciously alone in my cubicle, she'll definitely walk over. In a panic, I grab a fistful of Greg's shirt and tug him down under the desk with me.

"Uh—"

I put a hand over his mouth.

"Shh," I whisper. "We're hiding."

I can feel his smile forming under my palm. He's always been game for a ridiculous situation.

I withdraw my hand, and Greg mouths, *Erica?* I nod, and that's all he needs—he shifts around so he's shoulder to shoulder with me, our backs leaned against the inside of my desk.

It reminds me of a time in eleventh grade when I spotted someone I was avoiding in the high school parking lot. And I noticed Greg nearby, sitting behind the wheel of his Acura, so I slipped into the passenger seat, sliding down low so no one would see me.

"I'm hiding," I said in response to his questioning look.

So Greg slid way down, too, legs folded into the footwell. "Okay, then I'll hide with you."

"Ruby?" Erica calls from the direction of her office. "Is Ruby here?"

Greg shakes with a silent laugh, and he presses a hand against the side of my head, bringing it in to rest on his shoulder. He's patting my head in a *there, there* kind of way, still part of the joke. But his warm palm on my ear, and that familiar lemon scent—it brings me right back to the first time we kissed.

If it had happened only once, I might have thought it was a

fluke. We'd been friends a long time, we had too much history. Anytime someone asked if we were a thing, we said, *Oh God no, we know each other way too well for that!*

We were at the movies with a group of friends, sitting next to each other, and I leaned on him, more sleep-deprived than flirty. He pressed a hand to the side of my head, as if to say, *Get comfortable, stay awhile.* So I nestled in, cheek against his shoulder.

The music swelled just right at an emotional moment, and I turned my head toward him, at an awkward angle. It was dark, but he was already staring at me. There was something intense about it, like I caught him watching me sleep. The inches between us ached. And then our mouths brushed, his bottom lip pillowing between both of mine.

It was the briefest contact, but I felt it everywhere, a full-body unclenching. Like all my molecules sighed out the revelation: *Oh, this is what you've been missing.*

Then one of our friends made a joke, and I panicked and straightened up. We pretended to go back to watching the movie and acted like nothing happened for the rest of the night.

Under the desk, my lips tingle from the memory, and I jolt upright.

Greg tilts his head questioningly at me, our faces perilously close.

"Have you seen Ruby?" Erica's clipped tone carries faintly across the office.

"Oh," Sarah says, "she was here, but . . . maybe she went to the bathroom?"

"Tell her I'm looking for her," Erica says. "And I need that presentation after my next meeting, or else."

Greg raises his eyebrows and points sardonically at me. I try to smile, even though I feel like I've been chopping an onion.

He was a confused, experimenting seventeen-year-old then,

and he's concerned in a strictly platonic, I've-known-you-forever way now. And I *do* want to be friends with him. It's a good thing in my life, one that I held at arm's length for stupid reasons for too long.

I can fix it. We can make it work. I just have to try harder.

Greg pulls one leg to his chest, and he must feel the awkward shape of the box wedged inside my tote behind him. He peers into the bag.

"No, wait, that's—" I hiss.

"Hey!" Sarah raps her knuckles on the desk, and I jerk at the sound and hit my head.

"You okay?" Greg whispers.

Sarah's standing inside my cubicle now. From here, I have a view of her wide-leg trousers and chunky heels.

"Ooh, sorry," she says, kneeling down and grimacing. "I was just going to say—Erica left for her eight o'clock, you can come out now."

"Oh my God, *thank you*!" I say, scrambling out from under the desk and offering Greg a hand.

He takes it and lets me pull him up. "You good?" he asks.

"I will be, if I can finish this in the next hour." I wave frantically at my computer.

Greg shoves his hands in his pockets and nods up at Sarah. "Should we . . . ?"

"Oh yeah, I have that . . . thing to tell you about," she says, giving me a tight smile. "Bye, Ruby."

The two of them head for the elevators together, but I'm too busy tearing through this presentation to think much about it. And when Erica appears next to my cubicle, saying, "It's eight fifty-five, Ruby, where is it?" I can finally beam at her and say, "It's in your inbox!"

CHAPTER 23

After her presentation, Erica pings me:

erica.putnam:
Great work on that
Real life-saver. I'll remember how you took initiative
Keep it up and you're going places around here

Yes! Exactly what I needed! I did it!

Just in case Mom isn't paying attention, I take a screenshot and send it into the haunted DM. Good day at work! I write, and add a blushing face.

sampaguita72:
Good, that's what I'd expect from you

The curt reply makes me blink. I don't know why I'm surprised; I'd forgotten the times I'd bring home report cards filled with A's and hand them to her eagerly, and she'd barely nod and pass them back. One time I asked, "What do you think?" and she said, "That's normal. What do you want, a parade?"

ruby.ocampo:
Do you feel any different now?

sampaguita72:
Why do you keep asking me that?
Different how?

I have to close out of Slack and take a minute in the bathroom.

After the adrenaline from rushing out that presentation recedes, I slog through the rest of the day, melancholy and numb. And my mind wanders to earlier, under the desk—Greg so close, laughing together, sending me back to a movie theater ten years ago. I need to get my head on straight.

I play back the memory of Mark Winterson's arms around me, his astonished face gazing down at mine.

Everything's pointing in his direction. It might be Mom's best chance to move on. And maybe it would be good for me—someone who likes me. A chance for me to move on, for real. *Win-win,* like Mom would say.

I get up with my tote on my shoulder, like I'm popping out for coffee, and sit in the stairwell. Mark Winterson hates the elevator; maybe if I wait here awhile, I'll run into him.

And sure enough, he appears—I see the back of his head first as he walks up from below, his broad shoulders in a navy suit jacket. He rounds the corner of the landing between floors, looks up, and flashes his pearly whites.

"Just who I was hoping to run into." He raises the drink he's holding. "Got this for you. Strawberry fruit tea, no boba."

A hazy, flushed feeling comes over me, and I try to laugh it off, sliding the box out of my bag. "I'll trade you that for some shoes."

Mark Winterson's brows push closer to each other. "You don't like them? They don't fit? I can get another size."

"No, it's . . . it's just too much. And people talk."

"Ah," he says, walking up the steps toward me. "I should have thought of that. Sorry."

He hands me the drink and points to the stair beside me. "This seat taken?"

"Nah, saved it for you."

I slide the shoebox onto his lap and he drums his fingers on the top.

"Mark . . ." I start. "You said I could ask you anything?"

"Oh wow, just Mark, I've leveled up." His expression relaxes. "Sure, anything."

"Have you . . . been hitting on me?"

Mark Winterson clears his throat and sits up straighter. "I would never want to do anything to make you uncomfortable." His mouth twists into a bashful smile. "I was rectifying a wardrobe issue I caused. And now I'm checking up on a valued member of the team after a, uh, health scare."

I'm not sure what comes over me, but I stick one hand out, palm up, and give him a challenging look. "Maybe I'll feel worse later. Let me give you my number so you can check up on me some more."

His eyebrows go up, and he shakes his head, chuckling. "You're really something," he says as he unlocks his phone and passes it to me.

"So, hypothetically . . ." I punch in my number. "What if . . . I wanted you to be hitting on me? Would you want me to want that?"

He holds my gaze in that steady, searching way he has, and the heat rises in my cheeks.

"Strictly hypothetical!" I add. "Low stakes."

Those doe eyes give me a once-over, and he leans closer,

voice low so I have to strain to hear. "I can neither confirm nor deny until you sign some paperwork."

I burst out laughing, but his face stays serious. "Wait, for real?"

"Can't be too careful." He straightens his tie. "I could send you a DocuSign."

"Okay, so, just to confirm—it's not a joke?"

"Um, no." He leans forward, hands clasped together. "No, I'm quite serious."

Quite. It's like someone opened a window and let in a draft. I need to lie down.

"Let me think about that and circle back!" I squeak, hopping up and scrambling back to the eighth floor.

CHAPTER 24

Greg:
did you get your presentation done?

I'm sitting on the couch at home, where I planted myself shortly after work. I tried putting on the TV for a distraction, but my head has been circling around the question of Mark Winterson's paperwork.

On the one hand: It felt like he slid a contract for my soul out of his suit jacket. *A Wintersonian bargain!*

On the other: Maybe he's earnestly trying to be responsible about the uneven power dynamic between us? The image of him holding up one finger, saying, *I consider myself a feminist,* pops into my head.

I've been going back and forth about it for an hour, borderline spiraling. Batting away the image of Greg laughing in the dim light under my desk. Checking my phone to see if Mark Winterson texted me—but maybe after I basically ran away from him, he's giving me some space.

Finally I write back to Greg:

Ruby:
it went better than i was hoping, and it still didn't do it
maybe this is going to take years
maybe i actually need to get the promotion

Greg:
you could try other things on the list, in the meantime?
what's next?

But before I can reply, there's a knock on the door.

"Ruby, are you here?" Tita Wendy sings into the Ring doorbell.

"Oh, hi!" I pop up from the couch, still in my rumpled work clothes, and force on my brightest facial expression. I've been avoiding Tita Wendy ever since we talked to Mom's ghost together. I didn't want her to see how badly I'm failing at this too.

She's carrying a Tupperware with pinakbet inside—the familiar colors of my favorite stew, with orange kalabasa, green string beans, brown crispy pork. "Greg has such an appetite these days," she says by way of explanation.

She goes into the kitchen and opens the fridge, clicking her tongue disapprovingly.

It hurts sometimes, the way she tries to love me, because she's giving me so much and I can't ever pay her back.

And the thought of letting her down, the way I let down Mom—it makes it hard to breathe. Now that she's seeing me more directly—without Mom's stories about me as the filter, cherry-picking the accomplishments, downplaying the bad parts—maybe she'll finally see how disappointing I am too.

"How can I tell if I'm getting warmer?" I blurt out.

Tita Wendy turns around, startled. "Have you tried asking her?"

I nod, biting my bottom lip to keep it from shaking. "She doesn't know why she's here."

She sighs, and her shoulders relax. "She wouldn't. Death can . . . obscure that. Make it hard to remember. But maybe if you bounce things off her, see how she responds? Warmly or not? Maybe that would give you a clue."

She gives me a *What are we going to do with you?* look and pulls me into a hug. "I know this is hard. I'm so sorry." She pats my back. "But I know you're going to figure it out."

I give her a squeeze and step away. "Oh, I didn't even think of it, did you—would you want to talk to her?"

Tita Wendy shakes her head. "Oh . . . no. You know how much I loved talking to your mom. But it's painful this way. It's like when you say such a nice, heartfelt goodbye to someone at the airport, and then you see them randomly for a second again—maybe they realized they needed to use the bathroom before going through security." She laughs heartily, the way she used to when she and Mom would gossip at the kitchen table. "Okay, maybe not exactly like that, but . . ."

"No, I know what you mean. You're preemptively grieving again, already. You don't want to get too comfortable."

"Right." She smiles sadly. "I'm so sorry you're going through this, Ruby. I'm not sure what the best thing to do is, but—I'm here. Whatever you think of. If you want me to talk to her again, of course I will."

"No, no, I just wanted to offer, in case. I'll try asking her some things."

Tita Wendy gives me one more hug before heading out the door.

After she leaves, I open Slack on my laptop, download Mark Winterson's email intro to the staff as a PDF, and upload it into the haunted DM.

ruby.ocampo:
Mom, I've been talking to this guy at work. What do you think of him?

sampaguita72:
Is "talking" code for something else these days?

I can just picture Mom putting on her reading glasses and frowning at the email on her phone, holding it a bit farther away to be able to see.

sampaguita72:
Seems very successful
Exactly the kind of man you should be trying to attract
Wasn't I always telling you?

She certainly was. The tightness in my chest remembers.

Tita Wendy said to ask her things, so . . .

ruby.ocampo:
Mom, are you sad that I haven't risen higher than this position at work?

sampaguita72:
Of course I would be happy if you got a raise! I'll always want you to be better off than I was
But no, I'm not sad. I was so proud of you when you got this job.

The ache between my ribs gets more insistent. So maybe it's not about work at all, and I could drive myself up the wall trying to please Erica and never get anywhere. It has to be something else.

Maybe she wishes I were married. That had been her thing more consistently over the past few years. It was like she switched on a dime, after college, from panicking at any sign of me spending time alone with a boy to being disappointed that I didn't have more suitors calling. *But don't repeat my mistakes,* she'd say. *Don't marry for love, and definitely don't marry for passion. Marry for stability. Because he'll probably leave anyway, and then at least you get something out of it, after.*

There's movement on the screen again. sampaguita72 is typing.

sampaguita72:

Ruby, I'm worried about you.

You always seemed so lonely

Cut off from other people

This is new. And weird. Since when does she notice my feelings, or want to talk about them?

Death changes people, I guess? The thought passes through me with a shiver.

Maybe the question of *paperwork* can wait. Maybe I should keep going in order after all, try harder with the third item on the list: *BE WARM AND PLEASANT AND MAKE PEOPLE LIKE YOU AT WORK.*

ruby.ocampo:

Thanks, Mom. I'll work on that.

Good night

I can't help but scroll up and reread the part where she said *I was so proud of you when you got this job.*

I spent so long chasing those words from her, and now that I've got them, I don't know what to do with them. I reread it over and over, trying to make it sink in.

Tears quiver in the corners of my eyes while I take a screenshot, in case it disappears after she passes on.

And I pick up the phone and text Greg:

Ruby:

the next thing on the list is getting closer to everyone at work

being warm and pleasant and getting people to like me

making friends

not great at that, as you remember

Greg:

no that's easy

you should come to pub trivia night

He sends me the place and time.

Greg:

and you are pleasant, okay? and everyone will like you
you just have to believe it

My heart feels like it's stretched too tight, the way my face does right after I've been crying.

Then a couple more messages appear on my screen, this time from an unknown number.

Unknown:

Checking up on you, as requested.
(This is Mark, by the way.)

Even though the idea of signing a contract to date someone makes me feel insane, there's a rush of warmth in my chest.

I have to laugh at his use of proper punctuation in texts. It's like he was born with a tie on.

Ruby:

nice of you

I chew on my lip as I add him to my contacts, searching for a way to keep the conversation going without addressing the paperwork directly yet. What do I even know about him? *Dinner with Jack Welch? A dog named Ralph? Daddy issues?*

Ruby:

so do you still watch rugby?

He sends me a photo of a TV with what I assume is a rugby game on the screen.

Mark Winterson:

you're psychic.

Somehow I don't want to think about what Tita Wendy would say.

Ruby:

no idea what's happening on that screen

Mark Winterson:
i could explain it to you.

I consider saying: *You should explain in person sometime* or *Something to look forward to.* But the whole *contract for my soul* thing is holding me back, scared to ring a bell I can't unring.

An old thought works its way to the surface like a worm after heavy rain: *Wow, selfish of you. Couldn't even do this one thing for her when she does so much for you.*

And a new one is close on its heels: *It's not like it wouldn't also be something for you!* A highlight reel of moments when Mark Winterson made my heart flutter spins through my head, a carnival ride with too much velocity.

There are still other things you can rule out!

But here's this opportunity, right here!

I take so long to reply that he must get nervous.

Mark Winterson:
hope I didn't scare you earlier.

Ruby:
you didn't

And because that reads so blunt, sitting there by itself, I add:

Ruby:
hope you have a good night!

Mark Winterson:
you, too, Ruby.

Greg's voice echoes in my head, saying, *You can try again tomorrow.*

So I turn off the light in the living room and get ready for bed.

CHAPTER 25

At first, at least, I'm so glad I came.

At the bar, there's a funny collection of people from other departments gathered around the tables our group has shoved together. A bunch of the accountants, some people from Sales. Carol from Legal, who led a training the first week I was here.

The mood is light, and the trivia answers are flowing. Shouts and laughter rise up from the table, depending on the questions and how we do, and I cheer along as the beer in my stomach dulls my sharp edges. At first I think: *Why didn't I start coming to these a long time ago?*

I'm sitting between Morgan and Greg, conferring about the answer to a question. Across the table, Sarah checks her phone and her brow furrows. She comes around to our side and whispers something in Greg's ear, and he glances sideways at me.

"Sorry," he says, getting up. "Hang around. I'll be back."

And then they just . . . leave? They walk through the bar to the front, and unfortunately my seat has an unobstructed view as he opens the door for her and they slip outside.

A melancholy, faraway feeling overtakes me, like I'll always be on the outside of life looking in. I take a big swig of my drink, and the gnawing festers, becomes inflamed.

I can't believe I came here because Greg said to, and he just leaves to hang out with his new girlfriend! Like whatever, they're dating, but it's the principle of the thing! Bad friend behavior!

It reminds me too much of how he ditched me in high school. The disrespect of *discarding* me like that! Is he going to do it again?

But I did come to bond with everyone else. I should try to make the most of it.

The minutes tick by. Greg and Sarah are gone for over an hour. Our team keeps lobbing out answers, but I'm quieter, sinking into myself.

The host announces that the next category is "paranormal activity throughout history," and everyone groans.

"How do they come up with these niche categories?" Morgan gripes.

I have to laugh, because I actually know a lot about this from all my stress reading. After a streak of right answers, Al comes around the table to thump me on the back, and Adam from Accounting gives me a high five. Morgan's mouth hangs open in disbelief. "So this is your hidden talent!"

Morgan proceeds to crush the celebrity gossip category, and Al reaches over to fist-bump her. Our team wins, and while everyone cheers, I take a photo and send it to Mom.

sampaguita72:
Don't you have work tomorrow?

My heart sinks at how unimpressed she sounds, but she's still typing.

sampaguita72:
Aw, Al. I miss him.
Tell him I said hi

I glance over at Al and imagine saying that—

I used to be so good at not crying, but this whole situation is testing my abilities.

Then at the far end of the room, the door opens, and Mark Winterson walks in, looking broody under those prominent brows.

"Hey," Morgan says, nudging Carol from Legal beside her and pointing.

It's like all the sound stops—but, of course, it doesn't really. The room is still loud with other people's conversations and blaring music, but around our table, at least, everyone goes quiet as Mark Winterson orders a drink.

Morgan's watching him like she's keeping tabs on a poisonous spider. Did something change since we talked in the closet? She's not the type to hold back.

He walks over, beer in hand, and points at the spot Greg left open. "Mind if I join you?" And as he sits, he says low enough for the others not to hear: "Didn't realize you were going to be here. Hope you don't think I came to pressure you."

I laugh nervously and look up in time to see Greg and Sarah at the bar—they came back, apparently. And Greg locks eyes with me as Mark Winterson keeps on talking into my ear.

"Erickson encouraged me to come to these things." His warm breath tickles the side of my face. "Get to know everyone."

"Oh, yeah, yeah, of course." I smile like I'm having a great time and touch Mark Winterson's arm. "I didn't think anything of it."

Sarah nudges Greg to tell him something, and he leans closer.

I could really use a breather.

"Excuse me a moment," I say, pushing my chair back.

I hop up and weave my way through the crowded room to the exit, going the long way so I avoid the bar.

It's a relief when I get outside and the door shuts, muffling the too-loud music and overlapping conversations behind me. The neon sign overhead glows pink, and the sky is fading deep navy to black.

The noise of the bar picks up again—the door's open, and Greg's coming outside.

"Hey." He stops right in front of me, but it seems like he's struggling with himself again, trying and rejecting things to say.

"Spit it out, Greg!" I snap.

That makes him laugh, though it sounds a bit painful. "Does it have to be that guy?" He says it like a joke, but it gets my hackles up. *As if I owe Greg an answer!*

"He's not that bad," I shoot back.

Greg's staring at me, unfortunately puppy-eyed again.

And, fumbling for a joke, I add: "At least he doesn't live with his mom."

Greg scoffs. "So do you, basically!"

"I wouldn't call it *living,* exactly!" I shout.

We glare at each other, a moment of very intense, sustained eye contact passing between us. Some cars whoosh past on the road beyond the parking lot. Finally Greg looks away first.

"Sorry, Ruby." He's quiet for a while, arms folded across his chest. His Adam's apple bobs.

"Remember Owen?" he adds abruptly.

Unbelievable! "Reminding me of my shitty exes, what a power move."

"It's just—" His voice breaks, like we really are back in high school. "I can tell he's an Owen type. Looks good on paper, but . . . he's all wrong for you. He won't make you happy."

"You don't even know him!" The heat builds in my chest, and all the angry words I've rehearsed before I fall asleep at night are flying wind-whipped around my head. "What the fuck, Greg!"

I'm so agitated, I shove him, and Greg staggers back, eyes wide, like he didn't think I had it in me.

"Are you *judging* me right now?" I take a step forward and jab him in the chest. "What makes you an expert on what's right for me?"

And even though I'm furious at him, I have the insane urge to mash my mouth against his to shut him up—but I quash it, like I always do. "How would *you* know what makes me happy?" I shout. "When you just *dropped* me at the end of high school! And I *thought* we were friends, but then suddenly we weren't anymore, and—"

"When did we stop being friends?" He actually sounds confused, and it trips me up for a second.

I take a step back, arms crossed. "Great question, Greg!"

"I didn't . . . think we stopped being friends. I thought I . . . made some more friends, in addition?"

He's making me sound so petty and small. It's impossible to talk to him. "Forget it," I say, brushing past him to go back inside.

"Hey." He puts both hands on my shoulders and turns me to face him. "Ruby, you were always—" Greg makes a throaty sound, struggling for the words. His eyes meet mine in a way that makes the butterflies stir, and I'm gritting my teeth, telling them, *Not now, I swear to God!* "I need you to know that I'll always be your friend."

He's being very clear: I'm living in the shadow of something that ended a long time ago—or never started to begin with. We'll always just be friends.

I jerk away so his hands drop to his sides, and we stand there for a while in that tense, raw silence.

Behind Greg, Mark Winterson chooses that moment to peek his head through the door of the bar.

"Oh, sorry, were you in the middle of—?"

"He was just leaving!" I exclaim.

Greg shakes his head, but he takes his cue to head for the

door. He turns and mouths *Owen* one more time before he heads inside.

"Can I get you another drink?" Mark Winterson says, coming up alongside me.

I force a smile, even though I'm still shaking from yelling at Greg. "Thanks, but I'm going to head home. Work tomorrow."

"Let me call you a car." He takes his phone out of his pocket. "Least I can do, since I did ruin your shoes. And the replacement was probably a bit much. Sorry about that, again."

Mark Winterson taps around with his thumbs, the glow of the screen lighting his face from below. "Driver's on his way."

He shifts his weight from foot to foot, staring out into the distance.

"So, this paperwork . . ." I say. "What's in it?"

He rocks back on his heels, hands in the pockets of his suit trousers. "Statement of consent, establishment of boundaries." He says it so casually, he almost sounds bored. "Waiver of liability. Light NDA. All perfectly reasonable. More couples should do it, honestly."

The word *couples* kicks up a confusing mix of feelings in my gut.

"Can I, um, review it? See if I find the terms, uh—agreeable?"

Mark Winterson laughs. Maybe he can tell I'm reaching for language I heard fictional lawyers use on TV.

He bites down a smile and taps around on his phone. "It's in your inbox."

The car pulls up, and Mark Winterson hurries to get the door, closes it behind me, raises a hand as we pull away.

"Wait, was that—?" the driver says, doing a double take in his rearview mirror.

"No," I say. "Common mistake."

CHAPTER 26

I'm back home, scrolling through the document filled with places to initial and sign. My eyes scan the numbered sections and subsections, but it's hard to focus.

Maybe I should have a lawyer look at this. But where would I find one? Yelp? And that has to be out of my budget.

A text slides down from the top of my screen:

Greg:
did you leave?

I swipe it away without replying. He really pissed me off tonight—bringing up Owen, second-guessing my choices, gaslighting me about what happened in high school! And I'm even angrier at myself for not being able to accept reality as it is. It's my own fault I haven't moved on. I just need to try harder.

"Relationships can be dissolved in person (see clause nine, subsection two) by either party at will at any time, but clauses one, four, and five remain binding," I read out loud.

Mom always told me to *define the relationship early,* but this is ridiculous.

I jiggle my leg, full of nervous energy. Part of me wants to run screaming into the night.

When I'm agitated, it's soothing to review the evidence:

- This might be the key to freeing Mom from Slack.
- This could help me move past my immature fixation on Greg, so I can actually ease into our friendship again.
- I can't deny I'm attracted to Mark Winterson.

Maybe I'm resistant to it *because* he's the kind of guy Mom would want me to date, and I'm contrary like that. Because I think that means he can't really like me, by definition. But he's only given me signs that he does—and shouldn't that feel good?

This is the best thing for everyone. *Win-win-win-win-win.*

I tap through all the fields and sign. And then I call him.

"Okay, well," I say when he picks up on the third ring. "Guess you can explain rugby to me now."

Mark Winterson's booming laugh feels like the biggest compliment. "Best phone call I've gotten in ages."

His voice sounds lower on the phone than in person, raspier. I wonder what he's doing—if he's sitting on the couch in sweats, or lying in bed talking to me. The mental image makes my internal temperature rise.

"How are you spending the rest of your evening?" he asks.

I glance around my living room, at the dark TV and faded floral wallpaper and excessive amount of TKMART throw pillows on the couch. "No particular plans."

"Come over," he says, voice deep and smooth, and it sends a ripple of anticipation through me.

For a second, I try to weigh the consequences—but it's so quiet and lonely in this house, and the spontaneity excites me.

"I'll send a car for you," he adds. So I tell him the address.

*

The car glides through the night along the freeway, near-full moon hanging over the buildings of the West Side. It deposits me in front of a condo by the beach, a shiny modernist box in concrete and glass.

Mark Winterson opens the door, leaning one arm casually against the frame, and a smile spreads over his face.

"Come in," he says, taking a few steps back.

I slip off my sandals to be polite, even though he's still wearing his dress shoes. He's ditched his suit jacket, standing there in his shirt sleeves, yellow tie under his collar.

This condo is unreal. A full wall of windows that must have an ocean view when the shades are up. Living room furniture that looks like something out of an interior design magazine. An open-plan kitchen a chef would love.

He gestures expansively. "Mi casa es su casa," he says. "You want anything to drink?"

"I'm good." I cross my arms and take a lap around the large space. Everything is sleek and shiny—polished floors, marble counters, brushed-metal fridge. There aren't many personal touches anywhere. It's hotel-like that way, and there's a faint new-car smell.

Nerves prickle up and down my spine as I navigate around his leather sofa and dark wood coffee table. I can hear waves crashing, and I lift the edge of the shade a touch, revealing a glimpse of dark ocean outside.

"You had me sweating there for a second," he says. I turn on my heel and he's standing closer than I expected, holding a glass of whiskey in one hand. He stares into it and swirls the liquid around. "Thought I'd scared you off."

My heart jumps as he steps closer, and I will my mind not to slide back to that shitty movie theater from ten years ago. *Don't compare it like you always do. Let it be its own thing.*

"Well, here I am," I say, head tilted up to hold his gaze.

He sets his glass on the table, and I can practically feel the barrier of restraint that was between us trembling, about to come down.

"Here you are," he echoes, brushing my cheek with the backs of his fingers. Petting me, almost. Gazing at me possessively, like I'm his new favorite toy.

I catch his wrist, and his dark brows lift in amusement as I kiss the thin skin there, holding eye contact the whole time. His warmth beneath my mouth sends a thrill through me, like unwrapping a present I've been staring at for weeks.

He laughs as I let go of his wrist and pulls me closer by the hips. "You're full of surprises."

See? He wants you here.

I press my lips into the five o'clock shadow on his impressive jaw, inhaling that cologne smell I can't quite name. Something sharp and something soft. Tobacco and amber? Smoke and sandalwood? Whatever it is, it smells expensive.

Then he claims my mouth, and I can taste the bite of his whiskey with an undertone of acidic mint, like he gargled mouthwash when I was on the way over. His lips change position like they're on a timer, and a feeling nags at me, in the corner of my mind—it's too smooth, like he is, in general. Too studied, somehow, a routine he's gone through many times. Something about this kiss is like a (very nice) form letter.

You're overthinking it! Self-sabotaging again!

I pull back, trying to reset, and give him a flirty smile to cover my nerves. He brings out my pushiest self, and he seems to like it. Maybe I'll lean into that tonight.

I reach for his tie right below the knot, and his throat bobs as I tug him toward me and walk slowly backward. He catches up and slides his arms around my waist, kissing my neck until my legs hit the cold leather and I plop down onto the cushion.

"Tell me what you want," he whispers, leaning over me, hands on the back of the couch. "Order me around."

I'm always watching life with vague longing from behind glass, looking but not touching. Trying not to demand too much or be too difficult, never reaching out and grabbing. But somehow this bizarre situation makes me feel like I could be a different person.

I push on his chest so he leans back. "Get on your knees," I demand, and until this moment I would never have guessed I was the kind of person who would say that. Who'd feel something confusing and electric spark through me when he does what I told him, holding my gaze while he pushes up my tasteful midi skirt and strokes my thighs with the back of his hand. Who'd feel powerful for a second as he nuzzles me there with his nose, as he looks up and asks permission, tugging down my lacy black underwear.

But then his mouth is on me, and it turns out he can do some things that *distinctly do not feel like a form letter.* Where his kiss was impersonal, this feels like he has something to prove, heat-seeking, demanding. Every stroke of his tongue seems to say *mine mine mine.* A riptide carries me out to sea and I can't remember anything—how I got here, what I agreed to, what I was trying to accomplish, even my own name. And when he murmurs *Ruby* a little while later, I wonder distantly, *Who is that?*

CHAPTER 27

I get home at two a.m., thanks to another car Mark Winterson called, and doze off for a few hours before my alarm goes off.

I wake up in such a fog, I wonder if last night was a dream—but there's the contract in my inbox as a (somewhat jarring) reminder. My brain feels so tender and hazy, my first thought is: *I can't deal with running into Greg today.* I don't want to have to explain myself yet—and where does he find the nerve, anyway?—so I tell Erica I'm not feeling well and that I need to work from home.

At lunchtime, Greg texts again asking if I'm okay, but I don't write back. And then a message from Mark Winterson pops up on my screen: Come sailing tomorrow.

Oh sure, normal second-date stuff! I have to laugh out loud, and it's been so quiet in my house all day, the sound of my own voice startles me. But after a few minutes of agonizing, I write back: What should I wear?

*

When the car he sent to fetch me pulls up at the marina, Mark Winterson is standing at the curb, wearing a cable-knit sweater that reminds me of the rich guy from *Knives Out.*

"Hey, Ruby," he says as he opens the door and offers me a hand. He peeks his head inside and says, "Thanks, man," before closing the door and waving the driver off.

Mark Winterson leads me through a gate and down a long, narrow dock where boats are moored on either side.

"Here we are," he says, gesturing to the back steps of a gleaming white boat.

When we get onto the lower deck, he picks me up, spins me around, and kisses me. I'm breathless from laughing, lightheaded, smoothing down the too-short dress I decided to wear. For a second, I forget how nervous I am for this date.

"So," he says. "How do you like it?"

I shake my head, taking everything in. This back area is large enough for a couple of sleek beige couches outfitted with an assortment of blue throw pillows. There's a whole inside area ahead, and another deck above us.

"Yeah, wow, I . . ." My brow furrows. "Is this a . . . yacht?"

His smile stretches. "Sorry I could only get a small one on short notice."

I survey the second level, feeling slightly insane. "This is *small*?"

He lets out a short laugh. "It's my dad's."

Mark Winterson leads me inside to where the controls are. The . . . steering wheel? Whatever you call the thing that makes a yacht go.

He motions for me to sit beside him as he takes the boat out onto the water, narrating what he's doing for my edification while I nod along, overstimulated. The marina gets smaller and smaller behind us, and the wind whips my hair.

"Okay, this will do," he says, easing the boat to a stop. "I'll give you the tour?"

This boat is fancier than the fanciest hotel I've ever stayed in—clean lines, bright wood floors, and modern furniture in shades of beige and blue, like I'm inside a West Elm that somehow ended up in the middle of the ocean.

"There's, like, a dozen households' worth of couches on this boat," I say, dumbfounded.

Mark Winterson laughs as though he's humoring a child who said something strange.

The realization stirs, vaguely, that I go around all the time telling myself I'm rich, in an admonishing way. I'm aware of how much I have, especially compared to Mom when she was a kid. I grew up comfortable in a suburban house. I always had something to eat and a roof over my head. I splurged on an Erewhon smoothie that one time.

But I forget about actual rich people and how little I know about what they're up to.

As we're walking around, I keep snapping pictures to show Mom later.

"You're so cute," he says, giving me a one-armed side hug. "It's fun experiencing things through your eyes. Guess I take things for granted."

His tone rankles me. "Oh, well, it's not every day I go out on a *small yacht*." I take a couple more pictures of the view off the side for good measure.

Mark Winterson sits on one of the pristine couches, and I perch next to him, angling my phone to take a selfie with the ocean in the frame behind us.

"Where are you posting that?" he asks, strangely on edge.

"Relax, Mark, I read your contract." I pat his leg with one hand. "*Mutual consultation on posting photos of each other to social media.* I'm just sending it to . . ."

I nearly say *my mom,* thinking I can make up a fake story for him where she's still alive—the way Mom would edit the details of my life for new acquaintances she'd make sometimes, even when I was right there. A freelance graphic designer I was dating became *a creative director.* My completely average GPA in college became *nearly valedictorian, came so close but someone else got it, can you believe?* My closet of an apartment in New York that I shared with three roommates became *She's living with friends in Brooklyn, so trendy and glamorous, you know kids these days. She'll get it out of her system and move back soon, though.* It gave me an out-of-body feeling, the way Mom would edit around the facts, sew all her deepest wishes into their lining, embellish until the familiar details became strange to me.

But of course Mark Winterson knows about Mom. He's staring at me, eyebrows raised. "Send it to . . . ?"

"My aunt. So she knows you're real. She was asking about you."

He makes a sound halfway between a laugh and a cough. "Sure, that's fine. I am real, last time I checked."

His phone starts ringing, and he visibly startles. "Sorry, I was waiting for this one." He waves it in the air. "I should take it. Be right back."

Mark Winterson jogs up the stairs to the upper deck, and I settle into the couch to send Mom the picture of us.

ruby.ocampo:

Mom! Meet my boyfriend

I let that sit there for a few minutes. Maybe she'll be happy now. Maybe she'll find some peace.

sampaguita72:

Cute! You look good together. That's the kind of guy you should be dating.

Find out his credit score!

Then I send a burst of photos from the yacht.

ruby.ocampo:
I'm sure it's great

sampaguita72:
Oh my gosh! Is that real?

I press the phone to my chest. Maybe it will work this time. I have to be ready for her messages to be gone tomorrow. For *her* to be gone tomorrow.

It's what you've been scrambling to accomplish this whole time. It's what you want for her. You can't regret it now!

I force myself to take some long, steady breaths.

And then my phone buzzes with a message from my cousin.

Trisha:
Ate Ruby we're having another family party
Two weeks from today! Saturday!
You have to come okay! It's boring without you

She actually wants me there? I can't really argue with that.

But writing back and sounding normal right now is too overwhelming, so I mentally file it away for later.

A few more messages from Mom appear on my screen.

sampaguita72:
How much must that boat cost?
Is this his boat?

ruby.ocampo:
It's his dad's!

sampaguita72:
So impressive!
Seems like you've found a real keeper

She sounds happy—but somehow she's still here?

Okay. Okay, maybe these things aren't instant. Maybe I

need to stick with it, keep sending her photos so it seems like a serious relationship. We have technically only been dating for less than forty-eight hours.

My head flops back against the couch, and I glance around the room. On the coffee table in front of me are some navy folders with *Winterson Capital* embossed in gold. And I notice other objects around the room with the same logo: a baseball cap on the counter, a fleece draped over a chair, a tote bag tucked in a corner.

Mark Winterson comes back down the stairs, balancing carefully because he has a champagne flute in either hand.

"Sorry about that." He hands me one as he settles next to me, and we clink glasses. "Glad you're here."

I'm still on edge, between everything with Mom, and the opulent setting—not exactly in my element, here—and how prickly he was a moment ago. But now he's giving me that old soft smile.

I sip the champagne and realize I probably haven't eaten enough today, but I don't quite feel comfortable asking for a snack. Mark Winterson puts a hand on my knee and gives it an affectionate squeeze.

"Do I antagonize you too much?" I ask, giving him my best Bugs Bunny grin.

He smiles wider. "No, I like it. It gets boring, being placated all the time."

A reassuring warmth spreads in my chest. He likes my bad personality, and the *probing, slightly inappropriate* questions I ask. I guess I'll keep going.

"You gave me the basics of your résumé, but . . . tell me something I can't find out by googling you."

"Do you spend much time googling me?"

"A totally normal amount."

He seems to enjoy that idea. Maybe being googled is his love language. "What do you want to know?"

"Tell me . . . something you're insecure about?"

Mark Winterson laughs thinly. "You can't just come out and ask stuff like that. You'll never get a straight answer."

"Even if I signed a *light NDA*?" I set my champagne glass on a side table. "If you can't tell me now, when can you tell me?"

It takes me by surprise when he reaches for me and pulls me into his lap. "You've got me there."

He's quiet for a bit, head resting on my shoulder, arms around my waist. "This is going to sound pathetic," he starts.

"Try me."

"When I was growing up, I was just 'Grant's son' to everyone."

"Grant Winterson of Winterson Capital, I presume?"

He barely chuckles. "Yeah. My dad's this larger-than-life guy, for everyone in our social world. And in college, my cousin Zack—you'll meet him at some point—"

My cheeks warm at the way he's talking, like this is actually serious.

"Everyone was obsessed with him. And I was just 'that guy who tags along with Zack.' And now I'm . . . the guy who looks like some more famous, slightly taller guy?"

That makes me snort, and his chest shakes, too, reassuring me that I'm laughing with him.

"I'd love to break this streak," he says quietly into my ear. "Be known for something that's actually about me. Leave an impression that isn't secondhand."

"You want to make your mark," I say, and his laugh jostles me again. "Sorry, I'm terrible."

Mark Winterson plants a kiss on my neck. "No, uh, you're not wrong."

"So you'll turn TKCORP around, save this storied institution, be remembered for that?"

"More or less." He kisses the shell of my ear. "If I can prove myself to Erickson, secure my place here—maybe I can." Then he stands suddenly, scooping me up in his arms, and I shriek.

"Okay, now that you've grilled me"—he carries me across the floor, sun winking off the chrome surfaces inside the boat and the blue waves beyond—"I'm regretting that the tour barely glossed over the bedroom."

CHAPTER 28

Some time later, we're lying in the giant bed—what is this, a California king?—in the private room in the center of this yacht, sprawled across each other and exhausted.

Mark Winterson's hands are in my hair, stroking it distractedly while he is, for some reason, trying to give me financial advice. "Wait, so aside from your 401(k), you don't own *any* stocks?"

"The stock market sounds fake to me," I say breezily, trying not to sound as embarrassed as I feel. "Like, it just crashed that time."

"Your money could be doing more for you."

I shift so my cheek rests on his stomach like a pillow, getting a view of his jawline as he stares at the ceiling. "Money stresses me out."

He peers down at me, giving himself a fleeting double chin. "I'm sure you love money as much as anyone else."

My brain shuts down as soon as Mark Winterson starts talking about ETFs. When I think about financial instruments of any kind, my head fills with *fear fear fear.* Fear of losing what I have, all my money vanishing, because I don't understand these things, and I don't trust them, or myself. The way Greg lost his house, and his mom had to scramble. The way Mom would stash envelopes of cash in random places in case all the things we trusted to prop up our lives failed. The way she talked like that was a real possibility, like we had to climb and climb because the ground's not solid.

Mom was always so worried about something happening to me—she justified everything she did that way. *I want you to act right so you'll be safe and have a nice life.* She would regulate the order in which I ate the things on my plate for optimal digestion, because she read all these books that claimed gut health was the key to success. Every time I got sick, Mom would say it was my fault for not being careful enough.

Later, in New York, when I had more distance, I'd look back and think: Maybe because things felt so out of control after Dad left, it was comforting to exercise control over at least one other person. The way she'd say, *I'm scared of something happening to you. I don't want to lose you too.*

And then she goes and dies! God, what a hypocrite!

Tears are springing to my eyes for no reason, and before I can hide it, Mark Winterson is sitting up, cupping my cheek in his hand.

"I didn't realize this was such a touchy subject." He lets out an uncomfortable little laugh. "Are you okay?"

The echo of an almost-formed thought is still ringing in my ears, and I can't quite focus on being in this room with him. *Maybe "fear of losing" and "love" could be close enough to the same thing?*

"Yeah, just . . . emotional about money." I sniff and give him a weak smile.

Mark Winterson folds me up in a hug. "I don't exactly understand what happened here, but—are you going to be okay?"

"Yeah! Yeah, I'm fine."

"Okay, then." He looks at me like he's not sure. "In that case, I'm going to shower. We have dinner reservations."

He gets up, and a few minutes later, I can hear water running. My eyes dart around this unreal room and come to rest on one of those management books he likes—left face down on the nightstand, like he got a call in the middle of reading and abandoned it.

Mom raised me to never touch anything at another person's house without permission, and to this day I'm fascinated with people who can wander into someone else's home and casually pick things up, examine them, help themselves to food in the fridge.

But (a) it's someone else's *small yacht,* and (b) curiosity must override my superego. I reach for the book, peering closely at the underlined pages, trying to decipher Mark Winterson's spidery handwriting in the margins. He's underlined a passage about how high turnover can be good for growth, and dread sharpens between my ribs.

Mark Winterson comes back into the bedroom wearing fresh clothes, toweling off his wet hair. He crosses the room and plucks the book out of my hands, tossing it onto the bed with extra agitated snap.

"How important are layoffs to your management philosophy?" I ask, trying to keep my voice level and pleasant.

"Hey, let's be clear." He points at me. "No one said anything about more layoffs."

That is . . . not comforting, the way he just said that.

Mark Winterson scrubs the towel vigorously through his hair again. "But, yes, unfortunately, they're sometimes a necessary tool in the tool kit. Can't advance without some creative destruction."

"What does that mean?"

He makes a vague gesture. "That the market wants what it wants."

"Who is the market?" I get out of bed and start putting my clothes on—underwear, skirt, bra. "Have you met them?"

Mark Winterson gives me another indulgent laugh. "The individual choices of millions of people that move as their own force, take on a will of their own. And, you know—our shareholders."

My discarded shirt is flung over a chair in the corner, and I cut across the room to retrieve it, but he blocks my path with his body.

"Seriously though, Ruby." Mark Winterson grabs my wrist. "Don't go through my things."

"It was a book you left open!" I wrench my hand back. "I was curious what you were reading."

"I mean it." The edge in his voice makes me shiver.

"Okay! Okay, I won't." I rub my wrist. "Sorry."

I'm suddenly very aware that we're surrounded by ocean, and I can't exactly make my own way home.

CHAPTER 29

It's jarring, going back to real life on Monday morning. That moment on the yacht rattled me, but Mark Winterson was so charming at dinner that I forgot about it for a while. He laughed at my jokes, stole a kiss on the cheek, fed me some lobster. I took as many pictures of the fancy spread for Mom as I could, and afterward, we went back to his place again.

Now the TKCORP lobby is bustling, and that whole thing feels like a scene from a different world. Voices echo around the high-ceilinged room, and there's a bottleneck forming around the entrance to the elevator bank as people are slow to badge in.

There's Greg, up ahead—somehow I'd recognize the back of his head in any crowd. He's standing with Sarah, Morgan, Al, some of the accountants.

And I remember with a start that I went all weekend without responding to his texts, and I probably ought to talk to him.

"Greg!" I call across the lobby, and he turns and meets my eye.

But then Mark Winterson sidles up on my right and slips an arm around my waist.

"Hey, there you are," he says, kissing me on the cheek. Right here, in the middle of the lobby, in the bright light of day.

Wow, hard launch, okay!

My co-workers are all staring at me. I can practically hear Morgan's jaw drop.

"I looped in HR, of course," Mark Winterson says in my ear. "It's fine, there's nothing to worry about."

Greg's still turned this way. And it's strange, but I can actually see his face shift as though in slow motion, like he's registering the scene playing out before him on a delay.

He's usually so relaxed, always laughing at everything. All *life is too serious to take it too seriously.* But I can't remember the last time I saw him looking this crushed.

Sarah tugs on his sleeve from behind, and he follows her as they swipe through to the elevators.

I squeeze Mark Winterson's arm and say, "Late for a meeting!" before I dash across the floor, through the turnstile, and slip into the elevator.

But as the doors close, I realize the mistake I've made. We're all packed in here—my teammates, a bunch of the accountants, a smattering of people from other departments—and everyone is gawking at me.

Grace from Sales giggles and nudges my shoulder. "Damn, girl, didn't know you had it in you!"

Beside her, Sarah swats her arm and mouths something I can't make out. Somewhere in the far corner, Al coughs.

Greg's standing by the elevator buttons. I'm on the opposite side, trying to catch his eye over the heads of the people between us, but he seems very determined not to look.

Some people get out on the third floor, and I take the opportunity to loudly whisper: "Greg! Greg, can we talk?"

Morgan leans in, on alert for gossip.

"Um, yeah, sure," Greg says, glancing up. He's blinking a lot, dazed. "Stop by six for a second?"

The elevator dings for the sixth floor, and all the accountants pour out ahead of us. A couple of them give me a quick little up-nod. "Hey, Ruby," one guy mumbles.

Greg and I get out and linger in the hall before the entrance to the open-plan-office part of the floor. He stares at the industrial blue carpet for a long moment before gathering himself to ask: "Is this really what you want?"

"Um." I swallow hard, all the *win-win-win* reasons from last night looping in my head. "Yes?"

"Then everything's fine."

"Okay?" I squint into the sun that's coming through the tall windows behind him, with their view of the TKCORP parking lot and the old pool across the street. "Is it, though?"

Greg looks at the ceiling and sighs, like he's fighting with himself.

There are so many things I want to yell right now, but maybe they don't totally make sense. Things like: *What do you want from me?* And *Why are you acting this way?* And *I thought I was doing the thing that would preserve our friendship! Not ruin it again!*

He gestures behind him, not looking at me. "I should get to work. Bye, Ruby."

And he walks away while I stare at his back.

I run into the elevator and go straight to the bathroom on the eighth floor, tucking myself into the corner of the biggest stall so no one can recognize my shoes, like an old co-worker in New York taught me.

I don't know why Greg is acting this way, and I don't know why I'm acting this way, either. But as emotionally clogged as I am so much of the time, for some reason the tears are coming hot and ready, all this water springing onto my cheeks faster than I can wipe it off. I start laughing, even though I'm still crying. *What the hell, body?*

People come and go in here, politely ignoring my sniffling.

Someone slides a tissue box under the stall door, and I recognize Sarah's perfectly manicured hand. But I'm slow to get to the door, and by the time I open it, she's gone.

CHAPTER 30

The next week passes slow and strange.

After coming in so intense, wanting to spend all this time together, Mark Winterson is suddenly scarce, focused on some big project Erickson assigned. I send him a few texts, and some terse responses land hours later. A few days in, I start to wonder if I dreamed the whole thing.

Texting Greg is a similar experience—he takes hours, sometimes days, to reply, then says as little as possible. After work, I'm spending too much time alone with my spinning thoughts. I take longer runs around my neighborhood, down streets lined with jacaranda trees. The vivid purple blooms almost make me blush with their audacity. I'd forgotten about them while I was gone.

Unlike when I first moved back, I start jogging by Greg's house, hoping to find an excuse to talk to him. But I get too scared to knock the first few times I pass by—and the third time, Sarah's car is in the driveway, which scares me off for good.

The silent treatment reminds me of our years of not talking. By the time Friday rolls around, I'm so upset, I call in sick with a fake stomach bug.

And that afternoon, I get a text from Mark Winterson:

Mark Winterson:
come over tonight.

Ruby:
don't tell Erica
i'm supposed to have a stomach bug

Mark Winterson:
i'll never tell.

Ruby:
fine, but I'll drive

For once, instead of getting into a car he sent, I make my own way to his condo and park my old Honda on the dark street outside. Mark Winterson comes out onto his front steps and stops to stare at my car, light from his doorway framing him from behind.

"That's what you drive?" He puts an arm around me when I get close. "We'll have to do something about that."

But he turns on the charm again, and I almost forget about the weird dissonant moments lately. He puts on rugby and attempts to explain it while he cuddles up on the couch beside me, and I cut in with as many bad jokes as possible, and he plants kisses all over my face.

"Man, I could never live in the UK," I say, listening to the commentators. "I think the accents are too funny. And too attractive! I'd be inappropriately laughing all the time, and also in love with everyone."

"It's settled, then," he says, enveloping me in a bear hug, like he's going to physically stop me from leaving. "You're staying right here."

When I wake up in the morning, Mark Winterson is gone already, and I sweep a hand over the high-thread-count sheet beside me. There's a note on the nightstand.

> Had an early meeting. Sorry work's been crazy. There's croissants and coffee in the kitchen.
> I'll be back later—stay and we'll get lunch.

I brace myself and open Slack, checking to see if Mom is still there. And when she responds to my *Good morning!*, a rush of despair hits me.

Fuck. I am running out of things to try! Why isn't anything working?

I'm beside myself, mind racing, overwhelmed—and I can't even talk to anyone about it, since Greg is barely answering my texts.

There is still *BE CLOSER TO FAMILY,* which I leapfrogged over, before I go completely back to the drawing board.

With a pang of guilt over leaving my cousin on read for a week, I quickly tap out a reply to Trisha: Yes, I'll be there!

you better! she writes back. It makes me laugh.

But when I try to picture bringing Mark Winterson to see my family in San Diego, the stress in my body ratchets up. It's a visceral reaction, instant, like the snap of a rubber band. *Not happening.* Maybe it's just too soon.

I lie there staring at the ceiling, painted a pale shade of gray that's probably got a name with *pebble* or *dove* in it. And the memory I'd shoved down tumbles over in my head: how he grabbed my wrist, suddenly stormy, adamant about me not going through his things.

What is he hiding?

I slide out of bed, bare feet on the fluffy white rug by the bedside. *Time to snoop!*

I peek through his closets filled with pressed shirts and suits, ears straining for sounds of him returning, ready to scramble and put everything back the way I found it at a moment's notice.

I pad barefoot down to the living room, scanning Mark Winterson's bookshelves, thinking about when I'd spy on Greg's reading habits from a distance.

It all starts out normal enough, but the further I get, the more the sinking feeling deepens. Some classics. Some hefty novels I've always vaguely intended to read at some point. *Infinite Jest. Freedom.* The literary Jonathans. A couple books by Jack Welch—the title *Jack: Straight from the Gut* makes me snort. Some Nietzsche. F. A. Hayek. Milton Friedman. The complete works of Ayn Rand. Margaret Thatcher's memoir.

Hmm.

On the kitchen counter, there's a bunch of papers tossed around haphazardly, like he was searching for something and left in a hurry. A folder peeks out from underneath the pile, and I slide it out and flip it open, trying to remember the exact configuration he left all this in so I can re-create it later.

There's a bunch of official-looking documents—*Articles of Incorporation,* the papers say—and my cheeks burn with the knowledge that I should probably not be rifling through these. But it's strange. They're for a bunch of different companies with similar names. *GERBO I LLC, GERBO II LLC, GERBO III LLC.* It's a thick stack; there must be at least a dozen here.

How many companies does this guy have? Why does he need all of these? Is this some normal business thing I don't understand?

I'm sensing my limits here—a liberal arts person who lets the world turn without understanding what makes it happen. That whole money layer of everything that flies over my head.

The sinking feeling gets deeper while I slide the folder back where I found it.

When I finish and glance at my phone, the message on my screen gives me a start.

sampaguita72:
What are you doing right now?

Annoyance sparks through me, heart pounding, on the defensive. Mom always had an uncanny sense for when I was breaking a rule, like she could put up her own psychic reader shingle.

But the tension in my shoulders softens when I remember she must be lonely in there. She just wants to be involved.

ruby.ocampo:
I'm at my boyfriend's condo!

And then, anticipating what she'd say about me sleeping over, I quickly add:

ruby.ocampo:
I came over for breakfast
And he told me to hang out here while he runs some errands, isn't that sweet?

I wince—old habits die hard. I'm editing myself like I would when she was alive.

When I was in New York and we talked on the phone once a week, she'd ask for *all my news,* like only updates showing my steady forward progress could make her happy. She didn't want to hear *I stayed in binge-watching TV in my underwear again* or *I can't remember anything that happened at work this week, it's all a blur of screen glow and light back pain.* So I gave her only the most creatively curated updates. I'd paint a selective portrait of every guy I dated, designed for her to approve of him. Sometimes I'd find myself believing it, to the point where I'd lose track of how I really felt. And I'd avoid her calls altogether when I didn't have enough cheery news to share.

I walk around the condo taking photos for her: the spacious kitchen with its chrome appliances and marble countertops, the fridge filled with chilled bottles of Evian. The minimalist decor in the living room, the leather couch, the art on the walls that makes me wonder if Mark Winterson paid someone to pick it out for him. The polished hardwood stairs and the ocean view from his bedroom.

sampaguita72:

Wowww very very nice Ruby

Beautiful home!

Not like in here, so plain

Goosebumps rise along my arms. What *is* it like in Slack? What can she see? What did she say the other day, when I was talking to Erica?

Why don't you wear a more colorful top? Maybe put some flowers in your cubicle so they show up in your background?

Wait.

ruby.ocampo:

Mom, can you see Zoom in there?

sampaguita72:

Oh yes, it starts projecting on one wall every time you have a meeting

I cringe, thinking back on all the awkward calls she's had to sit through.

sampaguita72:

You were right, by the way

I blink a few times. I can't quite process that combination of words, coming from her.

sampaguita72:
Erica really isn't very nice

That message makes my eyes water. I reread it again and again, trying to absorb this thing I was starved to hear. It takes a while to sink in. And a question that's been nagging at me makes its way past my fingers and onto the screen:

ruby.ocampo:
Mom, why were you so critical of every guy I dated, but you also seemed unhappy when I was single?

Then my stomach drops, and I want to delete it. But Slack informs me that sampaguita72 is typing already.

sampaguita72:
Obviously I wanted to protect you from making my mistakes.

In life Mom would change the subject, or scold me for being nosy and disrespectful, or counter with an unrelated accusation directed my way. This is new, and my heart feels like a bird trying to flap its way out of a cage. Maybe we should have tried talking on Slack more when she was alive.

I realize I have my laptop here—for some reason, I grabbed my work tote when Mark Winterson suggested sleeping over. I guess I associate him so much with TKCORP, it was habit?

ruby.ocampo:
Want to watch a movie with me while I wait for him to come back?

Even though Mom declared early in my life that she didn't believe in romance anymore, she always had a soft spot for classic rom-coms. All through middle and high school, every Friday night, she'd sit down in front of the TV with a basket of clean laundry. We'd watch together, making running commentary until the clothes were all folded. She'd usually nod off well before the end credits, too exhausted to see the happily-ever-after she wanted so badly.

sampaguita72:
Oh, well, I'll have to check my schedule
So very busy in here

I can picture her smug little smile, the one reserved for when she thought she was telling a real zinger.

sampaguita72:
I should be able to make that work

I settle in on the couch downstairs with my laptop, start a call with no one else in it and share my screen, streaming one of her old favorites.

The movie plays, and Mom's running comments pop up on my phone. I write back, volleying jokes back and forth, giggling into the empty room. I can't see or hear her, but the realization hits me in a flush of guilt mixed with gratitude, an uncomfortable ache—*somehow I feel closer to her now than when she was here.*

sampaguita72:
This is nice
But I miss popcorn
Have some for me?

So I get up and search in the kitchen, scared of smudging any of the too-smooth surfaces. But I do find some microwave popcorn, and I take extra care choosing the most aesthetic bowl I can find in the cabinets, fluffing the mound of popcorn to look as appetizing as possible for the photo I'm sending her.

sampaguita72:
That's good

And my heart hurts at those simple words, the way I'd always scramble for these crumbs of validation.

CHAPTER 31

While I'm staring at my screen on Monday, drawing a blank on an assignment from Erica, I think about those documents in Mark Winterson's kitchen and find myself on the Wikipedia article for shell corporations, opening every source in a new tab. Then I have the sudden urge to look up Winterson Capital, and of course I go straight to the "Scandals" section, which sends me down another rabbit hole about their involvement in pushing risky mortgage-backed securities in the mid-2000s.

And I think about helping Greg and his mom as they carried boxes to their car, a foreclosure sign on the lawn. Tita Wendy tearing up and Greg putting a hand on her back, telling her it was going to be okay.

I think about the heat that crept into Greg's voice when he said we're not exactly in control and things don't make sense. And about the answers he might have been searching for in high school, when he'd stay up late reading and sleepwalk through his classes.

*

On Thursday afternoon, I come back from lunch to find a strawberry fruit tea (no boba) sitting on my desk with a note underneath it:

> *Sorry I'll have to miss you this weekend—work is crazy. I'll be thinking about you the whole time.*

I slump down in my seat, half relieved. At least I don't have to ask Mark Winterson to come to San Diego. He's busy anyway.

Erica raps her knuckles on the wall of my cubicle, reminding me it's time for the all-hands meeting.

The auditorium on the corporate campus is packed with people milling around, finding their seats. I spot Greg in the distance with Sarah and Morgan and Al, and shoulder my way through the crowd to catch up with them. They're all sitting in a row together, but there's one open seat at the end, next to Sarah.

"Can I . . . ?" I ask, pointing to it.

"Oh, uh—" Sarah gives me a stiff little glance. "Sure."

Do I smell, or something? I think as I settle into the folding theater seat.

Mark Winterson appears onstage, wearing one of those microphones that hovers in front of his mouth. "What's up, TK-CORP!" he shouts with real wedding DJ energy.

Sarah snorts quietly, and I slide down deeper in my seat.

He didn't mention he was going to be leading this. Though maybe I should have assumed?

And as charming as he is, somehow it does not translate well onstage, in front of a big crowd of people. His energy is ratcheted way up, but he's not really bringing anyone along with him. The room is silent, and his jokes are falling flat.

Mark Winterson is talking about TKCORP's future, trying to get everyone amped, but I can't make sense of what he's saying. It's that dense thicket of buzzwords again, and the words I do know seem vaguely sinister. *Transformation, new efficiencies, streamlining.*

"We're going to be growthmaxxing around here," he says with a sly smile, and that gets a murmur of laughter.

And the realization dawns on me: *Oh yeah, he's not just the person he is with me in private.* He's got this whole other side to him. And maybe he's *more* that person than the one I've gotten to banter and fool around with so far.

"You know what's bad for growth, by the way?" Mark Winterson says, grinning like a motivational speaker. "Unions!" He points at people in the crowd at random. His expression seems to say, *Ah ah ah, don't you go starting one!*

"A union would mean less money for all of you, believe me. Good thing we don't have one around here, right?" He actually winks.

It makes me cringe. What even is this speech?

I always vaguely thought well of unions. Tita Wendy was a proud member of the nurses' union, before her pivot. On the wall of the common room in my college dorm, someone had slapped a bumper sticker: *UNIONS—THEY GAVE US THE WEEKEND!*

When I glance down the row of my co-workers, they're all on their phones, messaging.

Greg's name pops up on Sarah's screen. There's Morgan's, and Al's, and Carol's, then Greg's again. They're all in a group chat together, without me?

Sarah seems to sense me looking, because she flips her phone face down.

I could really use some air. I slip into the aisle and powerwalk to the exit in the back, straight out of the building and into the grassy courtyard.

"Ruby!" Greg calls, and I turn to see him jogging toward me, work lanyard bouncing on his chest. "Wait up."

My heart rate spikes but I pretend not to hear him, and he trails after me as I cut a quick path to the parking lot.

Right before I reach my car, I spin to face him. "What do you want?" I demand.

Greg holds his hands up, palms out. "I wanted to say I'm sorry. About what I said at the bar. I was out of line." He takes a deep breath in, lets it out in a quick huff. "Obviously you'd know better than me what makes you happy."

"Took you two whole weeks to work that out?"

"Yeah, I'm not the sharpest." He squints at me in the bright sun, shading his eyes with one hand to see me better. "A bit slow."

His self-deprecating grin makes me soften a little. It's like the Greg I know is back, the one I was friends with when we were sixteen and things between us were simple. A strange affection swells up inside me like a balloon, and it scares me—I need to puncture it—so I ask in a rush: "Why didn't you tell me you were dating Sarah?"

Greg takes a sharp breath in and blinks at me a few times. All of his muscles seem to tense.

"Don't look so shocked I figured it out! You guys are always sneaking around together. Kind of hurt my feelings that you didn't mention it."

"Oh, um—" His brow furrows, and he seems way more nervous than I would have expected. "Sorry. Yeah, it's . . . complicated."

"Well, if you ever want to talk about it, I'm here." I try to smile gamely. "Here for your girl trouble."

"Oh, uh, sure. Yeah." He nods again. "For sure."

Damn, why is this so awkward?

"How's your mom?" Greg asks abruptly, leaning against my beat-up Honda.

"She's . . . still here." I chew on my lower lip. "I'm at the end of my rope, honestly."

Relief surges through me, and I realize how much I've missed being able to talk to him about this.

"Did you try everything on the list?"

I let out a long breath that puffs my cheeks. "There's being closer to my family. I'm going down to San Diego this weekend."

"Oh man, your Tita Rina's lumpia? Legendary." Greg sounds relaxed again, like normal. "Say hi to her for me." He met her a few times, years ago, when they came up to see us on holidays.

"Would you . . . want to say hi to her yourself? Maybe have some lumpia?"

Greg gives me a weary smile. "How can I say no?"

CHAPTER 32

Greg insists on driving us on Saturday—and he does take more of an active interest in maintaining his old Acura than I do my old Honda, so I don't fight him.

Just two old friends who are both in relationships with other people going down to San Diego! I tell myself as I get into the passenger seat. And it's a relief to have company as I tackle item #4: *BE CLOSER TO FAMILY.*

For the first hour of the drive, we crawl down wide Orange County freeways, stuck in traffic, vague anxiety about seeing my family swirling in my gut. Even though I'm relieved to be spending time with Greg again, I can't figure out how to fill the silence between us. He taps his fingers on the wheel and offers up some old gossip about mutual friends, but eventually he runs out and goes quiet.

Finally we reach the stretch of the 5 that runs along the ocean, an expanse of breathtaking blue to our right.

Greg glances over and asks, "You nervous?"

"I'm that obvious?" I lean my head against the window. "I don't know, I feel like I'm bad at family."

Somehow going to see my relatives always feels like a test of character—a spotlight shining on everything that's lacking about my life. The way Mom would pointedly say, *Jamie is dating a banker* or *Rosie graduated from med school* or *Why can't you be helpful like your cousins?*

"Why do you think you're bad at family?" Greg asks.

I never managed to put this feeling to words so bluntly, back when we were close.

"Mom always seemed unhappy with me, I guess."

Greg turns that over in his head for a while, focused on the road, sunglasses on. He looks even better than usual, somehow. My eyes skate over his smooth cheeks, his full lips. He's dressed casually today, and his dad's chain is out over his T-shirt. It seems like he got a fresh haircut for this occasion.

"I love your mom, but . . ." Greg says, picking up his thought after such a long pause, I assumed we'd dropped it. "But maybe . . . that wasn't a *you* problem. That she was unhappy."

I turn to face the ocean, chewing over what he said.

Mom always said I should try to be warmer, friendlier, more inviting—but in some ways, she was closed off and cold herself. Tita Wendy would rib her about it. *You're so aloof, hard to know,* she'd say, swatting at her with a rolled-up newspaper after she tried to introduce Mom to some of her friends and she gave them a chilly reception. The conditions must have aligned just right when Tita Wendy broke through Mom's defenses, like an eclipse or something—to be repeated only once every few decades.

I glance at Greg again, and with the ocean to my right and the sun in my eyes, flying down the coast, I have the sudden powerful urge to run a hand through the hair on the back of his neck. But it passes quickly, like always.

✶

As we walk up to Tito Rob and Tita Rina's house, awkward moments from years past play in my head.

We'd come down here once or twice a year when I was growing up, and I was always struck by how close all my other cousins were, more like siblings.

Mom wanted me to get closer to them—but then, from the way she acted, it also seemed like she didn't want me to get *too close.* The way she made excuses not to come herself. The way she'd constantly tell me to stay out of the sun, and lied about where she was from. The way she panicked when I was in kindergarten and I'd been spending time with another Filipino girl whose family came over more recently, and I'd started saying *peenk* instead of *pink.*

And I know, I can't blame her for everything. But somewhere along the line, I started to feel like I'm all sharp edges and uncomfortable pauses around my cousins, where they're warm and natural and fluid. I was clueless about all these things they just *knew*—card games at Christmas, how to dance, how to score 100 at karaoke. I was clumsy at everything, uncomfortable in my skin.

We go inside, and there's a cluster of Titos sitting around the TV watching basketball. I recognize a few of them, the rotating cast of older men who are vaguely related to me but aren't my mom's actual brothers, and whose names I would probably mix up, if you quizzed me. One time when I was twelve and I brought a Percy Jackson book to read at one of these things, the guy in the center of the couch asked me why I wasn't reading the Bible instead.

Through the screen door to the backyard, I see Tito Rob—my mom's actual younger brother—working the grill. We head out into the backyard, and he spots me and throws his arms out wide.

"Ruby!" he says, giving me a stiff bear hug, still holding the tongs he was using in one hand. "It's been too long. I haven't seen you since the, since the—" He was probably going to say *funeral,* but somewhere midsentence maybe he regretted bringing it up.

"Yes!" I say, patting him on the back. "It's been too long."

"Come on, help yourself, eat." He gestures with the tongs at the long table crammed full with aluminum casserole dishes. I make myself a plate, loading up on Tita Rina's famous lumpia. It's been years since I had these—the timing was always wrong when I came back from the East Coast for a visit. I can't help but immediately pick one up and take a bite.

The crunchy wrapping, the rich, savory filling—it's food like a warm embrace.

Mom would get annoyed any time I said something about Tita Rina's lumpia. *Who has the time to make that?* she'd say. *Of course* she *can, being married to someone who can help.*

"You're a worrier like your mom, ha?" Tito Rob says, catching me frozen in front of the food table mid-bite. He sets down a serving dish of barbecue skewers and points at me. "Ah ah ah! I can see it. You're worrying right now."

"You got me!" I say, doing a single finger gun with my free hand.

"You know, Roobs . . ." Tito Rob snaps the tongs together, fidgeting. "You're welcome here anytime. Whatever is happening. You're all alone up there—we worry about you." He reaches out to squeeze my arm with his non-tong-holding hand.

"Have some more," he adds, nodding toward the table. "Take some home, too, if you want."

Maybe I've been dense in the past—maybe I'd block out every little thing that showed they love me, selectively focus on the dissonant moments and ways I was coming up short. Maybe everything that's happened lately has heightened my senses, disoriented me so much I'm paying more attention.

But the mixture of worry and acceptance in his voice, and the gentle way he tells me to eat more—it sounds so much like

We love you, it's overwhelming, and tears intrude at the edge of my vision. I really have become such a crybaby these days.

Someone else comes up to talk to Tito Rob, and I excuse myself and hurry through the house, back onto the front steps.

"Ruby. Hey." Greg comes through the door and sits on the stoop, putting an arm around me and drawing me close, face pressed into his shirt.

"What is it?" he says quietly. "You can tell me."

"It sounds stupid," I mumble into his chest.

"Not to me."

I sit upright and take the tissue he hands me. "I think I've always felt like . . . Mom kind of hates me." It's embarrassing how jagged and blunt it sounds, how juvenile. "Like I know she loves me, but—also, she hates me. And I thought that meant they're going to hate me too. So I avoid them."

"No way they hate you." Greg wraps both arms around my shoulders and gives me a squeeze. "And I felt like your mom hated me too, honestly. So."

That makes me laugh, and he laughs too. We're jostling against each other, chests shaking, his arms still around me.

"It must be hard when it's like she wants you to be a different person," he says, voice low. The present tense gives me vertigo.

"But I'm glad you're this person," Greg adds, leaning back and brushing some hair out of my face. "I love her, you know?"

The blood rushes to my head, and I scramble to stand.

"I should go find Trisha!" I exclaim as Greg blinks up at me. "She wanted me to come, I have to say hi."

The second time Greg and I kissed, we were on the couch in my living room, trying to study. His grades were bad, and his mom begged me to help—and textbooks open beside us, we drifted into each other, fumbling fingers on my cheeks and fireworks between my ears.

But my mom walked in, and it wasn't a huge surprise that she freaked out. I knew by then what she thought of him.

The next day, I overheard her having an urgent, hushed conversation with Tita Wendy on the phone, but I could pick out only every few words.

Afterward, she cornered me and said, "Look, I love Greg, but he's not right for you. You want someone who can set you up for a nice life. Someone who'll lift you up, earn more than you. I don't think Greg's that kind of person. Trust me, I know what's best for you."

Who's saying anything about the rest of our lives? I wanted to scream. *I'm in high school!*

I was all ready to defy my mom—*We're in love! To hell with everyone else!*

But then things got weird. Greg acted like nothing had happened. He was distant, avoiding me. And it crushed me, but I was desperate not to show it.

I felt so stupid. *Oh. He wasn't even that serious.* I was the fool who fell harder and got bruised on the way down. Something shifted overnight and he was hanging out with all these new people—before I knew it, we didn't even have the same friends anymore. Soon we were barely speaking at all.

In his tagged photos on Instagram, I'd see him at parties with new friends—with other girls. And when we'd see each other because of our moms, our small talk got awfully strained.

One time I tried addressing it directly, and he clammed up and said, *We don't have to overthink it, okay?* So we never talked about it again, even though those two stolen kisses became my baseline, the one I'd subconsciously use to measure every first encounter with someone new.

But I'm over that now—it's ancient history. I'm dating someone who really likes me. I should have brought him today—

I will, next time! And I have the maturity and perspective to know that Greg was saying he loves me as a friend.

I swing by the food table and grab a couple skewers, biting into the blackened chicken. It's perfectly smoky, tangy, and sweet from Tito Rob's Jufran and Sprite marinade.

Tita Rina's sitting at a table they've set up in the yard, gossiping with my other aunties in rapid Tagalog and laughing. I've missed that sound, even though I don't know what they're saying. Weird how the texture and music of a language can feel like home, even if you don't understand a word.

She spots me and waves me over. "Ruby, it's been so long, glad you made it! Come here, let me see you!"

She launches into a stream of updates about all the cousins who are around my age: where they're working now, the cities they've moved to, all the engagements and babies on the way.

Across the lawn, Greg's crouched down next to Tito Rob and Tita Rina's younger kids, Gabe and Michael. Last time I checked, they were in fourth and fifth grades. Greg's talking to them seriously, gesturing to the Switch in Gabe's hands. Gabe hands Greg the game, and Greg sits cross-legged on the grass while both of my little cousins point and shout instructions.

Tita Rina's updates have wound to a close, and I take the opening. "Have you seen Trisha?" I ask.

She points to the backyard play set Tito Rob built at least ten years ago. "I think she's turned into a bat," Tita Rina says with a laugh.

And sure enough, there's Trisha, hanging upside down from the monkey bars, scrolling on her phone, hair almost trailing the ground.

My heart clenches as I cut across the yard toward her. *Little weirdo like me.*

"Hey." I sit down on the swing and bite into the turon on my paper plate—crispy egg roll wrapper covered in honey, creamy fried banana inside.

"Hey, Ate Ruby." If Trisha was excited to see me, she's not showing it now. She keeps scrolling on her phone, perfectly content to be upside down.

"Doesn't the blood go to your head like that?"

"Good for thinking," she says.

"What are you thinking about?" I ask around another mouthful of turon. "What are you into these days?"

Trisha sighs. "That's such an old-person question."

I laugh. "Sure, probably."

"Do you actually want to know, or are you just making conversation?"

"Um, yeah. I want to know!"

Trisha hesitates for a while. "I'm working on a project about self-limiting beliefs." She gives me a pointed look. "Seems like you would have a bunch of those."

Wow, burn. She wanted me to come because I'm a good research subject? *Most Neurotic Ate of the Year Award.*

But then again, she's not wrong.

"Okay. I'm interested. Tell me more. Is this . . . a school project?"

"It's my own thing. On TikTok." Trisha sets her phone on the ground, grabs the bars to hoist herself up, and drops back down on her feet. "You should follow me," she adds, and tells me the username.

She perches on the plastic slide next to me and launches into a detailed explanation, asking me a few loaded questions, and before I know it, I'm spilling my guts to her—telling her the whole story about Mom being a ghost in Slack, though I make her swear she won't tell her parents. She narrows her eyes at me. "Who do you think I am? Of course I won't tell them that." But she seems to believe me out of hand, asking thoughtful follow-up questions about the situation.

And when I get all the way to the end of the story, she gives me a sage little *hmm.* "I don't know, Ate Ruby," she says. "Maybe you're the one holding yourself back. You're so focused on who your mom wants you to be, but who do *you* want to be?"

It sounds so cliché and simple when she puts it like that, but I feel exposed and clammy in the open air of the backyard, realizing I don't have an answer.

"I'll have to think about it," I say, standing from the swing. "But I should get back on the road soon. Traffic is going to be killer."

I find Greg in the living room watching basketball with my Titos, chatting with them and reacting to the game like he does this every weekend. I really envy him, how he's good with people. How he can insert himself into a new situation and be at home.

CHAPTER 33

It takes us longer than I expected to make it back. There must have been an accident or something—traffic is at a crawl.

I'm spent from this afternoon, but the exhausted silence in the car feels comfortable. It's like we're back in high school, when Greg and I could spend hours together, doing the same things we'd do if we were alone.

The sun is going down by the time we take our exit off the freeway, and the golden early evening light makes the sky look like a matte painting in an old movie. As we come to a stop at a light, Greg says: "I'm hungry again already."

I laugh. "Didn't you have thirds?"

"It was that awkward 'late lunch/early dinner' time." He glances sideways at me. "Beach burrito?"

It used to be our regular thing—going to a drive-through after class, buying one burrito, sitting by the ocean, and passing it back and forth until it was gone. And I have that old fizzy feeling in my stomach, amazed that he wants to keep hanging out.

So we get our burrito, make our way to the beach, and find

a spot on the sand. The sun has dipped almost below the horizon, the chill of dry Southern California evening coming on.

I have the photos from the party on my phone, and soon I'll have to try sending them to Mom to see if that finally makes a difference. But I'm scared to find out, either way. I'm putting it off.

We sit there in silence, passing the burrito back and forth like when we were kids, the smells of avocado salsa and fatty chicken laced with salt air.

"How did you even end up at TKCORP?" I ask after a while. "Didn't seem like your scene."

"I wanted to coast, I guess," he says around a mouthful of food. "Do something that was easy for me. And numbers, you know . . ."

He shrugs. They always made sense to him.

"And I did it because . . ." Greg lets out a long breath. "I didn't want my mom to have to work anymore, at some point."

I hug my knees, fidgeting in the sand. "I'm sorry I said that thing about living with your mom. It must mean a lot to you to be able to help her out."

"Thanks," he says, passing the burrito back to me. It's notably shorter than the last time I had it. "I appreciate that."

That frustrating, unfinished conversation we had at the bar replays in my mind.

"Greg," I say as gently as I can. Maybe I can find a new way in. "You *know* something happened in senior year. Why did you stop talking to me?"

He lets out the longest sigh. Impressive lung capacity—must be all those lunchtime gym trips. "Because . . . I read the room. And for a while, it kind of hurt to be around you. That was my own issue—it wasn't your fault. And giving you space seemed like the better friend thing to do."

Read the room? What the fuck is that supposed to mean?

I'm scared to examine it too directly. The melancholy in his voice, and how pained he looked when he saw me with Mark Winterson in the lobby—a dizzying, ground-shifting feeling rears up, like I've been reading him wrong for years. I can't stand to think it all the way through; I need a safer topic.

"So what do you do at the gym?" I ask around a bite of burrito.

"Lift weights."

"Damn, Greg, who even are you?"

"It makes me less depressed."

"You're depressed?"

"Isn't everyone?" He smiles to himself and looks out at the ocean. "Got into it a few years ago when that was more of a problem. It's better these days."

It makes me think about how much I missed, avoiding him all these years. I wish I could have been the bigger person and gotten over it sooner, so I could have been a friend to him when he was going through that. He made a dumb mistake when he was seventeen, and I just can't let go of a grudge.

I love her.

The warmth of acceptance in his voice when he said that, steady, unbending—I feel like I don't deserve it.

I lean my head on my raised knees and look at Greg. He shifts to get more comfortable on the sand, and his dad's gold chain glints in the moonlight.

"What do you remember about your dad?" I ask.

"Not a lot," he says, staring at the water. "His vibe, mostly? Calm, reassuring, even-keeled. So I try to be like that when I can." He chews on his bottom lip. "It's mostly snippets of things, not full memories. A shirt he wore. A flash of his smile. Some random things he said." Greg makes his voice deeper. *"Real men know how to cook."*

I nudge him playfully. "Guess you didn't take his advice? When do you ever cook?"

He laughs a little sadly. "I—" For a strange moment, he hesitates. "Yeah, I should get on that."

The silence stretches out, waves crashing. The burrito is gone now, and I crumple the empty wrapper in my hand.

"Okay." I can't put it off anymore. "Let's see if this gives Mom some peace."

There's a tight knot of dread in my gut as I choose the photos to upload. For a few weightless seconds, I sit there holding my breath.

ruby.ocampo:
Mom? Are you still there?

And then the words pop up on the bottom of the screen: sampaguita72 is typing.

sampaguita72:
Where else would I be?
Is Rob still working that same job? He hasn't gotten a promotion yet?
Rina's going so gray, I can't believe she hasn't started dyeing her hair!

All the same things she would nitpick in life. The questions that would frustrate me and make me zone out on the phone from New York, saying *mm-hmm* at regular intervals.

ruby.ocampo:
Do you feel any different?

sampaguita72:
Why are you always asking me that?
Do *you* feel different?

Does she even realize where she is? Does she remember that she's dead?

I'm so frustrated, tears are welling up. *I've tried nearly everything! Am I ever going to get her out of there?*

"Hey." Greg puts a hand on my shoulder.

"It didn't work!" I drop my phone in my lap and press the heels of my hands over my eyes.

Greg rubs my back, and we sit like that for a while as the waves crash. "It must be hard to have to just . . . try things," he says quietly. "Shots in the dark. Rummaging through all the corners of your life."

"Not as hard as it must have been to raise me alone! And I can't even do this for her! What if—what if I never figure it out!" The dam breaks and I'm crying again. Mom would hate to see me like this. *Have some character,* she'd say, *some dignity!* But here I am, an undignified hot mess, losing another round of Trying to Be a Better Person.

"What if she's trapped in there forever?"

"You know . . ." Greg starts again quietly, like he's trying not to spook me, his knuckles tracing a slow path up and down next to my spine. "I wonder if my mom was wrong. When she said—" He hesitates, and I get the sense he feels bad saying something to contradict his mom, even though she's not here. "Maybe your mom's unfinished business doesn't have anything to do with you. Maybe it's not something you can fix."

I don't know what to do with this idea—don't know where to put the things it makes me feel. I stand abruptly and brush the sand off myself, offering Greg a hand up.

"Thanks for coming," I say as I pull him to his feet.

"You're welcome." Greg laughs, but there isn't much joy in it. "You can stop thanking me. It's okay. We've known each other forever."

An uneasy silence hangs between us on the drive home, and when he turns into my driveway, we both sit there, not moving. I can barely stand to be around him right now, but I also don't want him to go.

Greg stares at his hands on the wheel and takes a deep breath in.

"He's not good enough for you," he says finally, like he's been workshopping that in his head, all the times he's been silent over the past few days. "And—and I don't know who is, but—" His voice is ragged, a way I'm not used to hearing him. "But he's definitely not."

I'm so surprised, I have to laugh. "What are you even talking about?" I've been thinking about Mark Winterson in aspirational terms for so long—the Guy Mom Would Want Me to Date, from the moment I laid eyes on him. "Seems like he's better than me by most metrics."

Greg's eyes tick over to me. "Not by any of the ones that matter."

The mood in this car has gotten weirdly intense, all of a sudden, and part of me is frustrated verging on angry. *You're dating someone else! I'm trying to move on from you! Why are you making it so hard?*

So I give him a tight smile and say, "Good night, Greg," before I clamber out of the car and shut the door.

CHAPTER 34

There's nothing left on the list to try. I don't know what else to do for Mom now. And things with Greg get weirder every time we hang out. *He's not good enough for you* loops in my head, and I resolve to avoid him for a while.

It's Sunday afternoon, and I'm lying on the couch, staring at the wall and moping when Tita Wendy stops by.

She slips off her shoes—sneakers a streetwear blog would envy—and breezes through the house to the kitchen, Tupperware in hand. I can see she's made laing, another one of my favorites: taro leaves and pork in a thick sauce of spicy coconut milk. Even better as leftovers, because all the flavors have had time to mingle.

Guilt creeps over me like a rash as she finds a place for it in the fridge. I should learn to cook so I can bring her food sometime. I'll add it to the to-do list, once I figure out how to free Mom from Slack.

"How've you been, Roobs?" Tita Wendy asks when I join her in the kitchen.

"Oh, I'm okay!" I sigh, wavering about whether to burden her with this. "I just . . . don't know what else to do."

Tita Wendy gives me a sympathetic look and rubs her palms up and down my arms. "Think about it some more. I'm sure it will come to you."

I shake my head, and she pats my arms gently, clicking her tongue. "I'm so glad you and Greg made up," she adds. "He was getting insufferable."

She collects her purse from the kitchen table, where she'd dropped it, like she's about to head out.

"Tita Wendy, you really don't have to keep making me food!" I add in a rush. "It means so much to me, but I don't want to make extra work for you."

Her mouth forms a surprised little O. "But I'm not—"

"I know, I know, you just made too much."

"No no, uh—Greg asked me not to tell you, but . . ." Her mouth curls into a knowing smile, and she raises a hand as if to deflect incoming objections. "A mother reserves the right to make a judgment call."

"He asked you not to tell me . . . ?"

"Greg made this," she says with a casual flick of her hand toward the fridge. She laughs. "I haven't really cooked in years!"

The floor of the kitchen spins, and I brace myself on the counter, trying to seem normal.

"He got interested in it a few years back, when he was going through a rough period. Heartbreak, I think? Some kind of girl trouble—not that he talks to me about it!" Tita Wendy smiles like it's really a funny story. "He needed a hobby. And he seems embarrassed about it for some reason—who knows why." She shakes her head, and the wistful look on her face says, *That boy is hopeless.* "But it works out for me, anyway. I love not having to come up with dinner every night."

So every time one of them brought me food . . . Greg actually made it? This information is too much to process. It's like my body can't absorb the idea of him caring for me like that.

"Anyway, I've got to run." She gives me a quick kiss on either cheek. "But we're nearby in case you need anything."

I need to lie down, and after the door closes behind her, I slump back onto the couch.

Greg's been feeding me for months, and he didn't even want me to thank him. An aching mix of guilt and gratitude sticks in my chest.

I grab my phone and start writing him a text: hey thank you so much—

But then I delete it, because he didn't want his mom to say anything, and I don't want to make things weird for them.

Instead I put on some rice, lie back down to stare at the ceiling while it cooks, and heat up the laing once it's almost ready.

I take some photos of the steaming plate in front of me, searching for the best angle, and send one to Greg with the message: sooo good!

And just in case it makes him uncomfortable, I add: your mom really is the best cook.

CHAPTER 35

All of a sudden, Mark Winterson seems to want me around more often. He asks me to sleep over twice during the week—unprecedented!—*and* on the weekend.

But the more time I spend with him, the more I notice strange things. On Tuesday, he keeps getting calls all evening. While we're eating at a restaurant, he gets a text that makes him visibly agitated, and he walks outside, telling me to stay put and that he'll be right back. And when he returns, his eyes are a little red, and there's some pink in his cheeks.

On Thursday, he starts putting on his clothes at two a.m., and when he notices that I'm awake, he says he needs to go to the office for an emergency—something about how TKCORP's operations are global, so he's never really off the clock.

And on Saturday night, we're lying in bed when his phone starts buzzing on the nightstand, and he hurries out of the room to answer it. Whatever he's saying sounds urgent, but I can't quite make out the words.

He comes back and gets dressed in a hurry while I keep my eyes squeezed shut. His footsteps recede down the stairs, and there's some distant clattering, the sound of him moving around below. I hear the word *Fuck!* distinctly at least once. There are a few moments of silence, followed by the rumble of the garage door opening and closing. I pad over to the window in time to see his sleek black Mercedes driving away into the night.

What on earth?

I get up to pace around—there's no way I can sleep now—and wander down to his office. The first thing I notice is the glow of his monitor. His computer has been left on, screen unlocked, open to his email.

And even though it feels wrong, every strange thing that's happened lately, all bundled together, propels me across the floor to his keyboard, where I search the words *DocuSign Relationship Contract,* looking for the same one he sent me.

And *oh my God,* there are so many! His whole dating history laid out here, relationship contract after relationship contract. Following each one, a few weeks after the first email, there's a follow-up to the same address—*Update to: Relationship Contract.*

"Contract terminated in person," I read out loud. "Irreconcilable differences."

My fight-or-flight response kicks in, and Greg's voice pops into my head, saying, *Dude seems like he'd talk to you for twenty minutes about the texture of his business cards.*

I'm staring at all the names of the women who received this contract before me, and on a whim, I toggle over to the browser to google them.

But . . . oh my God. In the browser, he's—I bite my finger to keep from screaming—*still logged in to his bank account.*

There's the landing page with all his account information, like he left in a frenzy.

My first thought is: *Holy fuck that's a lot of money!*

And my second thought is: *Huh. That's weird.*

There's the same amount, recurring, over and over. So many transactions for $9,999. *Nearly ten thousand dollars!* An eye-popping sum to me, on its own.

A bunch of those transactions are deposits into his account—all from the weirdly named LLCs I stumbled across the other day. *GERBO I LLC, GERBO II LLC, GERBO III LLC,* on and on. And shortly afterward—a couple days, usually, it looks like—there's an outgoing wire transfer in the same amount, $9,999.

With trembling hands, I lift my phone to take a picture—and I manage to get it before I hear the garage door rumble below. *Shit, shit!*

I move the windows on his screen so they're the way I found them, clear the search from his email, put the computer to sleep, and race up the stairs, diving into bed, heart beating so loud I'm convinced he'll hear it from the ground floor.

I lie there rigid as Mark Winterson's footsteps come up the stairs, and as he shuffles around, getting undressed again. My heart rate has slowed by the time the bed dips and he climbs in. He edges closer, curling up around me, and tosses an arm over my stomach as I focus on taking slow, steady, sleeping-person-sounding breaths.

Of all times, why does he want to spoon now? Maybe a little corporate malfeasance makes a guy needy.

After a while, I carefully slide out from under his arm, moving slowly so I don't wake him. I gather up my clothes, creep downstairs, and get dressed. And I grab a pen and hover over a block of Post-its on the counter, trying to invent something that will keep him from getting mad or suspecting anything is wrong.

Headed out to an early workout class! See you later.

xoxo,
Ruby

And then I slip out the front door and run to my car, driving home as fast as my 2002 Honda Civic will take me.

CHAPTER 36

I need to break up with Mark Winterson. Sure, maybe there's a chance, gnawing at my gut, that some new relationship milestone would be the thing to help Mom move on. And I don't 100 percent understand what I saw in his bank account, but between all the weird things that have happened since we started dating, I can't stay in this relationship. I have to bail.

Unfortunately the goddamn contract specifies that the relationship *cannot be terminated by electronic means,* including phone calls. At the time, when I skimmed over it, I thought, *Good, he won't be able to dump me with a text.* That's happened to me a couple times before, and I wasn't exactly a fan.

But I didn't imagine I'd be lurking in the stairwell, hoping to intercept him. Or that I'd be constantly texting him asking to meet up and getting evasive replies. Hey this project is crazy, I'm probably not going to make it home at all tonight, or I'm at an offsite and won't be back till late. I even wait outside his place in my car one evening, but when midnight approaches and he still hasn't shown up, I throw in the towel and head home. Who knew breaking up with him would be this much work?

Days pass, and now it's Thursday evening, and I'm the last one at the office, finishing a research memo Erica asked for. I'm going through it with a fine-tooth comb, making sure there's nary a comma out of place. I've been staring at the screen for so long—I need to look at something else for a few minutes, so I get up and pace around the empty eighth floor.

Some new flowers on Sarah's desk catch my eye, and after double-checking that no one else is around, I lean into her empty cubicle. There's a tiny heart-shaped card dangling from the bouquet, this time with a handwritten note inside:

Picked these ones myself!

Happy two months

Love, G

But that's not Greg's handwriting? It's too neat and looping, where his is more of a scrawl.

I hurry back to my desk. Maybe it's time to get out of here.

I'm so antsy on the drive home, fingers tapping the wheel as I pass by the high school, by Sterling Field, by the boba place I used to go to with Greg. And—

Wait. There's Greg?

He's standing outside the old diner we would go to sometimes after class.

I hit the brakes irresponsibly, and the car behind me honks. With a grimace and a sheepish wave, I make a left into the diner parking lot. The asphalt is littered with bright purple petals from the jacaranda trees around the edge.

Greg's gone now, but there's Morgan and Sarah, heading inside. And a few more people from work I recognize are also getting out of their cars and drifting over: more of the accountants, and some of the people I saw on pub trivia night. Adam holds the door open for Carol.

I follow them inside, and there are a few dozen more people from work, gathered around a series of tables they've pushed together in the center of the dining room. Some of them I never work with, but I recognize them from when we were in school together. It's empty in here, other than this crowd—it's a wonder the diner stays in business.

There's Greg, back turned to me, talking and gesturing at a piece of paper. Next to him, Morgan has her laptop open, and—I move closer to see—there's a very detailed, color-coded spreadsheet on her screen.

Sarah sees me and reaches across the table to close Morgan's laptop.

"Hey!" Morgan says, before she turns around and startles at the sight of me.

Wow, I'm the jump scare.

"Ruby!" she squeaks. "Hi! What are you doing here?"

"I, um . . . come here often?"

Greg turns toward me, and the tension on his face is hard to read.

"Okay, that's a lie, I just . . . I saw you guys and felt left out?"

I look from face to face uncertainly. Everyone is eyeing me like a stray dog who wandered in—or maybe a coyote.

Steve the Project Manager nudges Greg. "We can't tell her!" he whispers—or at least, he probably thinks he's whispering, but he's bad at it. "She's dating management!"

Greg sighs wearily, the way he does when he's heard something too many times.

Sam from Sales sneezes, and some cards he was holding in one hand scatter. Sarah dives for them, but before she can snatch them up, I grab one by my foot.

There's a lot of text on it, but my eyes gravitate to a few words across the top:

AUTHORIZATION FOR REPRESENTATION

It all falls together—the time I thought Greg was handing out business cards at the reunion. All the times he stayed late for mysterious reasons. Mark Winterson's weird remarks at the all-hands.

"You guys are forming a union?"

Greg stands and pulls me to the side, by the pie case.

"You can't tell anyone. And I mean *anyone.*" The urgency in his voice, and the stern look on his face—it's an unfamiliar side of him.

"Or you'll what?"

"Or—" Greg glances at the ceiling and lets out a long breath that puffs his cheeks. "Or it'll kill me and I'll haunt you."

I laugh despite myself. "Wow, too soon."

"It probably would kill him, honestly," Sarah pipes up from where she's sitting. "Greg really made this happen. Brought all of us together. We've been working on this for years."

My heart swells with pride for him. "Damn, Greg, you've been busy!" I exclaim so vigorously, it makes him laugh.

I want to shout: *See, Mom! Greg does apply himself when it counts!*

"You have to keep this to yourself, okay?" His eyes are pleading. "We're so close, and—" Greg glances at Sarah, and she gives him a meaningful look. "It matters for everyone here. For everyone's jobs. And we're racing the clock, trying to get this together before the next round of layoffs hits."

"You think there's one coming?"

"Yeah." Greg sounds so tired. "Much worse than the last one."

Time slows, and I'm very aware of everyone I spend most of my waking hours with, watching us from the tables.

Al is peering over here sadly, and my chest tightens at the idea of him losing his job. Carol and Morgan are whispering to each other. Sarah's arms are wrapped around her middle like she has a stomachache. From the seat beside her, Grace from

Sales puts an arm around her shoulders, and as Sarah leans into her, Grace plants a light kiss on the top of her head.

Wait. *Love, G*?

So much for my psychic link with Greg! I read this situation completely wrong.

Greg is standing with his arms crossed in front of me, and my heart hurts, thinking about him being unemployed and Tita Wendy having to worry about their mortgage payments, after they already lost their house once.

"Look, I'm not going to tell Mark Winterson anything." My eyes dart between Greg and the group at the tables, sizing me up. "I've been trying to break up with him."

"You have?" Greg says with sudden enthusiasm.

"You've been *trying*?" Carol from Legal arches an eyebrow. She seems out of place in this diner, with her sleek blond bob and black pin-striped pantsuit, her short pumps and skeptical expression. She has a permanent let-me-speak-to-the-manager voice going on.

"Yeah, he's been . . . hard to pin down recently." My heart seems to beat louder and louder, the longer I stand in front of everyone. And a wild idea starts to form in my head. "Maybe I could help you."

Morgan turns in her seat, peering at me curiously.

"I . . . found some weird stuff at Mark Winterson's house," I say. "It seems like something strange is going on."

"Strange, like . . . ?" Sarah says.

"Financially?" I laugh nervously. "Like . . . is this a crime?"

Morgan's eyes widen. Carol's jaw drops. Greg looks like he's seen a ghost.

"It's that thing you were talking about—" Sarah starts, turning to Greg.

"We've already told her enough!" Steve the Project Manager cuts in. "How do we know we can trust her?"

"Let her finish," Greg says firmly. "I've known her my whole life, okay? If you trust me, you can trust her."

"Sorry to interrupt!" A woman with an apron around her hips and a pad in hand comes by. "Are we ready?"

Morgan picks up a menu, but Carol cuts her off, orders enough fries for the whole table, and gives the waitress a tight smile that says, *Please leave now.*

"Ruby?" Carol prompts. "What are you suggesting?"

Adam from Accounting pulls out an empty chair, gesturing for me to sit. So I do, scooting in nervously.

"Maybe I could put off breaking up with him for a couple weeks. And try to notice what I can, in the meantime. And tell you about it. Maybe get you something you can use."

I glance at Greg, still standing behind me, looking skeptical and confused.

The list of my self-limiting beliefs that Trisha made me write is running through my head:

I am selfish
I am lazy
I am a mess

Maybe I can accept myself. Use my inertia, be selfish and messy for a good cause.

"I mean, lord knows I've stayed in relationships past their expiration date before," I add. Around the table, that gets a couple nervous laughs. "Maybe I can put that to good use. I got myself into a weird situation, but . . . maybe I can use it to help you guys out, before I extract myself from it."

Greg walks around the table so he's facing me, expression flat, annoyed. "What exactly are you saying?"

Sarah looks concerned, and Morgan looks like she's about to reach for some popcorn.

"Maybe I can spy on him for you guys. Or throw him off your trail. Buy you some time, at least."

"Are you sure about this, Ruby?" Al asks.

Greg scoffs and looks at me like I've lost it. "Are you kidding? That's insane."

"I'm dead serious, Greg!" And then I start to sweat, thinking of the paperwork. "Um, there's just—there's this thing I signed."

CHAPTER 37

Carol from Legal peers at my phone through her reading glasses, scrutinizing the contract.

"There is in fact nothing *light* about this NDA, Ruby," she says, gaze flipping back up to me.

"He had you sign an NDA?" Greg actually looks like he wants to kill someone on my behalf. Regrettably for me, my first and most powerful thought is, *It's kind of hot.*

"Why did you sign this?" Carol laughs. "Was the sex that good?"

"Carol!" Rebecca from HR scolds.

Greg's scratching his neck like he has a rash.

"She can't tell you without breaking the NDA," Steve the Project Manager cracks.

"Wow, hostile work environment!" I snatch my phone back and shoot Steve an acid glare.

I'm ashamed enough to last a lifetime already, but the idea of this random dude from high school judging me makes me see red. I want to make him squirm right back. "I'd give him a six out of ten," I add.

Sarah cackles. "Brutal." She glances over at Greg, who's looking very interested in the ceiling tiles. "Sorry," she says.

"I'm an idiot, okay!" I exclaim. "No thoughts, head empty."

Morgan nods knowingly. "I remember being like that. It's relatable. Losing our minds over a hot man who is ultimately kind of terrible—I mean, it happens to everyone."

Al furrows his brow. "Does it?"

"God, what is this, *Melrose Place*?" Diane from Complaint Resolution says under her breath.

"Hey," Greg says. "Ruby's willing to take a big risk for us now, okay? Ease up."

"Why don't we vote on it?" Sarah says. "Whether we trust Ruby to, uh . . . work with us on this."

"What happens if we don't trust her?" Steve asks.

"Then I'll sign an NDA about this too, and you can sue me if I break it."

Everyone laughs, and I feel lighter for a second.

"All in favor of trusting Ruby," Sarah says, "raise your hands."

The moments when everyone is thinking about it, trying to make a decision about me, seem to stretch on forever.

And suspended in that moment, even though I've been settled on breaking up with Mark Winterson for days, a pang of guilt hits me—because of all the things I've tried, dating him is far and away the one Mom has been happiest about. A panicked, lizard-brained part of me squeaks, *What if marrying him was the thing that could make her move on?*

But hands start going up, one by one. Morgan's and Al's and Sarah's. Rebecca's, tentatively, then Carol's too. All the accountants, Grace and Sam from Sales, some people on other teams I haven't seen since school.

I twist backward to look at Greg, who's been pacing the whole time and is once again hovering by the pies. His hand goes up, reluctantly. There's something complicated in the way he's staring at me, and I can't tell if it's directed at me or himself.

In the end, there's only a handful of detractors. It almost makes me tear up—a literal vote of confidence.

"The ayes have it," Sarah says.

Greg lowers his arm. "Okay, I think we're good here. Ruby, let's talk? I can fill you in on everything."

In the time it takes us to get to the playground, an evening fog has rolled in, and the glow of the streetlamps in the distance is all fuzzed out and hazy. You can't even see the school building on the other side of the field. It's like Greg and I are in our own little world, pushing ourselves back and forth on the swings, wondering where to start.

"You should break up with him," he mumbles.

"Excuse me?"

"Just break up with him!" Greg exclaims, an unfamiliar edge in his voice.

A contrary impulse overtakes me. I want to shout, *Don't tell me what to do!*

He tugs at his hair with both hands, like he's losing his mind. "I felt like I needed to defend you back there, but . . ." His hands drop into his lap. "This is ridiculous. It's a bad idea."

I take a deep breath. Maybe we should reset. Find a different way in to talking about this. "How did you even end up organizing a union?"

"Kind of by accident? A bunch of us were talking about how things had been going at work, and I said we should form a union, half as a joke."

"Nothing like living out your joke suggestion."

He laughs and shakes his head like it's the craziest thing. "But Sarah went to college with someone who works for one of the big unions who could represent us. We met with her, and I talked to people at work about it, and I started to realize . . . people wanted to listen to me? And I started to think, the more I talked to everyone . . . maybe there's something we can do here."

"So capitalism isn't a meritocracy, and we're not really in control and things don't make sense—but you believe in the union?"

Greg's smile gets wider, recognizing his own words thrown back at him. "I like it better than the alternative. Wherever things are going, we're here in the meantime, with one another—all of us, day to day. We're all we've got. We'd better make the most of it."

"You said you're close to going public with it?" I prod. "How close?"

Greg rocks himself back and forth in silence. And then, with a deep sigh, he pulls out his phone.

"You know TKCORP is massive," he says, tilting the screen horizontally and holding it out in front of me. It looks like he's pulled up the same spreadsheet Morgan had on her screen earlier.

"Maybe fifty thousand people?"

"Yeah, across all offices. We're starting by unionizing headquarters first, and hopefully other offices can follow, one by one. But even that's like five thousand people. Huge. That's why it's taken years. Kind of a miracle we've managed to keep it a secret this long."

He scrolls down the spreadsheet with one finger. "We've been going around to everyone we can, getting people on our side in different departments."

Every row in the spreadsheet is a name, and beside each one is a number and some notes. It seems like every single person who works at the main office is in here.

"Can I see?" I ask, and he passes the phone to me.

"The colors show who's talking to who," Greg says, leaning closer in his swing and pointing. "Everyone gets a rating based on how likely we think they are to support the union—'one' is most likely, 'five' is least."

I scroll down slowly, skimming the notes about conversations the union members had with each person. They really have been busy.

Finally I reach my name, and there's a *three* next to it, with some comments attached.

Five, she's dating management (Steve)
Two, she's cool (Greg)
DO NOT CONTACT (Carol)

My heart warms at what Greg wrote, even though the doubt stings at the same time.

"We need half the people in the office to sign cards before we can have an election," Greg says as I pass his phone back. "And we're basically there."

"That's amazing!"

"But if you go public with only that fifty percent secured, you'll probably lose. Management is going to pull out all the stops to turn people against us. They've already started—you saw."

Greg looks down at his feet, shuffling them in the dirt. "Every week we put it off is a gamble. If they find us out, they'll probably lay us all off before the bigger wave. We're holding out until the company retreat that's coming up, because that'll be big for us—everyone from the departments we've had trouble reaching will be there, in one place."

"I still can't believe you got twenty-five hundred people to sign cards."

"Helps that a lot of us went to school together. All that social overlap across departments." The corner of his mouth turns up. "Why do you think the accountants throw so many parties? Good recruitment strategy."

"Is that why I never get invited?"

"You think I haven't wanted to invite you?" Greg lets out an exhausted laugh. "I'm relieved you know now, honestly. I'm sorry I didn't tell you, before you started dating . . ." He trails off and waves a hand.

"Why didn't you?"

"You were going through a lot. And I figured it didn't exactly fit with your mission? Trying to live the way your mom wanted. I didn't want to derail you." He sighs again, staring out into the fog. "Maybe like a week or two before that all-hands, we realized Mark Winterson was going to be a problem. He started showing up to every work-adjacent social event he could, trying to catch any union gossip, figure out who was involved. He's Erickson's guy. The one doing his dirty work."

I stop swinging, all these weird moments from the recent past flashing back through my mind. "Okay, what should I be looking for?"

"I don't want you looking for anything."

"Greg, I'm doing this!" My grip tightens on the swing, chains digging into my skin. It's hard to explain, but when everyone's hands went up, it was like I could see the answer to Trisha's question shimmering just out of reach: the outline of who I want to be. "I'm always going around feeling like I'm this numb host for *tasks* and *unmet goals* and *failures.* But here's a mess I made that I can do something with, for once!" My voice has slowly been getting louder and louder, and now I'm shouting. *"So tell me how I can help!"*

Greg blinks at me, like he wasn't expecting this outburst. A little smile creeps onto his face, and I shove him reflexively, which sends my swing rocking from side to side.

He stares at his feet, fighting himself again, but eventually telling me must win out. "There was something in the books—

these recurring payments to a vendor I didn't recognize, coming up over and over. Same amount, each time. I tried to get more information about them, my boss ran it up the chain, and we got a bullshit excuse back. Right after I asked, that vendor disappeared for a while, and another weird one popped up. But when I mentioned that one, my boss told me to stay in my lane."

"How about this for proof?" I ask, pulling up the photo I took of Mark Winterson's bank account. It looks like it was taken through a screen door, the way the image distorts, but when I pinch to zoom, it's still clear—all the transactions for $9,999.

His jaw drops. "How did you get this?"

"He literally left himself logged in when he bolted out of the house at two a.m. This isn't exactly *Ocean's Eleven.*"

Greg runs a hand over his face. "I don't think it's enough on its own, yet. But it's definitely something." He moistens his dry lips in his mouth. "Just be careful, okay? Don't let him catch you."

He looks so worried about me, I can hardly stand it—I lean over and ruffle his hair, and he closes his eyes like it's painful. "I really hate this," he says quietly.

There's so much hanging unspoken in the air between us. But I keep thinking about everyone at the diner, and how clear-headed I felt for once, after years of fumbling around in a haze.

"I'll break up with him after the company retreat," I say. "That's two weeks—I've stayed in relationships I shouldn't have for way longer than that. Like there was Owen . . . Miles . . ."

"Jamie," Greg adds, ticking off his fingers. "Brian."

"All right, stop helping! What are you, my permanent record?" I whack him on the arm. "We don't talk enough, as a society, about the downsides of having lifelong friends."

"I'm not that much better?" Greg says with a weak laugh. "Averaging, what? Three or four girlfriends a year."

I do love some self-awareness.

"Yeah, you're kind of a fuckboy," I say wistfully. "Who knows if you've ever really liked someone."

"Ouch. That's harsh, Ruby." Greg sounds more wounded than I would have expected. "I've been trying! Every new relationship, I go in hopeful. But maybe . . . my heart has just been somewhere else." He hesitates for a moment, kicking the dirt under his swing. "I'm also not dating Sarah, in case you didn't figure that out." He squeezes the back of his neck with one hand. "I just couldn't think of another explanation on the spot, when you pointed out we were sneaking around. And I didn't want to blow our cover."

There's a rush of blood to my head, and I feel uncomfortably weightless, like I jumped off something tall. But all those old wounds and years of silence weigh on me; I need more confirmation.

"So when you said he's not good enough for me—"

"He's not!" Greg scoffs. "It's just a fact."

I give him a playful little shove. "Are you jealous?"

He takes the deepest breath in, lets it out real slow. "Ruby," he says like this is the most obvious thing. "Of course I'm jealous. I try to keep it low-key, but . . . there might not be enough adjectives in the world to describe how jealous I've been."

I have to laugh, even though the butterflies I usually keep tamped down are starting to riot. "Greg, I have . . . a lot to think about right now. It's—"

It's going to be hard enough to act like nothing is different when I'm around Mark Winterson. I have to deal with one thing at a time.

"Can you hold that thought for two weeks?" I ask.

Greg stares at the ground for a long moment, but then he nods slowly. "Yeah, I mean . . . I've felt like this for a while. What's another two weeks?" He reaches for my phone. "You have Signal?"

He adds me to the union chat and shows me how to mute notifications and set it so the messages disappear after twenty-four hours. "Check it when you're not with him," he says, jaw tense.

Then Greg stands, tugs me out of my swing, and wraps me in a hug, pressing me tight to him like we're not going to see each other for a year. His hand cradles the back of my head, fingers in my hair.

"Two weeks," I say again. "And then we'll have a long talk."

Greg huffs out a laugh, a small puff of air against my cheek. "Looking forward to it."

We go to our separate cars and absurdly follow each other home, mine after his down the same sleeping streets, stopping at the same red lights. When I park in my driveway, he slows, window down, and gives me the saddest little wave.

At home, I open the Signal thread, and there are all these messages rolling in. My first real group chat.

Al:
talked to some guys from the mailroom finally. They're in.

Sarah:
i had coffee with Lisa from Supplier Relations and she's working on spreading the word on that team

Morgan:
and hey, look at us
can't believe we have an undercover agent

Ruby:
LOL
i'll do my best

And Sarah sends me a side message, individually:

Sarah:
thanks for joining us
here to talk if shit gets weird
and i'm sure it will

My thumbs move to type but it's like with Mom's messages—I'm overwhelmed with too much feeling for pixels on a screen, too many things I want to say to tame with twenty-six letters, even with special characters and emojis. But I just write back:
thanks sarah!

And then a text arrives from Mark Winterson, asking if I can come over this weekend.

CHAPTER 38

When I get to Mark Winterson's place on Sunday afternoon, I stop outside the door and take a few deep breaths before ringing the bell.

Okay, you've got this. Don't think about Greg. Now is the time to compartmentalize and pretend you're in love with Mark Winterson.

I ring the bell, and it takes him a while to answer. I'm about to text, but the door finally opens, and there's the man I've spent all week searching for, looking like he hasn't slept in days.

"Sorry," he says, "I know I said I wanted to teach you tennis today, but . . ."

"Mark, honey, what's wrong?" I'm trying to put all the sweetness I can into my tone, and he gives me a confused glance. *Shit, did I overdo it?*

But then he shakes his head and rubs his eyes. "Been working some late nights on this Erickson project. Maybe I should take a nap before we head out."

"Do you want me to leave? Come back later?"

"No, stay," he says, pulling me in by the wrist.

He leads me over to the couch, and when I sit down on one end, he puts a pillow in my lap and rests his head on it.

"Sometimes I just feel like I'm in over my head," he mumbles.

God, tell me about it.

From this angle, he seems like a soft, breakable thing, not imposing at all. I put a hesitant hand on the top of his head, and he nestles into it.

A weird little swell of affection kicks up—I guess these things don't turn off on a dime—and my anxiety spikes, realizing I don't quite understand what to do here. Should I get him to talk more about Erickson?

"Like there are these—" He yawns. "These expectations and there's no way I'm going to meet them."

"I feel like that all the time."

He opens his eyes. "Why do *you* feel that way?"

Whatever I felt a second ago ebbs back again.

"We're talking about you right now," I say, running my fingers through his hair, and his eyelids flutter closed.

"Sometimes I think—*Fuck, I'm screwed.*" A smug smile creeps up on his face. "But I always pull it off in the end."

We're really not the same, after all.

"Does Erickson put a lot of pressure on you?"

He curls up a bit more and presses his cheek into the pillow. "Yeah," he says, voice thicker with sleep. "But it's because he thinks I have potential. And he trusts me."

"Did you know him before you started working here?"

"Mm-hmm. He recruited me. He's, um." He swallows. "He's a friend of my dad's."

"Oh, so you've known him for a while."

He rolls onto his back. "I know what you're thinking." There's a defensive edge in his voice.

My thoughts are just *GERBO GERBO GERBO.* "I doubt that," I say evenly.

"I earned this, okay," he bristles, shadowboxing with an argument he assumes I'm going to make. "I work hard."

"You're stressed," I say, stroking his hair. "Let's talk about something nice."

He curls back up on his side. "For example?"

My mind is drawing a blank, and my superego is shouting, *Don't say GERBO!*

"Tell me about something you like."

A tiny puff of air comes out of his nose. "Attention."

I laugh in spite of myself. "Don't you get enough attention?"

"Your attention specifically." He nuzzles his nose into my wrist. "It feels like an accomplishment."

My heart waffles, and a distant voice in the back of my head shouts at the rest of me, *Come on, really? You're going to fall for that?*

"You have my full attention," I say, kneading his earlobe between my thumb and forefinger, and the corners of his mouth curl up.

Mark Winterson opens his eyes, looking overcome with affection.

"Do you have anything to wear to a wedding?" he asks, and I nearly choke on my spit.

"A wedding?"

"This weekend. I had a plus-one when I RSVP'd, but . . ."

Oh God, what happened to the last girl?

"Anyway, I still have it. I didn't update them." His eyelids drift shut again, like it's too much effort to keep them open. "Would you come with me? Sorry it's last-minute."

"What's the dress code? I . . . might not have anything."

"It won't be a problem," he says vaguely.

But before I can ask him to explain, he's snoring already, out cold.

CHAPTER 39

I sleep over at Mark Winterson's house again on Tuesday, and once again he leaves in the middle of the night. But when I creep downstairs and search his office and living room, there's no sign of papers anywhere—it's like he's never printed out a thing in his life. His computer is locked, and of course I don't know the password. I pace the room, biting my nails. *Why did I think I could be some kind of spy?* It's not like I have relevant skills.

I'm scanning every surface of his office, like that will yield a clue. The leather and chrome chair that looks very Modern Design, the red and blue Persian carpet, the cringe mini samurai sword sitting on the desk by his computer.

I take a picture of the mini sword and send it to Sarah with the caption, What did I get myself into?

Sarah must be a night owl, because the dots that show she's typing leap up right away.

Sarah:
i'm trying not to judge but
hahahahahaha

Ruby:
YOU'RE JUDGING
MY TERRIBLE TASTE IN MEN
IT SEEMED LIKE A GOOD IDEA AT THE TIME OKAY

Sarah:
i'm laughing with you!
you pointed it out!

On autopilot, I open Slack for a second instead of Signal. And a message from Mom pops up at the top of my screen.

sampaguita72:
Ruby, what are you doing right now?

I nearly jump out of my skin.

sampaguita72:
Your green light came on
Isn't it late?

She really has a sixth sense for when I'm fucking up!

ruby.ocampo:
Just getting a midnight snack!
I'm going back to sleep in a second!

sampaguita72:
Are you sure you're all right?
How are things with that boyfriend of yours?
You haven't mentioned him in a while

Oh God, that's right—with everything going on, I've fallen off with updating her.

ruby.ocampo:
Oh things are great! We're going to a wedding together
this weekend

sampaguita72:
Oooh fun! Gosh I envy you
Maybe you'll catch the bouquet!
I regret that I didn't get to see you get married

Oh God oh God. Is *marrying Mark Winterson* the thing that would help her move on? Is there a way I can give her the illusion we're heading in that direction *and* spy on him at the same time?

But then again, maybe Greg was right: I don't know what will free her from Slack, or if it even is something to do with me. I get back into bed and squeeze my eyes shut, willing myself to sleep, but I lie awake the rest of the night.

Later that week, Greg is on the eighth floor talking to Sarah, but he keeps glancing over my way.

I feel so antsy, I can't sit still anymore, so I get up and shut myself in the copy room. And a few minutes later, there's a soft knock, and Greg slips inside, shutting the door behind him.

There's a knot of stress in my chest, because *oh God I'm balancing too many things emotionally right now,* keeping up too many ruses at once—for Mark Winterson, for Mom. But it's not like anyone can see us in here.

"You okay?" he asks, wrung out.

I laugh unhappily. "Are you?"

We stare at each other for a long moment. The light in here is dim. One of the overhead bulbs burned out and no one has gotten around to replacing it yet.

"Don't think I've really slept since we talked the last time." Greg smiles like it's funny, and his voice drops lower. "I hate the idea of you over there with him. When I thought this was actually what you wanted, it was one thing, but . . ."

I throw my arms around him, hugging him so forcefully, he lets out a surprised gasp. But he eases into it—hands on my back, his chin on my shoulder—and I'm flooded with relief, like stepping into a hot shower after a long day.

"Hey," Greg says. "It's okay." He squeezes me tighter.

His fingers knead the muscles between my shoulder blades, working out the tension around my spine. It's like Greg knows what I need, still, unspoken. Even in high school, my back would always be tense—too many hours bent over my desk studying—and he would sit behind me and work my sore spots with his thumb. Apparently he still remembers.

I take a step back, crossing my arms. Something he said has been bothering me. "Why did it hurt to be around me? At the end of high school."

Greg stares down at the carpet, and the long pause that follows nearly makes my heart stop. "Right after we kissed . . ." He heaves a deep sigh. "I overheard you and your mom talking."

Suddenly it's hard to swallow. "You overheard us?"

"It must have been, like, a day or two later? I was passing by, and the window was open, and . . . and instead of walking on like a normal person, I . . ." His eyes go up to the ceiling, clearly embarrassed. "I crouched in your bushes for a while to listen."

I have to laugh in disbelief.

"Your mom was saying I have my head in the clouds, I'll never go anywhere, I'm a bad influence. That I'm not the kind of guy you should be trying to date. And you said, *I know, Mom. We're just in high school, it's not that serious.*"

"I said that to placate her!" It feels like someone has turned up the thermostat in this room about ten degrees. "I needed to calm her down! And we *were* in high school. Why didn't you give me a chance to explain?"

He runs a hand through his hair. "I knew you weren't going

to go against your mom. And I didn't want to be the one to make you."

It hadn't ever occurred to me that he might think that, and now I'm flipping through years' worth of memories, reviewing them in this new light.

"I told myself: I like you too much, but it's not going to work," Greg goes on. "And my feelings are just going to create problems for us."

"Why didn't you ever talk to me about it?"

"I guess, in my mind . . . I thought you rejected me already." He lets out a defeated little laugh. "Didn't want to run a race I couldn't win."

I remember now—Greg was like this with a lot of things. Like that time I asked what he wanted to do when he got older, and for once he didn't answer with a joke. Maybe he was sleep-deprived, or the moon was in a strange phase, but he said that if he could do anything, he'd want to be a professor. It made sense for him, the way he read voraciously, like he was hunting for something.

After that, whenever I tried to bring it up, he'd deny it, find a way to deflect. And then one time, after I'd needled him enough, he spit out the truth like the words burned him: *It's not realistic, okay! I don't want to play a game I can't win. I'd rather not even try.*

I'm so frustrated—I'm so mad at him, deciding this all on his own!—that tears spill out onto my cheeks.

"Hey." Greg steps closer and cups my face in both hands. "Ruby. I'm sorry. It was—it was the wrong thing, looking back."

He wipes away my tears with his fingers, and I try to muster a reassuring smile.

"I thought you were over it already," he says, voice raspy. "I thought I would get over it someday."

It's clear now from the tremor in his voice that he never really did. All the times I judged myself for not being able to move on, all the years I felt pathetic—he was feeling the same, right there with me.

"I just thought . . . I knew where I stood," he says, eyes searching mine. "I wanted to be respectful. Not ruin our friendship because I got carried away."

A bitter little laugh shakes out of me. "It's possible you went overboard."

"I see that now." He scoffs, and his thumb strokes my cheek. "I was wrong. I'm sorry I didn't fight for us back then."

We're standing so close in this tiny, dark room. It would be so easy to lean in and press my lips to his.

Suddenly the Xerox machine behind me springs to life, making a horrible metallic shriek. I pitch forward, hands on Greg's chest, and we tumble to the ground so I'm on top of him, blue light from inside the machine shining on the walls, the top moving back and forth frenetically, its buttons glowing in random patterns. The machine spews out a stream of paper, and it flies against the wall, landing in a pile in the corner.

"Jesus!" I scramble to my feet.

"Maybe you leaned on a button?" Greg picks himself up and studies the display screen, hitting the side of the machine—but it keeps making that *ka-klack-ka-klack* sound and spits out more paper, as if to spite him.

I glance at my phone, conscious of how long I've been away from my desk, and there are about a million and one notifications.

sampaguita72:
WHAT ARE YOU DOING

Oh God oh God oh God. *How does she know?* What else can she see?

sampaguita72:
WHAT ARE YOU DOING WITH GREG IN THE XEROX ROOM?

In the corner of my eye, something moves—a security camera in the far corner, turning jerkily in our direction.

I look back at the spitting copy machine and realize with creeping horror—is that *her*? In the cameras, in the copy machine? Is the haunting spreading outside of Slack?

Erica opens the door. "God, what is happening in here! Such a racket! What did you do to the machine?"

Al comes in behind her, and he and Greg take turns inspecting the display and hitting the sides of the copier.

The machine is still spitting out paper, flying upward toward the ceiling, white sheets floating down in lazy spirals.

"Ruby, don't just stand there—call maintenance!" Erica shouts, fingers plugged in her ears to drown out the whining copy machine noise.

I nod and speed down the hallway, barely watching where I'm going, heart in my throat.

CHAPTER 40

"Oh, Ruby!" Erica calls after me. "Don't you have your offsite now?"

I pivot on my heel. "My . . . offsite?"

"Yes, did you forget? Mark told me about it." She points at me. "Good opportunity for you, a VP taking you to a meeting! Get down to the lobby, don't mess it up!"

I have no idea what she's talking about, but I grab my bag and rush downstairs, head still reeling. And through the big glass doors I can see Mark Winterson, leaning against his black Mercedes S-Class.

The doors part between us, and his grin gains in wattage as I step toward him.

"You asked for me?"

"The wedding is this weekend." He goes around to open the passenger-side door. "When did you think we were going to get your dress?"

I can't quite process what he's saying. All I can think about, as he starts to drive, is (1) I need to calm Mom down, and (2) *Holy shit, she can access way more than Slack!*

ruby.ocampo:
Mom! Mom, nothing was happening!
Greg was comforting me because I was upset

But oh God, I hate telling her I'm upset. Back in New York, sometimes my roommate would come home crying—someone was mean at work, or she fucked something up, or both—and she'd already be on the phone with her mom as she came in the door. I'd marvel at that, being able to call your mother sobbing, half coherent. The idea of having someone on the other end of the line who wasn't furious that you didn't have it together, who would help you *feel better.*

sampaguita72:
Why were you upset?

Of all the strange impulses right now, I *do* want to call Mom and cry. But what would I even say?

Somehow Trisha chooses that moment to text me.

Trisha:
hi ate ruby, how are you doing with reframing those self-limiting beliefs you listed out?

It makes me feel hysterical, thinking about how I've *reframed* my messy situation.

Ruby:
i've been working on it!
how's school?

Trisha:
such an old person question
but it's fine
oh have you tried affirmations? those can help

Affirmations?

This man is no match for a messy bitch like me!

Like that?

But before I can puzzle over it too long, more Slack messages slide onto the top of the screen.

sampaguita72:

Is it that man you're dating?

Is he cheating on you?

My stomach twists. I'm going to break up with him soon, but what if seeing us dressed up together at this wedding will help somehow—convince Mom I'm on the right path in life? I don't want to ruin this for her yet.

ruby.ocampo:

I'm probably just being jealous for no reason!

You know me! So irrational!

"You okay?" Mark Winterson asks, putting a light hand on my arm at a red light. "Who are you messaging so furiously? Should I be worried?"

"Haha!" The backs of my thighs are sweating against this leather seat. "Just my aunt! She worries. Very protective."

He arches an eyebrow, glancing sideways at my screen before starting to drive again. "That looked like Slack?"

"Yeah, we have a family Slack!" I slip my phone into my purse. "Such big families we have."

"Mm," he says, brow creasing. "When do I get to meet them? Your aunt knows I'm real now, but—" He gives me a pointed glance. "How do I know she is?"

"Oh, I don't know," I say, desperately trying to regain that flirty tone that used to come easily with him. "Have you earned it yet?"

Mark Winterson frowns, his eyes on the road. "How exactly would I earn it?" he demands. Then softer, he adds: "I'd like to," and my heart aches.

I notice we're entering Beverly Hills, and it dawns on me

that I don't have the most basic information about what I'm getting myself into.

"Wait, so whose wedding is it?"

Mark Winterson adjusts his grip on the wheel. "My cousin Zack's."

"Ooh, the famous Zack!" I say, remembering his story from the yacht.

"You, um—you might have seen him around. He works at TKCORP, too."

"What does he do there?"

He hesitates like he's been dreading telling me about this for some reason. "He's the Senior VP of Finance."

Oh God. That would make him Greg's boss's boss's boss's *boss.*

"Senior VP of finance?"

"Yeah—senior, already! He's, like, twenty-nine. Barely just learned to shave." He laughs unhappily. "Can you believe it?"

I know from glancing at Mark Winterson's driver's license that he's thirty-one. I wonder how much of his waking life he spends ruminating on the fact that he's an *associate* vice president.

"So are you guys . . . still close?"

He runs a nervous hand through his hair. "He's a character. You'll see."

We're making our way up Rodeo Drive, and I can't help staring at all the shiny, glittering storefronts, like jewelry boxes all up and down this palm-tree-lined street.

The car turns in to a parking garage, and we head underground. After he parks, Mark Winterson doesn't move right away, and we sit there in silence.

He reaches out to caress my cheek, and I bite back my fight-or-flight reflex. "You always seem closed off." His fingers come to a rest under my chin, tilting my head to meet his gaze. "Do you not trust me?"

"No, of course I do."

He narrows his eyes at me. "What are you hiding in there?"

"What makes you think I'm hiding anything?" The sweat is gathering behind my knees, and I try putting on a goofy voice. "What you see is what you get, baby."

Mark Winterson traps my chin between his thumb and forefinger. "Mm yeah, I don't think that's true. I think you don't trust me." He traces my bottom lip with the pad of his thumb, and I feel panicked and slightly turned on (*mind and body really at odds here!*).

You're just extending a relationship longer than you should and gossiping to your friends about him! Not such a huge departure from the past!

"But that's okay." His hand drops back into his lap. "I get the sense you've been through some shit. I do hope I can earn that one day, though."

The earnest look on his face is like a knife in my gut. *Am I going to be able to pull this off? Should I end this now?*

"Okay," he says, opening the driver's-side door. "Time to shop."

CHAPTER 41

When we emerge into the sunlight, I take as many photos for Mom as I can—selfies of our reflections in the Gucci window, in the Prada window, multiple views of the street. Mark Winterson humors me and snaps a tourist picture of me flashing a peace sign in front of Saint Laurent. When he hands my phone back, chuckling, he says, "One day you'll get used to this," and goosebumps rise on the back of my neck.

He laces his fingers between mine and tugs me into one of the boutiques, the kind I always felt too nervous to enter. It makes me think of watching *Pretty Woman* on the couch with Mom while she folded laundry, bowl of popcorn on the coffee table in front of us. She loved that movie, watched it again and again.

And now Mark Winterson is leading me around a fancy clothing store, and a saleswoman wearing a matching black knit skirt and top with white piping approaches us. "Mr. Winterson, pleasure to see you again," she says brightly, and I wonder how many of the girls with contracts in their inboxes—nullified except for clauses one, four, and five—he's dressed for an event before.

"Please," he says, chortling. "Call me Mark. Mr. Winterson is my father."

I raise a finger. "Could I use your restroom?"

When I get inside, I realize this has to rank among the nicest bathrooms I've ever been in: bright tile, mood lighting, sleek wooden end table with a diffuser sitting on it. Wait, is that . . . a TKCORP aroma diffuser? *Maybe my copy worked on someone!*

My head is spinning, running back the events in the copy room. Mom can see Zoom. She got into the Xerox machine and the security cameras somehow. What else does she have access to?

I sit on the closed toilet seat and write:

ruby.ocampo:
When you said it would be better for me to date Sam from Sales because he makes more money—how did you even know that?

sampaguita72:
I can see it

ruby.ocampo:
What do you mean?

sampaguita72:
I noticed it
I was trying to tell you and Wendy! You don't listen!
In here there are all these long hallways and doors and more and more rooms, and I get bored sometimes, go walking
And in one room—you wouldn't believe it
Everyone's pay information! Right there in one place!

I can just picture how her eyes would light up at gossip this juicy.

And this means . . . maybe, theoretically, she could be the key to finding something on Mark Winterson. Something that could help the union, if I ever work up the nerve to ask her.

It's not like it was easy to ask her for help in life, to begin with—and how could I explain what I'm doing and shatter this illusion for her?

And what if a Slack admin sees?

Until this moment, I thought if someone peeked into the haunted DM, they'd think I was crazy—that I'd created a bot with my mother's personality as an elaborate coping strategy, maybe. But now I'm tripping over into breaking some serious company data-policy rules.

I guess we can start with that problem first.

I open Signal, panic growing between my ribs, and start writing to Greg.

Ruby:
i just realized my mom has access to all the company systems
what else should we be looking for? if we can get into anything

He's typing for a while, and I feel my stomach swoop, wondering what he must be feeling.

Greg:
holy shit, okay
i think the books we're getting in accounting aren't accurate anymore but a real ledger probably exists somewhere. if they don't want to run things totally into the ground, they have to be keeping track. you could try searching for spreadsheets on mark winterson's work drive?

Ruby:
can the slack admins see my messages with my mom?

I need to know before we try this. And I'll deal with how impossible it feels to ask her for help when I get there.

Greg:
i'll have ahmed from IT message you
he's with the union and he set the company up on slack
way back—they left the admin rights with him

I stuff my phone in my bag and flush the toilet, washing my hands for good measure and resetting my shoulders before walking outside.

Mark Winterson is sitting in a cushioned chair, legs crossed, reading a print copy of *The Wall Street Journal.* "You good?" he asks.

"Yeah! Must have eaten something weird." I come up beside him and he stands and slips an arm around my waist. He leads me around the room, asking me what I think of the dresses on display, but my head's not in the game. I end up mumbling, "Wow, that's pretty," over and over again.

"I don't think I can afford this," I say, examining one of the price tags.

He gives me a withering look. "You think I'd take you here and make you pay for it?"

My head has been in a million places, and somehow I hadn't quite put together that he's about to drop thousands of dollars on my wardrobe for this wedding.

"I'd like to see you in this one," Mark Winterson says, plucking a beige dress off the rack.

The woman who works here takes it from him and leads me into the fitting room. And after I've carefully slipped into the beige gown with gossamer fabric and delicate beading, paranoid I'm going to rip it if I breathe the wrong way, I check my phone again.

There's a group DM on Signal where Greg has already explained the entire situation, and Ahmed says he's going to check it out and report back.

I let out a long, very careful breath and come outside, doing a full turn in front of Mark Winterson's chair.

The saleswoman hovers next to me, pointing to the detailing on the dress. "Each bead has been carefully affixed by an artisan in rural Tuscany."

He purses his lips, index finger resting on them, giving me a once- and twice-over. "Mm, it's a bit plain," he says finally. "Think we can do better."

"If you want to make more of a statement, I have just the thing." She bustles away and brings out an iridescent green dress with an elaborate cutout back.

"Could be fun," he says.

"Sure! Fun!" I chirp.

Back into the fitting room I go, holding my breath as I slip out of this artisanal dress and rehang it, terrified of accidentally popping off a bead or two.

And standing there in my underwear, I open the chat.

Ahmed:

so I checked out your Slack DM

it's the strangest thing, but all the messages are a blur

when I try to access them

take a look for yourself

He sends me several screenshots, and sure enough, all the text in the DM between ruby.ocampo and ruby.ocampo is obscured behind a gray haze.

Ahmed:

i checked several other people's DMs with themselves

for comparison—yours is the only one like this

same thing across multiple devices

how did you do that? Pretty genius hack

Ruby:

oh gosh, it's a long story

I'm sweating even though it's frigid in this dressing room. The little hairs on my exposed back stand on end. *We're actually safe from being seen in there.* Something about this haunting must obscure our conversations from the admins.

I could ask Mom for help. I *should* ask. People are counting on me to figure this out.

"Ruby?" Mark Winterson calls from outside the dressing room. "You good?"

"Do you need help?" the saleswoman's voice chimes.

"Just a minute!"

I struggle braless into the dress, and it squeezes me like a tube of toothpaste.

"Stunning!" the saleswoman exclaims. "A vision in green."

"Mm." Mark Winterson squints. "Of course, you're stunning in everything. But not quite right for this occasion."

"All right, something more classic but not too plain," the saleswoman says. "And it's a wedding, so no white or black. How about . . ."

She disappears into the back and returns with a navy floor-length gown with a plunging back.

In the dressing room, I'm halfway out of the green dress, but it's so skintight, I feel like a molting snake. I could use a breather, so I sit for a second and open Slack on my phone.

I'm being selfish and messy for a good cause! Does that count as an affirmation?

I hold my breath like I'm about to dive into a pool and start to type.

ruby.ocampo:

Mom, I'm trying to find something. Could you help me?

Can you see Mark Winterson's work drive on there? Do you have access to that?

Just to rule something out, for my peace of mind.

I'm walking a narrow tightrope here, trying to ask for help and not ruin this for her at the same time.

sampaguita72:
Hmm let me see

She doesn't write back right away, and Mark Winterson is waiting—I can practically see him tapping his foot, sitting in that chair—so I shimmy out of the green dress and into the navy one.

He's chatting with the saleswoman when I emerge, making her laugh, and a weird knee-jerk jealousy sparks through me.

What is wrong with me? I shouldn't care who he flirts with now.

"Wow." Mark Winterson holds a hand out and tugs me closer, beaming in a way that makes my heart hurt. "That's the one."

Alone in the dressing room again, I let all the air out of my lungs. But when I check my phone, Mom still hasn't written back.

ruby.ocampo:
Mom? Are you okay?

sampaguita72:
Be patient, all right! It's a long walk down this hall

I get changed and check my phone again. Still nothing, but I don't want to rush her.

So I join Mark Winterson in the front and ignore my spiking anxiety when I see the four-figure price come up at the register. But he hands over his AmEx black card like it's nothing.

We go to a wine bar afterward, and I say my stomach is bothering me and excuse myself to the bathroom again so I can check my phone.

sampaguita72:
Ah yes I think this is it! I see it! I'm in!
But what are you looking for?

I chew my bottom lip, gaming out how much I can tell her.

ruby.ocampo:
Do you see any spreadsheets?

sampaguita72:
Ruby, what are you doing? Why are you poking around in this man's drive for spreadsheets?
Going through his emails, his texts, I could understand, but this is strange even for you

Even for me. Well, she's not wrong.

ruby.ocampo:
You know how people used to have little black books? I think maybe he's doing that, but in a spreadsheet

sampaguita72:
In a spreadsheet! I don't understand you kids these days
Is this it? It's the only spreadsheet in here.

My eyes bug out at the file that's appeared in my private Slack channel. File name: gerbo.xlsx. But when I try to open it, nothing happens.

ruby.ocampo:
Were you able to see inside?

sampaguita72:
No, it asked me for a password
But look! I also found this

Another document pops up in the channel: password_reminders.docx.

This fool!

I open it, and it's not a list of plaintext passwords—it's a series of cryptic hints to jog his memory, little riddles only Mark Winterson would understand.

> GERBO doc: Dad motto first two + first deal Erickson told you about + heartbreak year four digits

Man, this guy is more sentimental than you'd think.

I can't exactly just come out and ask him any of this—I'm going to have to back into it somehow. And how am I going to figure out the first deal Erickson ever told him about? There's not exactly a casual way to go fishing for that.

For a second, I think wistfully about breaking up with him. But then I'd never be able to live with myself when he lays everyone off.

Amid all my failures and all the ways I feel helpless in my own life, here, finally, is a problem I have a chance of fixing. And as things spiral more out of control around me, I need to cling to the things I can actually change. Didn't I see an inspirational Instagram post once that said something like that?

I come back out, and Mark Winterson slips a bottle of Tums out of his leather briefcase.

"You're suffering, huh?" he says, depositing a few chalky tablets in my palm.

"Oh, I'll live." I pop them in my mouth and chew dutifully. "Always had a weak stomach."

He wraps his arms around me, hugging me from behind, and whispers in my ear: "Hope you're feeling better by this weekend."

CHAPTER 42

"Charming little bed-and-breakfast," I say as we enter our hotel room on the ground floor of a converted Craftsman home in Napa Valley. It's Memorial Day weekend, and Zack's wedding festivities stretch over three days: rehearsal dinner tonight, ceremony tomorrow, brunch Monday morning before we drive back.

I sit on the four-poster bed and bounce, soaking in the cool from the central air after the long drive.

"It's a boutique inn, technically," Mark Winterson corrects, sitting next to me.

I give him a stink-eye to rival Mom's, and he laughs at himself.

"Sorry, I'm insufferable." He pushes my hair back and plants a kiss on my cheek. "Amazing that you put up with me."

Why does he have to make my life harder by being self-aware?

But a little part of me is relieved he's warming to me again, after the chilly drive up here. I kept trying to ask him about his relationships with his dad, with Erickson—with his cousin, just for variety—but his answers were evasive bordering on annoyed, and he was driving so fast the whole way, it made me queasy. Eventually he put on an audiobook about the history of IBM and we sat there for hours listening to it in tense silence.

"How's your stomach doing?" he adds.

I asked him to pull over a few times on the drive so I could use the bathroom—setting the stage to explain why I'm not up for doing much on this romantic getaway. I've been trying to be *more sparing* with physical intimacy, ever since I decided I was going to stab him in the back. And I've actually managed to avoid sex entirely since then, given how work is consuming his life lately. Even when I come over, he'll be falling asleep or have to leave suddenly. If I still legitimately wanted a relationship with him, I might even be sad about that.

Part of me hopes, in a far-off way, that he'll naturally lose interest. After all, if his inbox is any indication, he's a short-term serial monogamist to the point of absurdity. None of his relationships last longer than six weeks, and if he sticks to his usual pattern, we're cruising to the end.

The company retreat is happening in a few days; I'll break up with him after. And that means this weekend is my last, best chance to get his password. The pressure of it weighs on me, and that stomachache is becoming genuine.

He must notice I look ill, because he asks: "Need me to get you anything from the pharmacy?"

"I think I'll manage," I say with a weak smile.

"Maybe you should see a specialist when we get home." He pats me lightly on the back, like he's burping a baby. "Let's get dinner, then? If you feel up to it."

"Oh, don't you have a rehearsal dinner? I don't want to keep you. I'm sure I can figure something out."

"Nah," he says, offering me a hand up. "I'd rather hang out with you."

A ripple of tenderness and guilt passes through me as I take his hand.

We make our way to the hotel restaurant on the back patio of the house—a farm-to-table, upscale place. The seating arrangement is cozy and intimate: two woven deck chairs angled beside each other, facing a small round table with a view of the vineyard.

I'm usually too embarrassed to ask for substitutions, but Mark Winterson orders for me, perfectly entitled and relaxed as he specifies *exactly* how plain he wants the chicken to be. And it's weird to see how people listen to him.

But as the evening wears on, he seems increasingly distracted, constantly sighing and running a hand over his face. I wonder if there was some other reason he wanted to skip the rehearsal dinner, and I was just a convenient excuse.

It's putting me on edge, and suddenly all the anxiety I've been shoving down hits me like a wall—about lying to him, about when he inevitably finds me out and sues me into financial ruin. About what's going to happen to everyone at work. About *what's going to happen to Mom if I get fired and lose access to TKCORP Slack!*

"Nervous about tomorrow?" I finally ask.

He blinks at me, startled, like he just remembered I was there.

"Sorry," he says, rubbing both eyes with one hand. "Just—you know. Family." And he gives me a tiny smile that lets me know he's intentionally turning my own cryptic answer back on me.

"I do indeed," I say, raising the ginger tea with honey and lemon he ordered for me in a mock toast.

How am I ever going to find out his password this way? If I can't get him to talk, what am I even doing here?

I have to soften him up, I think as I watch the sun go down over the green hills in the distance. And maybe to do that I have to seem softer—like a safe place for his secrets to land. I have to channel the part of me that likes him a little bit to put on a more convincing performance.

"It's okay." I reach over and run my fingers through the hair on the back of his neck, massaging the tension there. "We don't have to talk about it."

He lets out an appreciative hum, and his eyelids flutter closed, soaking it up. "There's also some business I have to take care of this weekend," he mumbles.

"At a wedding?"

He smirks like it's cute I'm so clueless. "Whole board's going to be here. Some big suppliers. Potential investors. Erickson's tasked me with a little persuasion. Smoothing the way for something he wants to do."

"I see. Big assignment." I give the back of his neck a squeeze, and he leans his head into my palm. "Anything I can do to help?"

"Make me laugh, like you always do." Mark Winterson bends forward and kisses me lightly on the lips. "Make me look good." The evening is mild, but I get a chill up my spine.

We head back to our room, and part of me is dreading what comes next. But he seems so exhausted as he sits on the bed and wrenches off his tie—this business tomorrow must really be weighing on him. And when I come out of the bathroom after doing my skincare routine, he's already fast asleep.

The next morning, I spend over an hour getting ready, the words *make me look good* bouncing around in my head. Finally I step out of the bathroom in the dress he chose and spin around so he can take in the full effect—but the dire look on his face makes me freeze on the spot. You'd think he'd just learned about a massive earnings shortfall.

"No," he says abruptly.

"No?"

"This doesn't work. It's too much." He waves an agitated hand in my direction. "Too much makeup."

My knee-jerk reaction is to laugh. I worked hard on that winged liner!

"It's just your nerves talking, it's going to be fine," I say breezily, grabbing the clutch he bought me off the bed. "Let's go, I want to see the grounds." I need to get some photos for Mom before the ceremony.

"Hey." He grabs my arm and his fingers dig into my skin, stopping my forward movement. "I have enough to worry about today, all right? Would you just fix it?"

He releases me and I take a staggering step back, heart racing.

"Please," he adds, voice softening a touch. "My mother has opinions about these things."

Oh. I hadn't quite put two and two together. *I'm meeting his parents.*

"Fine!" I say, cut down to size, embarrassment scalding my cheeks. "Fine, just—just give me a few."

Back in the bathroom, my hands shake as I fumble with the makeup remover.

When I come back out, face redone, Mark Winterson looks relieved.

"Thanks for humoring me," he says, recovering some of that charm. He pulls me closer and kisses my temple. "I just want to show you off to everyone."

I never knew, until this moment, that these emotions could coexist in my body: a twinge of tenderness; a roiling, white-hot fury; a weaselly little flattered feeling, even though I should know better.

He puts a hand between my shoulder blades, forcing me to stand straight. "Good," he says, and my chest burns. "Remember to smile."

CHAPTER 43

It's a short drive over to the venue where the wedding is being held—a mansion on another vineyard. When we pass through the main house and out to the back, a breathy little "wow" escapes from me before I can worry about sounding like a bumpkin.

Rows of Chiavari chairs are set up underneath strings of lights. The lawn gives way to impressive manicured gardens, complete with topiaries and a *fucking hedge maze.* My inner child wants to kick off these teetering heels and go running off into it.

I wave Mark Winterson over to take some pictures with me against this backdrop, and he obliges, a hand resting possessively on my lower back. I'm still angry at him, but I lean my head on his shoulder, trying to be convincing for the photo, and his warm palm on my bare skin muddies my thoughts.

As we're making our way to our seats, Mark Winterson gets caught up talking to someone, and I claim a spot on the groom's side and send Greg a photo of the whole setup.

Ruby:
look at this shit
there's a hedge maze!

Greg:
damn, you've got me beat

He sends a blurry photo from the outside of a Ramada Inn, freeway off-ramp visible in the distance, and I resist the urge to snort.

That's right, I remember—he's also at a wedding right now. Adam from Accounting is tying the knot with his high school sweetheart, and lots of TKCORP people are going. Big weekend for marriage, I guess.

Ruby:
idk yours might be a better time
i heard the accountants like to party

Mark Winterson extracts himself from his conversation, and I stash my phone in my clutch and beam up at him.

I sit *spine straight, shoulders back* through the ceremony—the generic exchange of vows, the inside-joke-laden readings from their friends. It's not lost on me that Mark Winterson's cousin is also taller than him, and maybe that doesn't help with whatever resentment he's harboring.

All morning I've been turning the components of his password over in my mind, rethinking my approach. I have to take it slow, ideally wait for alcohol to do some of the work for me. I've ranked everything in order of how drunk I want him to be:

1. Ask about his relationship with his dad, in hopes that I can finagle a way of getting him to talk about his dad's life philosophy and that motto. (He should be buzzed, slightly tipsy.)

2. Get him to talk about his relationship with Erickson—though finding out about the first deal they ever discussed might be more of a needle in a haystack. (Ideally at least three drinks in, given what I've observed of his tolerance.)

3. Ease more delicately into asking about his dating history, to find out what heartbreak could have been so formative that he'd think of it as the one and only "heartbreak year." (Preferably when he's shitfaced.)

"Thanks for coming, again," Mark Winterson says as we get up after the ceremony. "Might have to leave you alone for a bit to do that room-working. You'll be all right?"

It stings that he doesn't want me on his arm for the whole thing, after he made such a stink about my appearance. But I gather myself and make finger guns at him. "Always be closing, right? Gotta chase that senior VP title."

Then I worry I'm pushing my luck with making fun of him, but he laughs, genuinely. "Yeah, you get it."

Mark Winterson takes my arm as we cross the lawn to the area where cocktails are being served, and he spots some people he recognizes. "Frank! Linda!"

An older white couple in a tux and gown turn around.

"Mark!" The man shakes a finger at him. "I've known this one since he was in diapers."

"Old family friend," Mark Winterson clarifies.

He introduces me as his girlfriend, and Frank and Linda's exaggerated reaction of delight sets my teeth on edge. "Take care of Ruby for me for a second? I'll be right back," he says, and slips away.

Wow, he actually parked me with babysitters.

"What's your background, Ruby?" Frank asks, tipping his glass of rosé up in my direction.

"In . . . marketing?"

"Oh, I mean—" Linda swats Frank on the chest. "I suppose we're not supposed to ask where you're from!"

Here we go, my body knows this drill—patient smile, stomach clench.

I'm so bored of this, my constant free-floating angst about everyone else's confusion over my racial/ethnic identity. But it's part of the texture of my life. It came up more on the East Coast than here, but still, you'd be surprised, depending on the composition of the room you find yourself in (or tastefully appointed backyard, as the case may be).

It comes with a low-level seasickness, knowing that one of the first things people perceive about you isn't stable. And when you realize a surprising amount of people have opinions about what you must *actually be,* or which side you are *more,* and the opinions all contradict, you start to feel like you'll always be *almost* something, *almost but not quite,* that there is no option where you can be *authentically* whatever you are. And you hear so much about how important authenticity is these days. It's what people want, what algorithms want, it's supposedly what sells. But I've spent most of my life thinking I should fold myself up and make myself neater, less confusing. That if I tried harder tomorrow, maybe I'd finally find a way.

"My mom's from the Philippines and my dad was white." It's what I've said all my life, rote, but my heart snags, realizing the tenses are technically all wrong now.

"Oh, I love half-Asian babies!" Linda exclaims, as though we're discussing a trendy dog breed.

"Like . . . in general?" I am notably not a baby.

She nods, and her silver ringlets of hair and heavy gold earrings jiggle as one unit. "Oh yes, one of my sons married an Asian woman, and the baby—so cute, these mixed babies! I love to see what comes up!"

I never know what to say when people come out with comments like this. *It's just something I'm living with whether I like it or not, but, uh, thanks?*

At that moment, I see Sandra Winterson swanning by in a lavender gown and wave like I'm seeing an old friend.

"Lovely chatting with you, please excuse me!" I sidestep away from Frank and Linda and hustle across the grass. "Hey! Sandra!"

"Oh gosh, Ruby!" She grabs two champagne flutes from a passing waiter. "I think we should toast to you," she says, passing me one. "When we were in high school, I never would have guessed you'd end up with my brother."

My brow wrinkles. "Why's that?"

"Oh, I don't mean anything about you!" She waves a dismissive hand. "I mean, it's about *him.* I feel like he's . . . different, lately. Don't tell him I told you, but I haven't heard him talk about someone this way since . . ." Her smile flickers, and she seems to catch herself and reset. "Haven't heard him talk about anyone this way in years. So—cheers!"

Sandra raises the glass and downs most of it (but, like, delicately, somehow). So I drain mine, too, wanting to be polite.

"Can't stop and chat, unfortunately! Bridesmaid emergency." She deposits the glass on the tray of a different passing waiter. "But I have a feeling I'll be seeing more of you soon."

I squint as she hurries away, trying to make sense of what she said, but then my eyes land on an incredible sight: the Senior VP of Finance putting Mark Winterson in a headlock on the other side of the grass. Getting to witness this has to qualify as a *small win.*

I hitch my gown up with one hand so I can move quickly, balancing on the balls of my feet so my heels don't sink into the grass.

"Hey! Knock it off, kids," I say as I get closer, right as the groom seems poised to give Mark Winterson a noogie. I get a rush of this strange, almost maternal affection toward him—if

I ever see a therapist, there will surely be plenty to unpack about this entire experience.

If I even have a job and healthcare then. Or if Mark Winterson hasn't found me out and sued me into oblivion.

The Senior VP of Finance lets him go and straightens up, flashing me a toothy smile. "And who have we here?"

Mark Winterson grabs my hand and tugs me closer. Territorially, maybe.

"Let me guess," his cousin says, pointing a finger at me. *Oh no, not one of the guys who wants to guess.* "Are you Mexican?"

"Zack," Mark Winterson says.

"I'm just making conversation! What, Mark, are you woke now?" He points at me. "Did you make him woke?"

"Not . . . that I know of?"

"I love Cancún—beautiful people there. So, am I right?"

"Sorry to disappoint," I say with an airy wave of my hand.

"Oh, okay, I see." He laughs. "So mysterious."

Is this recently married man . . . trying to hit on me? Or is this just how he socializes?

Mark Winterson looks a bit murderous. Interesting dynamic these two have.

"Mark, lighten up," Zack says, and glances at me again. "Can you believe this guy studied *political economy* in undergrad? What even is that?"

I give him a weak laugh, because at least he seems to be done guessing.

Zack gives Mark Winterson a friendly whack on the arm. "Hey, man, no hard feelings, right?"

"Yeah, yeah, it was a long time ago. Glad you guys are happy."

That piques my curiosity. Mark Winterson does not sound very happy about this long-ago thing.

"Zack!" a man's voice booms. "Congratulations!"

Another older couple drifts over to us, and from the strong

family resemblance and the way Mark Winterson drops my hand suddenly and his jaw tightens, I take it these are his parents.

"Yes, Zack, you and Clarissa look so good together," his mother says, dabbing at her eyes. Her gray hair is pulled into a slick updo and her makeup is indeed understated. Her clothes are, too, but in a specific way that makes me certain they cost a fortune.

"How's business, son?" his father asks, thumping Mark Winterson on the back.

"Oh, lots going on. Been burning the midnight oil."

Mark Winterson seems uncomfortable, and there's a bit of an awkward silence, so like a fool I blurt something out to fill it. "It's true, he, like, barely sleeps."

His parents look at me with mild confusion.

Oh shit, maybe he didn't tell them we're dating? As an old hand at hiding things from my mom, I should really know better.

"Or, I mean, so I've heard! It's, uh—legendary, at the office, how hard your son works. You raised a real *winner,*" I add, looking his dad in the eye. "You must be so proud."

Mark Winterson beams like this is the nicest thing anyone has ever said about him.

"Good, good," his dad says, clapping his son on the arm. "I always say, ex nihilo—"

"—nihil fit," Mark Winterson finishes for him. "Nothing comes from nothing. I know."

Hellooo, low-hanging fruit! It takes all my strength to stop myself from punching the air. One down, two to go.

"You must be Ruby! Such a pleasure," his mother says, extending an imperious hand for me to shake. Then she steps back, shoulder to shoulder with her son, and says as though I can't hear: "Different than the girls you usually bring around, Mark. Maybe you're maturing."

She sips her champagne while he laughs nervously.

Extremely strange vibe these people have. Not sure how I feel about being the mature choice.

"Would you excuse me?" I say, fighting the urge to curtsy. "I'm going to find the ladies' room."

This wedding is like an endurance exercise, and I could use a break. I head in the direction of the main house and duck behind a topiary animal in a spot of shade—a bear standing on its hind legs.

After taking a few deep, calming breaths, I peer back around it, checking on the Wintersons.

And another man I recognize is wandering down the lawn toward them: Winfield Erickson, the CEO of TKCORP. I've seen him only through screens—some of his town hall meetings were posted to YouTube last year, and I watched them from my desk in New York, because Mom was worried about her job.

"You know new leadership can mean layoffs," Mom said at the time, on the phone from across the country. "That's when it's even more important to put your nose to the grindstone, work as hard as you can. They'll notice it. It will be worth it, when they're making decisions about who to let go."

The way she talked, it was like hard work could get her everywhere. Like buckling down and suppressing your desires and complaints for a little while longer would keep you safe—just one more late night, just another big push, try harder, come on, almost there, *almost there*—

A wave of anger hits me so hard it turns into nausea as I watch the CEO greet the group and clap Mark Winterson on the back. Then the two of them turn and start walking toward the hedge maze, so I hustle across the lawn as quickly as I can in these precarious heels.

CHAPTER 44

It's tough, following someone in a hedge maze. Every time I reach a fork, I strain to hear what direction their voices are coming from—until I realize Mark Winterson's dress shoes leave a distinctive imprint in the soft dirt, and I relax about losing them. But I still have to make sure to stay far enough behind that I don't run into them, and that's tricky too. I turn every corner with lots of clandestine peeking around. It would probably be funny, if I weren't so stressed.

Their voices are suddenly too close, so I stop cold in my tracks for a few minutes. It seems like they're standing just on the other side of the hedge that separates us.

"Who's that girl you're with?" Erickson says, voice gravelly, garnished with a gross little chuckle. "Surprised you'd bring a new fling to one of these."

My cheeks burn, and my scalp tingles. My constant low-level fear that people are talking about me, once again bizarrely actualized.

"She's not a fling." Mark Winterson's voice comes through the hedge.

Aw, that dork. A pang of guilt twists in my gut. He liked me because he thought I was genuine and no-bullshit, and I've been bullshitting him quite a bit.

Erickson guffaws. "Doesn't seem like your type. Weren't you dating a model? Is this some kind of reverse quarter-life crisis?"

"I'm a bit old for that." There's a sound like feet kicking at the dirt. "She cheers me up. She's funny." Mark Winterson becomes a real chatterbox talking to this guy, compared to how he was with his parents. "And she really listens."

Hearing him say that makes me a bit woozy. Or maybe it's that last glass of champagne and these vertiginous heels.

"And it's cute how much she doesn't know about the world," he adds. "Kind of fun to show her things."

Anger spikes through whatever tender feeling I was just experiencing.

"You don't have to explain yourself to me, kid!" Erickson's laugh sounds like it's laced with the traces of an old smoking habit. "So . . . did the falcon come in for a landing?"

My ears perk up. That sounds like code for something juicy—though I wouldn't put it past these guys to literally be interested in falconry.

"Yes, two falcons. Sent them both off on the new flight path. Hopefully that's more discreet than last time."

"Good, good. And how about our . . . little problem?"

"I think the annual retreat will be a good time to figure out who's behind it. We're setting a trap, basically—getting some loyal employees in place to tell us who's asking them to sign cards."

Oh shit, the union—the retreat! I have to warn them. But when I pull out my phone, I have no bars out here.

"You've arranged everything?" Erickson presses on.

"Got some of our most ambitious employees together, coordinating in a private Slack channel. Promised them promotions if they participate."

"Good, good," Erickson says, and there's a sound like he's thumping Mark Winterson on the back. "Very organized. But watch out for your paper trail."

He's doing this all in Slack? So Mom might be able to see?

"Should we head back?" Erickson asks.

Oh fuck! I hadn't quite considered that stalking them into the hedge maze might involve them chasing me *out* of the hedge maze at some point.

I kick off my shoes so I can run ahead, bare feet in the Napa Valley soil, heels dangling in one hand and the other hiking up my dress, making snap decisions about what direction to take at each fork I hit because I can't remember the way we came in. Their voices get fainter and fainter, and eventually I realize I must have lost them, but I also seem to have run deeper into the heart of the maze.

There's no Google Maps to help me, but with some trial and error, I manage to find my way to an exit on a different side.

I wedge my feet back into my shoes and head through the gardens toward the sound of the party, past a topiary elephant that's giving me a judgmental stare. And when I round the corner to get back to the lawn, I practically collide with Mark Winterson.

"Hey, there you are!" He slips an arm around my shoulders, and I want to sink into the earth. "I was looking for you."

"And this is . . . ?" Erickson's standing a couple feet away, swirling a glass of some dark brown spirit.

"This is Ruby Ocampo—she works in Marketing."

The image of a business card flashes through my mind:

Ruby Ocampo from Marketing

Not a Model, Not a Fling

"She's second-generation TKCORP." Mark Winterson lets me go and lifts his glass in a jaunty toast. "Her mom worked here too! For almost thirty years."

"Is that right?" Erickson sounds disinterested.

It hits me in the face, right then—how Mom threw her whole mind and body at this job, and to the people at the top, it barely registered.

"Yes, she loved this company. She really—" I swallow hard, trying to stop my voice from wavering. "She really gave everything to it."

"Oh." Erickson's salt-and-pepper brows push closer together. "Oh God, do you mean the woman who died? I saw the GoFundMe. Carmela?"

"Adela," I snap. She worked there for nearly two-thirds of her natural life—*and is still trapped there*—but this man doesn't even know her name.

I look at Mark Winterson for help, but he's staring at me like I'm *being a problem.* "Excuse us a moment," he says, taking my arm and tugging me off to the side.

"Hey," he whispers sharply in my ear. "The last thing I need is for you to make a scene right now. Don't be so sensitive."

And wow, this tells me everything I need to know. I changed my mind. Now I don't feel guilty for a single thing.

✶

I peel off for the bathroom again at the soonest opportunity, lock myself in a stall, and open Signal. And I see that Greg's messaged me a bunch of pictures from the wedding.

There's Adam dancing with his new wife in the middle of the floor; all the accountants sitting around a table, doing shots; Sarah next to them, leaning her head on Grace's shoulder and flashing the camera a peace sign.

There's Al and Morgan, line dancing. There's Carol, looking absolutely sloshed, pink in the face, laughing with Sam from Sales. There's Greg, mouth open like someone grabbed his phone from him, and he's asking them not to take a picture. His tie is loosened, knot sitting low under his collar.

I feel my heart constrict, wishing I were there with them. And there are a couple more messages from him, sitting there.

Greg:
erica's here too
she was bawling during the ceremony for some reason

So I write back:

Ruby:
knew she was a crier

Then I hesitate, thumbs hovering, words crowding my head faster than I can type.

Ruby:
hey so i overheard something

And as clearly as I can, I explain everything I found out about the trap at the annual retreat.

Greg:
oh shit
thank you

He's typing for a minute, stopping, typing again.

Greg:
(and for the record, i still hate this)

I almost laugh out loud, but I stifle it.

Ruby:
your feedback has been recorded

Greg:
but seriously you're a lifesaver

A little bud of warmth sprouts in my chest. For once, I did something right.

CHAPTER 45

It's eleven p.m., and Mark Winterson is at least four drinks in. It's probably the right time to probe about his relationship with Erickson. But when we get back to our room at the bed-and-breakfast, he says he needs to read on his phone for an hour to wind down.

"Come here," he says, and pulls me closer so I'm nestling against him, head on his chest. His heartbeat pulses in my ear as I notice the title at the top of the page.

"*Capitalism in America: A History*?" I scoff. "Some light bedtime reading."

My head rises and falls with Mark Winterson's laugh. "Alan Greenspan's droppin' bars in this one."

My God, I really do have terrible taste in men.

I'm starting to zone out when a very interesting push alert slides onto the top of his screen. It's a Telegram notification. He flicks it away before I can read it, but I could swear the sender name was *Win.*

Winfield Erickson.

Mark Winterson turns off his phone and sits up suddenly,

forcing me off him and onto my own pillow. He turns off the bedside lamp, so the only light in the room is the faint glow from his phone.

In the middle of the night, while Mark Winterson is snoring steadily, I tiptoe around to his side of the bed and disconnect his charging phone—*oh so carefully,* barely breathing. He snorts in his sleep, and my heart nearly stops. But he rolls over with a deep snore, back turned to me, and I finally exhale.

He still uses a passcode—I made fun of him for it when I noticed a couple weeks back.

"Maybe I'm old-fashioned, but I hate the idea of handing over my biodata," he said, running a hand through his hair.

"I would have thought you're one of those 'scan your palm at Whole Foods' guys."

He shuddered, playing it up for a laugh. "I don't know, call it a phobia."

Whatever you call it, it's convenient for me, because after watching him open his phone out of the corner of my eye at every opportunity, now I can do it too.

With shaking hands, I open the Telegram app. If there were messages from Erickson, he must have sent disappearing ones, because I can't find them. There's just a thread with *zackthagod*—bro, really?—that seems to go back weeks and weeks. Fumbling open my phone with my other hand, I find the screenshot from his bank account and check the date stamps. And on Mark Winterson's phone, I scroll up to around the same time in the Telegram thread.

zackthagod:
i'm drunk who up
just kidding

falcon is in flight
mark, you tracking that sucker?

mwinterson:
yup, falcon received
the bird will be heading south after a brief rest

zackthagod:
thanks man
clarissa says hi

I'm still puzzling over how weird their family dynamic is, but this seems like it means something. I hold his phone out in one hand and take the steadiest photo I possibly can with mine in the other.

Mark Winterson suddenly rolls over, flinging out one arm that comes close to grazing my leg, and I hold in a yelp as he settles with a hefty inhale-snore, arm dangling off the bed. I plug his phone into the charger, arrange it the way he left it, and slip back to my side, lying on the farthest edge of the mattress.

Then I remember I still have those photos from the wedding for Mom, so I send them into the haunted DM.

sampaguita72:
Beautiful couple! You look so good together
And those grounds! How much must this have cost?

I wait awhile, staring at the wall, before messaging her again.

ruby.ocampo:
Mom?

sampaguita72:
You're still up?
Did you drink too much? I told you, you should always

stop drinking by 9 p.m. if you want to get a good night's sleep

She's still there.

Mark Winterson snores loudly again beside me.

There's no way I'll ever marry him. I have to face it: This won't be what frees Mom from Slack, and I have no clue what will. I'm going to have to end this charade. Sooner or later, I'm going to have to tell her this isn't going to work.

CHAPTER 46

The next evening, I'm home again, drumming my fingers on the kitchen table, putting off the conversation I don't want to have.

The company retreat is in a couple days. Greg won't ever ask me to get more information—he doesn't want to take advantage of this situation he hates—but the mood in the group chat is tense. Everyone is stressed about the trap, and how little they know about it.

I have to ask Mom for help again. And I can't think of a good way to spin this that lets me avoid telling her what's really going on.

ruby.ocampo:
Mom, can you look something up for me?
I need to know if Mark has been saying anything strange
in one of the private Slack channels

I cringe after I hit *send.* And then the messages come popping up, fast and furious.

sampaguita72:
Ruby, tell me the truth
What are you doing?
Are you in trouble?
How can I help you?
You never tell me anything
You have to talk to me so I can help you

Ugh, God, I don't know how to explain this. Mom is going to peek inside that channel where he's setting the trap and see some of TKCORP's *most ambitious employees* talking about the company retreat and the union. I can't think of a lie this time—I'll have to be honest with her.

I start typing: Mom, things at work are . . .

I pound the delete key on my laptop.

sampaguita72:
I can see you typing! I know you're there!

I'm sweating now. If I tell her the truth, she's going to accuse me of exploding my life *all for Greg! For that boy who doesn't have any ambition! Dragging you down and making you just like him!* She'll turn it into another speech about how she was right all along and he's a bad influence.

But Mom is messaging me again, impatient with the long silence.

sampaguita72:
You know it was hard for me, breaking into corporate life
People didn't exactly treat me with respect

I sink deeper into my seat at the kitchen table, settling in for the story I've heard so many times before.

ruby.ocampo:
I know, Mom

sampaguita72:
I was so terrified all the time. Alone here, scrambling

ruby.ocampo:
I know, I remember

sampaguita72:
Let me finish! You think you know everything
I'm trying to tell you, I was wrong when I said that
I was so tired when I was alive, out of my mind with stress
I wasn't thinking clearly
I was doing this so you wouldn't have to
It does make me sad, seeing how you're living, staying late at the office, running around in circles
I wanted more for you than this

All my muscles are clenched, and I'm willing the tears gathering in the corners of my eyes not to spill out.

ruby.ocampo:
Aren't you the one who told me it's good to keep your head down
Aren't you the one who told me

I stop and flex my fingers, breathe in, breathe out. The barrier between my thoughts and my fingers is becoming dangerously thin.

ruby.ocampo:
Every time I complained about work, I remember you'd tell me
about how you knew you had to work twice as hard to be taken seriously
and you were just glad to be participating
and because you did it, it's normal

and how grateful i should be
i am grateful!
i know how much worse things could be!
and that i'm the problem and it's probably my fault i can't
thrive here, okay! i get it!
i don't know what to DO with it, now that i've got it!

I'm dizzy, putting that knot in my chest into words for the first time.

sampaguita72:
Always so dramatic
You make me sound so bad!

So now she's gaslighting me!

ruby.ocampo:
Every time you'd sigh and say, "i wish you would . . ." or
"why don't you . . ." or "why can't you just . . ."
you think those things just pass through me? you don't
think every single one gets under my skin?
do you even realize how much power your words have
over me?

My head is spinning. I'm going to throw up.

sampaguita72:
It's your life, Ruby!
I was so afraid all the time, just trying to hold things
together for you!

And there it is, right on cue—the guilt creeping back in, like a puddle seeping into a sock. It seems like we always end up back here. But I'm so agitated from this conversation already—a truly unprecedented level of honesty between us—it's like my fingers barrel ahead on their own.

ruby.ocampo:

Mom, why didn't you approve of Greg? Why were you so insistent I shouldn't date him?

Oh God, we're going there.

sampaguita72 is typing

The words vanish, appear, disappear again. It feels like hours pass, but the clock in the corner of the screen says it's been minutes.

I can practically hear her sigh.

sampaguita72:

Because Greg is too much like us
He and Wendy, they struggle like we do
And he seemed content with the way things are—no drive to change his situation

She's wrong about him. I know he has drive, even if it's not the way she expected.

sampaguita72:

And I didn't want you to have to struggle
I wanted you to have the best
I thought the path to a good life for us is so narrow
That there are only a few ways to get there, and this job is the surest one
And marrying well can't hurt

A fresh pang of guilt roils through me.

sampaguita72:

So what are you saying now? You want to quit your job?
Break up with this man?
Go ahead! It's your life

I sigh, hands hovering over the keyboard. I'm exhausted, but right now there's a task at hand.

ruby.ocampo:
It's a bit more complicated than that, Mom
And I'll need your help.

I explain about the union, and the looming layoffs. I add that Al is involved, playing on her sympathies. But I can't bear to tell her the whole truth, up to a certain point—that I'm willingly continuing to date a man I suspect of some kind of corporate fraud. I'm still editing the way I used to, but it's the best I can do for now. Gritting my teeth, I tell her that I have some doubts about what Mark Winterson's been up to lately, and I really like him, so I'm just trying to rule out his involvement in this scheme.

sampaguita72:
All right then. Was it so hard to tell me?

She has no idea.

But her green light goes off, and several minutes pass before it comes on again. In the haunted DM, a list of every private Slack channel that I don't have access to appears.

sampaguita72:
Do any of these look like the one?

It's a long list—TKCORP is a huge company, after all, with tens of thousands of people in our Slack—but my eyes finally settle on a channel called #future-managers.

And Mark Winterson's voice reverberates in my head: *Some of our most ambitious employees. Promised them promotions if they participate.*

God, he can be so cringe sometimes. That has to be it.

ruby.ocampo:
Can you see who's in this one?

sampaguita72:
I'll take a peek inside

Several minutes later, Mom resurfaces:

sampaguita72:
Oh! Oh!

She sends a few clapping emojis.

sampaguita72:
I think I figured out how to take a screenshot! If I raise my hands like a fake camera and press the shutter, it does something!

A few screenshots appear—of the recent conversations in there, indeed discussing the union and the upcoming corporate retreat, and of the list of members in the group.

ruby.ocampo:
Thank you thank you thank you!

sampaguita72:
Well? Can you tell if he's involved?

I bite my bottom lip, peeling off a bit of dry skin.

ruby.ocampo:
It doesn't seem like it? He's in the group, but he didn't say anything.

He must have delegated that out to someone else—maybe being careful about his paper trail, like Erickson said.

I don't have the heart to end the fantasy for her yet. To cut off that hope completely.

And Mom isn't stupid, but she had a habit, in life, of not looking too closely at stories she wanted to believe.

CHAPTER 47

The day of the company retreat finally arrives, and my heart is in my throat as I walk through the glass-roofed atrium of the hotel where they put it on every year. The floor is packed with booths and people I've never seen before, teams flown in from other offices, everyone with lanyards around their necks.

It's been a TKCORP tradition to hold this event for as long as I can remember, with professional development sessions organized along different tracks and grand proclamations about *investment in human capital* in all the company literature. Mom was so proud when she was asked to present, one year.

A bunch of union members are clustered in a group across the floor, and I start moving toward them—but then Mark Winterson steps into my line of sight.

"Whoa, didn't mean to startle you. You okay?" He steadies me, and leans in to whisper in my ear. "I got a room upstairs."

"Why?" I blurt out.

"Because I can." He slips an arm around my waist and tugs

me closer. "And it's my fault—I know I've been distracted—but we . . . haven't in a while. Couple weeks at least?"

I laugh nervously. "Did you consult your ledger?"

Mark Winterson chuckles dryly and presses me into a side hug. "Just wanted to show you I can make time for us." He puts a key card in my hand, folding my fingers over it. "Text me."

As he strides away, I turn the key over in my hands, staring at the paper sleeve that says *Room 505.* I'm going to have to meet him there. I realized, sometime on the long drive back from the wedding, that I don't even need to find out his heartbreak year—I just need to get the first deal Erickson ever told him about.

If I have those two parts, I can try every year of his life along with them. There are only thirty-one possible combinations, and I don't think Excel will lock me out if I've tried too many times. And this is probably my last, best chance.

Maybe it's not clear what I can do for Mom anymore, but at least I can see this through. And then I can break up with him. This will all be over soon.

Rising up above me on either side, all the floors of the hotel are visible in cross section—conference rooms on the third and fourth floors, guest rooms above, every room letting out onto a walkway with a view of the convention floor. You can see everyone coming and going from pretty much everywhere you stand. Tough location for clandestine operations.

And thanks to that design, I can see some of the #future-managers approaching Al and Grace on the fourth floor. If they're following the script laid out for them in the Slack channel, the #future-managers are asking them if they've heard anything about the union, acting like they want to sign cards.

And Al and Grace are making a show of acting confused, while a group of accountants is on the floor below, chatting up a group from the Logistics Department about the union. They all step into an empty conference room together, and some of the tension in my shoulders releases.

On the other side of the fourth floor, Morgan and Steve are going into another conference room, followed by Carol and Sarah and—my heart jumps—Greg. We haven't really talked since the copy room, confining ourselves to scattered texts, passing nods in the halls, furtive glances.

And Mark Winterson emerges from the stairwell nearby and goes into the same conference room everyone just went into. Oh fuck!

I wait a few minutes to see what might happen. Then I open the union chat and write:

Ruby:
you guys doing okay?

Sarah:
we were getting somewhere
there are people from all the departments we haven't reached yet in this mixer

Carol:
but then Mark Winterson showed up

Greg:
yeah, he's just hanging out? making weird small talk

Steve:
he must know he's cock blocking

Morgan:
Steve! Gross

This would be a great time to create a diversion. I take out my phone and text Mark Winterson:

Ruby:

wow these sessions are a grind!
could use some of that stress relief you were talking about
meet you upstairs?

I peer up at the fourth floor again, leg jiggling with nerves. And lo and behold, Mark Winterson emerges from the conference room, smiling at his phone.

So I run for the elevator, heading to the fifth floor.

When I enter room 505, Mark Winterson is reading on his phone again, lying on the bed in his shirtsleeves and navy suit pants, wiggling his black-dress-socked feet. His jacket and tie are thrown over the back of a chair in the corner.

"There she is," he says, putting his phone on the nightstand face down and extending an arm out toward me. "Come here."

I climb onto the bed beside him, and while I'm still balanced on my knees, he reaches for my waist and tugs me close—and in the process of trying to maintain my balance, I end up straddling him.

My sensible A-line work skirt strains, bare knees pressed into the cool hotel duvet beneath us. The laminated card at the end of my conference lanyard whacks him in the face, and he laughs as I mumble "Sorry" and toss it back over my shoulder.

From this angle he looks soft and vulnerable, gazing up at me all dopey and content. It makes me dizzy, the way mental revulsion and sexual attraction get all twined up in each other when I'm around him these days.

His hands are on my hips, keeping me in place, and his fingers drum idly along my lower back. "Ruby, I need to talk to you about something."

My stomach clenches, bracing for him to ask me why I'm spying on him for an unrecognized union.

I slide off him and lie on my side, propped on one elbow. "Sure! Anything. Shoot."

He rolls onto his back, staring at the ceiling. "The first time we had lunch, I was kind of using you."

I'm so surprised, a laugh bursts out of me, inappropriately loud. "Is that so?"

He chortles like it's a cute story. "I was going to ask you about your co-workers. Find out which ones are, let's say, less essential."

A chill runs up my spine, and he shifts back onto his side so he can look me in the eye.

"But that's only how it started." His thumb and forefinger encircle my wrist, the lightest handcuff. "I wanted to be honest with you about it because my feelings changed. A lot. It surprised me. The more I saw of you, the more I couldn't stop thinking about you. What I'm trying to say is—"

Mark Winterson lets a ragged breath out. He actually seems nervous. "You really got me. Hook, line, and sinker. At first this was just a fun distraction, but I haven't felt like this since . . . since . . ."

The echo of what his sister said piques my interest. "Since . . . ?"

He shakes his head and seems a bit pained, like he's mad at me for making him feel something.

I groan. "Come on, you can't do that. I'll tickle you and make you sweaty."

He has mentioned several times, over the six weeks we've been dating, how much he hates being sweaty.

I reach for his armpit, and he clamps his arms against his sides.

"I hate this story. It makes me sound like a loser."

I give him my most innocent look. "I won't judge."

Mark Winterson closes his eyes like he's getting a migraine. "Remember Clarissa?"

"Zack's wife?"

He grimaces. "She was my girlfriend in college. Thought we were going to get married, for real."

My gasp is genuine. "And she dumped you for your cousin?"

"I found out she was cheating on me."

"Oh my God, Mark, that's awful." I'm trying to focus, but my brain is screaming *Heartbreak year!* "How old were you, even? When you found all that out."

"Like twenty? And Zack was a fucking *eighteen-year-old freshman,* but she said he obviously had more drive." Mark Winterson runs his hands over his face. "And then I still had to see them at family gatherings a few times a year. Totally humiliating."

"That's terrible." I put a hand on his arm and rack my brain for something comforting to say. "You seem very driven. Also, you're *way* hotter than him. Like, objectively. Hands down. No question."

Mark Winterson laughs in a way that is probably meant to be self-deprecating, but he's obviously delighted to hear it. "You're funny."

"Nah, just calling 'em like I see 'em." I give him my best Bugs Bunny grin. "You're smarter than him too. And better personality, for sure. He seemed like a dick."

"Don't girls like that, though?" His smile is taunting.

"Do they? Seems like a big population to generalize about."

"Oh, okay, didn't realize you were a social scientist." Mark Winterson chuckles and glances at the ceiling. "Anyway, it was long enough ago that it's a bad look for me to still be mad about it. Everyone else is like, *Obviously they are a better fit, they're really serious, blah blah.*"

So is that why he's doing whatever he's doing? Going balls to the wall to impress Erickson and become his number two so he can outshine his cousin?

The things I've read about him slowly fit together with the story he just told. He started his undergrad at UPenn, where Zack graduated (I learned from Google), and where he must have met Clarissa. But partway through undergrad, Mark Winterson somehow transferred to the London School of Economics.

There's an uncomfortable wobble in my stomach as I recognize the similarity. I got my heart broken and moved across the country. He moved across an ocean.

"Anyway, it stings a lot less now," he says with a small smile, squeezing my wrist again. "Thanks for that."

Mark Winterson's phone buzzes on the nightstand, and he grabs it.

"Shit, I have to go," he says, rubbing his eyes. "Sorry. I would have wanted to—"

"It's okay!" I say, sitting up too fast.

Fuck, I didn't ask him about his relationship with Erickson, I realize as I watch him cross the room and redo his tie.

"You probably noticed I'm working a lot lately," he says, putting his jacket back on. "It won't always be like this, but—we're trying to figure out this deal. It could be big for the company."

"Like a merger?"

"More like risk management." He pauses as he's adjusting his tie in front of the mirror, and meets my eye in the reflection. "I can't exactly talk about it."

"Must be a lot of pressure. Working on Erickson's project."

"Just don't want to disappoint him. And I found out today—" He laughs, but he doesn't sound like he's having a good time. "I actually have to go to Vegas this weekend to meet with the other side. Seal the deal."

"Oh, fun, I love Vegas," I say reflexively, remembering when

Mom and Tita Wendy took me and Greg out there with them in eighth grade. Something about how glitzy and unreal things were was weirdly comforting to me.

Mark Winterson sits back down on the bed and plants a kiss on my temple. "Come with me, then."

Just one more late night. Just one more weekend. Almost there, almost there.

His phone buzzes again, and he frowns at it and stands.

"Bring a bag to the office tomorrow." He points at me. "We'll leave early. I'll arrange it with Erica."

"O-okay," I say in a daze. "See you tomorrow."

The heavy door closes behind him, and I slump backward onto the bed, staring at the round ceiling light, thinking, *exnihilo_____2013!*

CHAPTER 48

The sessions are over for the day, and the union is unofficially holding a karaoke night in a third-floor conference room. Diane from Complaint Resolution conveniently happens to run the party planning committee, and she organized the whole thing.

After Mark Winterson and I parted ways, I attended a few sessions to keep up appearances, then spent a good long while hyperventilating in the bathroom as *exnihilo______2013, exnihilo______2013, exnihilo______2013!* looped over and over in my head.

And by the time I show up, the conference room is bumping. Karaoke seems to have ended, but someone has plugged their phone into the sound system, and now it's transformed into a weird office version of a high school dance. Someone got hold of a disco ball, and its lights spin around the dim room.

Carol from Legal is cutting the rug with Bob from the Houston office—I know from the group chat that she's been talking to him all day about unionizing there next. And damn, she has moves! I wouldn't have guessed. Sarah is leaning back against

Grace, nestled into her arms, and they're swaying gently from side to side. Al is standing in the back, earnestly trying to carry on a conversation with a few people from the Supplier Relations team—but based on their body language, it seems they can't hear him over the music.

"Hey!" Greg comes up alongside me and clinks his beer bottle against mine. "Shouldn't we be celebrating?"

I swallow hard, and his eyes flit nervously around my face. He leans in so he can talk into my ear. "Congratulations on your recent breakup?"

"Can we, um—" I shout over the music, gesturing for the door. "Can we go outside and talk?"

"Oh! Of course. Sure." So I follow him out of the conference room and down the walkway to an outdoor patio.

It's pleasantly warm outside, early summer evening coming on, the scent of jasmine in the air. The silence hangs tense between us as cars whoosh past on the freeway in the distance, streams of red and white lights coursing in opposite directions.

Greg leans on the railing, shifting a few times like he can't get comfortable. "You're not breaking up with him," he says finally. A disappointed observation, not a question exactly.

It's like the bottom of my stomach has dropped out, but I still feel such an intense drive to finish what I started. Maybe if I can find the right words—maybe he'll understand—

"I want you to know that I did everything I could here," I start, grip tightening on the railing. "I still need part of his password. He asked me to go to Vegas with him this weekend."

Greg blinks a few times. He looks at me like I'm getting smaller and smaller, vanishing in the distance, even though I'm still right here. "How much more are you going to extend this?" he says quietly, like he's already bracing himself, becoming resigned. Coming up with a strategy to protect himself in advance, maybe, before he can lose something again. "Do you even want to break up with him?"

"Greg—" I reach for him, but he takes a step away and gives me a long, searching look, like he doesn't recognize me anymore.

He scoffs and shakes his head. "Ruby, I love you, but I can't *hold that thought* forever."

"You think I'm doing this for fun?" I yell. I'm so frustrated, I can't explain fast enough—all the words are wrong, and Greg looks so hurt, and everything is going sideways.

"I mean—I can't—" Tears are trembling in the corners of my eyes, and I take a sharp breath in, trying to hold them back. "I don't know what to do for Mom anymore. I couldn't follow through there. And I don't want—I just—I can't stand to fail at this too!"

Greg pulls me into a hug, and some of those tears break free. "Hey, shh, shh. You're okay. It's okay." His lemon smell wraps me up, and one hand runs up and down my back. "I know I can't fully understand what you're going through," he says, voice raspy. "But you don't have to do this. You don't have to do anything else."

"It's not okay!" I pull back, wiping my cheeks roughly with my palm. "I can't just—just *squander* this chance! I'm doing this for you too!"

He laughs desperately, no joy in it. "I don't want you to do this! You don't have to get his password. We'll figure something else out."

"Do you have a better idea?"

"Ruby—" He runs an agitated hand through his hair. "Let's back up, go back to your mom for a second. What if you tried being honest with her? Really honest. Put all your cards on the table. Say you can't figure out what her unfinished business is and explain everything you've done so far."

"And how will that help? What if that makes her feel even worse, on top of everything she's been through?"

Greg puts his hands on my arms. "Maybe compared to everything she's been through, whatever you say can't be that bad."

He's not making sense. I jerk out of his grasp, even though the look on his face is making my heart break.

"Don't go," he says. "Please."

"It's just one more weekend."

Greg stares at me for a long moment, until something in his head seems to click into place and he looks away. "Call me when you're ready to talk, then," he says and walks back inside, leaving me on the balcony by myself.

CHAPTER 49

It's Friday afternoon, and Mark Winterson is driving his Mercedes like a maniac.

We're on a two-lane road snaking through the Angeles National Forest, headed around a blind curve, and he's decided to hop into the wrong side to overtake multiple cars in a no-passing zone.

"God, where did these people learn to drive?" he mutters to himself, designer sunglasses glinting in the light. "They're barely going the speed limit."

It seems like a rational response to slow down when you're taking hairpin turns three thousand feet up into the San Gabriel Mountains, but what do I know? If another car came around the bend and hit us head-on, we'd probably tumble down the side of a cliff.

Finally, he gets back onto the right side of the road, and I stare at the craggy mountain face rising up above us, waiting for the terror to leave my body. The mountains are strangely green because of the rain we've had recently, and tall stalks of foothill yucca with crowns of pale yellow flowers whip past us on the side of the road.

"My mom called that one Our Lord's Candle," I say, voice wavering, pointing to the yucca blooms. "Doesn't it look candle-like?"

"It does," he says, smiling like he just remembered I exist.

And then it occurs to me that I should probably update her, at least.

ruby.ocampo:
Mom, Mark and I are driving out to Vegas!

I can't stand the idea that there's nothing I can do for her anymore. I'm still sharing updates with her, hoping against hope that something will be the difference-maker. Maybe seeing that we're going on vacation together will make her think it's really serious? Put her at ease enough to let go?

But I'm not holding my breath the way I used to as I upload a photo of Mark Winterson in profile, speeding through the mountains.

sampaguita72:
Good! You should be having some fun!
What did I tell you? Life is short
I'm glad you cleared things up with that boyfriend of yours
He seems good for you

My stomach clenches tighter than it already had from Mark Winterson's driving.

"Your aunt doing all right?" he asks.

"She's great." I wave the phone vaguely before sliding it back into my purse. "She just has lots of opinions about where we should go."

"I think I've got it covered," he says with a condescending smirk.

Okay, Ruby. Focus. How do I steer the conversation in the direction of Erickson without being too obvious?

But Mark Winterson punches the gas, taking a curve too fast, and all I can think about is clinging to the sides of my seat.

We make it down to flat land, and the mood relaxes. On either side of us, the desert stretches out, baked brown earth and pale green scrubby brush, jagged shapes of the mountains hugging the horizon in either direction. It feels like we're passing into another world together; for a long time, we let his audiobook do the talking, and neither of us speaks at all.

It's the golden hour when we pass the World's Tallest Thermometer glowing on the side of the road, the bright red that stands in for mercury hovering just under one hundred degrees. AVOID OVERHEATING, an orange sign warns, signaling the start of the Baker Grade. TURN OFF AC NEXT 16 MILES.

The sun sinks lower in the sky as Mark Winterson weaves—pushing 100 miles per hour, air conditioner blasting—around the older cars that are straining to climb the steep slope. Another sign whizzes past, saying ELEVATION 2000 FEET.

"Why aren't these people moving!" He sighs, exasperated, adjusting his grip on the wheel as his gold watch catches the light. ELEVATION 3000 FEET, another sign says, so soon after the last one. We pass a truck with its hood popped open on the side of the road.

Every time I'd drive out to Vegas with Mom and her old station wagon would struggle up this incline, she'd pinch my arm and say, "Ruby, make sure you end up with a man who drives a car that can go ninety up the Baker Grade with the AC on." *Weirdly specific advice, but okay,* I'd always think. But now the irony makes me feel faint.

After a while we pass into Nevada, coasting downhill again,

and the lights of Las Vegas come into view. I remember how magical it seemed the first time I made this trip, sitting in back with Greg while Mom and Tita Wendy chatted up front. For the rest of that weekend, our moms switched off watching us by the hotel pool while the other one went to gamble.

I remember how refreshed Mom looked, lounging poolside, sipping a cocktail. How she said, *Even if it's just a fantasy, I love coming here because I get to feel rich.*

As we cruise down the Strip, I glance at Mark Winterson, his profile lit by the glow of the neon lights. I'm not going to make it through this weekend unless I compartmentalize. Pretend he's a nice guy and we could potentially have a nice time.

We check into our room (on the fifth floor, low enough that Mark Winterson can take the stairs) and do some exploring: wandering around the food court on the second level, strolling down the passageway that connects this hotel to the others on the strip.

On the way back, we pass through the casino floor with its blinking lights and electronic pinging sounds. The smell of cigarette smoke makes me nostalgic.

"Oooh, I love slot machines," I say, clapping my hands together. "The twenty-five-cent ones."

Mark Winterson laughs like I'm so quaint.

"They're weirdly soothing!" I protest. "They're almost, like . . . meditative. What was that thing your mom was talking about at dinner? Mindfulness?"

"I don't think that's what that means." He chortles. "I hate games where it's just random. Need it to be at least a little bit about skill."

I guess that tracks, for someone who seems to believe he's in control of his own destiny.

We head back to our room and get ready for dinner, neon

signs dancing outside the large window. I open my overnight bag and pull out a sundress, and Mark Winterson clears his throat.

"So I made reservations . . ." He trails off and gestures toward the dress. "That doesn't quite fit the vibe, I think. But I brought something for you to wear."

"Oh!"

He opens his big hard-shell suitcase and takes out a garment bag, and I can see a second one hiding underneath it.

"What's that one?"

He grins and closes the suitcase. "A surprise for later."

I don't think I've ever been to dinner somewhere quite this fancy in my life. There's a giant crystal chandelier hanging from the ceiling that looks like it must weigh more than I do. Tasteful moldings adorn the walls, and silver carts pass by loaded with opulent desserts and an entire bakery's worth of bread. There are flower arrangements stationed all around the room—it feels like someone is about to get married in here.

Mark Winterson orders appetizers for both of us, and an amuse-bouche that involves some kind of foam comes out first, followed by a caviar dish that appears to be literally topped with a thin sheet of gold.

"There's gold in them-there caviar," I say in an old-timey voice, waving my fork for emphasis.

Mark Winterson gives me a thin smile. Maybe he's getting tired of me. My jokes aren't so novel to him anymore.

Our meal progresses, and he seems tense, chewing his food and staring into the middle distance. The longer the silence stretches out, the harder it gets to shove down my rising panic.

You could search for the rest of your life and still not figure out how to free Mom! She'll be trapped there forever!

And Mark Winterson is going to find me out and sue me! He's going to ruin me—bury me! What the fuck am I doing here!

Goosebumps rise on my back, exposed in this dress he picked out for me to wear. (Starter kit for being Mark Winterson's girlfriend: Invest in more than one backless bra.)

I've been admonishing myself to stand as straight as possible all night, and the tension is building between my shoulder blades.

"Anything to drink?" the waiter asks.

"Whiskey, please!" I say, and when it arrives, I throw the drink back as quickly as possible, then order another.

Mark Winterson raises his eyebrows. "You okay there?"

"Just stressed from work." I point at him. "You must be so stressed! Big deal in progress. Aren't you going to have a drink?"

He straightens his jacket. "Gotta keep my wits about me for tomorrow, unfortunately."

I swirl the liquid in my glass, finish it off, and flag the waiter down for one more. Around the time the main course arrives, I start to feel calmer. Certainly looser.

"It was interesting meeting your parents," I say. "Your dad . . . seems like a tough cookie?"

He scoffs, corner of his mouth tilting up. "Yeah. He thinks I'm too soft to make it in this business. Loves to remind me." He pitches his voice lower. *"You'll never get anywhere if you want everyone to like you, Mark."*

I make sure to give him an appreciative laugh. "Erickson seems to think you're getting somewhere? Having you come out here. Giving you more responsibility."

Mark Winterson fidgets with his silverware. "He's one of my dad's best friends. They're pretty similar." He takes a long gulp of water and sets it down heavily on the table. "Except he actually believes in me."

Oh God, what a setup. Erickson must have him wrapped around his finger.

Another fake business card flashes in my mind:

Mark Winterson

Terrible Driver
His Own Man, Definitely NOT That Celebrity
Hella Daddy Issues

That third drink is really catching up to me. Everything feels a bit funnier. *He's going to sue me! Haha!* And I don't even want to think about how much this meal costs. When the dessert cart arrives, I actually clap a hand on Mark Winterson's shoulder and exclaim, "Shut up!"

The noise in the dining room seems to get louder, and my head starts to feel like it's a balloon filled with helium, fixing to float away.

I take another selfie to send to my "aunt"—my eyes closed, head resting sloppily on his shoulder while he smiles stiffly, hand raised in a wave—and upload it into the haunted Slack DM.

sampaguita72:
You look so good together!
Hope you're having a good time!

I'm so drunk by the time we're heading back to the room, I can barely walk. I'm holding the wall for balance, but the floor doesn't seem to want to stay in one place.

Maybe I shouldn't have come with him on this trip. Maybe I really am in over my head.

Then the world tilts as he scoops me up off my feet and carries me inside.

CHAPTER 50

When I pry my eyes open the next morning, I have an earth-shattering hangover. The sun is stabbing me through my skull.

And Mark Winterson is sitting in a curved hotel chair, fully suited, looking broody. Facing the bed, like maybe he was watching me sleep. He's leaning forward, elbows on knees, turning a velvet box over and over in his hands. But then he notices I'm awake and slips it in his jacket pocket.

Part of me thinks distantly: *Huh, that's strange?* But I'm in too much of a haze to really process it.

"Hey." The soft brown eyes that make him seem so attentive catch the copious natural light in this hotel room.

"What time is it?" I mumble blearily.

He checks his watch. "Just past noon."

"Do you have your big meeting soon?" I rub my tender eyes.

"Had it already." He smiles, and that dimple pops again. "Went great."

It dawns on me that I'm just wearing a T-shirt and

underwear—one of his T-shirts, I see, and I don't remember how I got into it.

"What . . . did we do last night?"

"Nothing." He laughs. "You were out like a light. It was a struggle to get you out of that dress and tuck you in. Here—"

He goes to a room service cart parked by the window, pours some coffee into a mug from a silver pot, and delivers it to me in bed.

I feel ten percent more human as soon as I've taken a few sips, even though it's a bit weird that he's just standing there watching me drink.

"So I've been wanting to ask you something," Mark Winterson says. He takes the box out of his jacket pocket.

Everything seems to slow. Suddenly all the coffee in the world couldn't be enough to brace me for this. It's like I have pins and needles in my stomach, my chest, the inside of my brain.

He goes down on one knee and peers up at me earnestly, holding the box out and popping it open. Nestled inside is a ring glittering with more diamonds than I've ever seen in one place.

"Get the fuck out," I squeak.

"I mean it. I haven't felt like this about anyone in years. Or maybe ever." He runs a nervous hand through his perfectly tousled hair. "And I know it probably seems sudden. But . . . we're here in Vegas, and—Ruby Ocampo, will you marry me?"

My brain is a total fog. I can't feel my fingers, and it's hard to get enough air in my lungs.

"I—I didn't think you'd be a shotgun wedding person," I stammer. "Thought you'd want something fancy. Maybe at a vineyard. With all the chairs?"

His brows lift. "Not sure chairs figured into it for me. Do *you* want all the chairs?"

That makes me laugh despite my mounting panic.

"I mean, at least for me," he says, putting a hand over his heart, "I'm not going to be more sure than this."

He sets the open ring box down beside me on the comforter, like maybe looking at the dazzling specimen will convince me.

A sick feeling of relief seeps into my sore muscles. *Here's something I can do to fix Mom's situation.*

It could be my last chance to help her move on. And when will I have an opening this clear again?

Mark Winterson's still down on one knee, his absurdly handsome face turned toward me.

"And I've learned, in life—" He reaches for my hand and rubs a thumb along my palm. "You shouldn't hesitate, once you're sure."

What does marriage even mean, with divorce rates as high as they are? I can go through with it and then immediately work on getting out of it.

You liked him well enough for a while, right? You can fold yourself up into this shape for a bit longer? Grit down, persevere, almost there, almost there—

My heart beats faster, and my head aches. I close my eyes and see Greg hiding under my desk, beside me on the swings, hugging me in my kitchen. I promised him: Just one more weekend. I feel like I'm going to throw up.

I'm saying goodbye to him, if I do this. He'll never forgive me.

But can I stand always wondering if this one decision is the reason Mom gets stuck at work forever? Can I live with myself if I knew I had the chance and didn't take it?

"Ruby," Mark Winterson says, squeezing my hand. "Are you all right?"

"Yes! Yes, my answer is yes," I blurt in a fevered rush.

Mark Winterson grins, relieved, and throws his arms around me, hugging me tight, kissing me. He slides the ring onto my finger, and I feel nauseous.

"Fantastic," he says, standing and brushing his hands together like he's dusting them off. *A job well done.* "I have to take care of one more work thing. Our appointment at the chapel is at two-thirty. You should eat something." He nods toward the room service cart, a silver domed lid sitting on a tray.

"And I got you a dress." He retrieves that mysterious second garment bag and holds it up. "There's a veil in here. And . . ."

He opens the closet and takes out a bouquet densely packed with pink and yellow blooms, and sets it down at the foot of the bed.

Wow, he really had this all planned. It's kind of scary.

"Get dressed and wait for me on the casino floor downstairs? You can meditate at the slot machines," he says with a crooked smile, taking out his wallet and handing me a few hundred-dollar bills like it's nothing. "I'll come get you."

CHAPTER 51

After Mark Winterson leaves, I cry in the bathroom for a while. My head is so foggy and it hurts to think. I keep trying to examine the problem from all angles, but once I've turned it all the way over, I forget what was on the other side. I can't hold the whole thing in my mind at once—Greg, the union, Mom's ghost, GERBO, this giant ring on my finger.

Just do this one thing. It's not that bad. Just grit through it, hold on, almost there, almost there!

Finally I get myself together and retrieve the dress. It's stunning—gauzy and transparent across the shoulders, opaque from the bodice down, flowing elegant and satiny to the floor. And, of course, there's a low-cut back.

He must be a back man, I think to myself as I turn around in front of the mirror.

The whole time I'm doing my makeup and hair, I can't stop thinking about Greg—laughing next to me on the couch, holding me while I cried on the stoop, staring at me under the broken light in the copy room.

I want to message him—I want to call and hear his voice—but what could I possibly say that won't make him hate me now?

I sweep my hair into a tight bun, shellac the whole thing with hairspray, and insert the comb of the veil into its base, flipping it back so it floats behind my head.

Mark Winterson even brought heels for me to wear with this. *He really had it all planned out.* But no one will see my feet anyway—and after last night, all my muscles are sore, from my brain down to my toes, so I slip on the sneakers I brought with me instead.

I take a photo of the ring on my finger for Mom, and a mirror selfie of myself in the dress, clutching the bouquet. My throat is tight as I tap out the message:

ruby.ocampo:
Mom, guess what! He proposed! We're getting married!

Her reaction is instant: multiple GIFs of fireworks, followed by a cascade of dancing and champagne-popping emojis.

sampaguita72:
Ruby!!! That's incredible news, congratulations!!! I'm so thrilled for you!
I wish I was there to see!
You look stunning! Send pictures of the ceremony!

She seems happy, and yet she's still here. Clearly it's not enough if I don't go all the way through with it.

I meet my eye in the mirror, feeling like I'm getting dolled up to face a firing squad.

It will be over soon. Just do this one thing and then you'll know you really tried whatever you could.

I feel like I'm having an out-of-body experience as I walk down the hall, holding this giant bouquet, obviously dressed for a wedding. People keep smiling at me. A woman getting out of the elevator says, "Congratulations!"

The elevator doors open on the ground floor, and I spot Mark Winterson and the CEO of TKCORP, heading toward the sportsbook.

They walk down past several rows of leather couches before settling in the front, turned away from me, facing the wall of televisions showing nine different sports at once. I trail after them and duck behind the couch they're sitting on, while their attention is on the screens.

"Good work, kid, I mean it," Erickson says. "We're taken care of now, whatever happens. And once you finish cleaning things up, we can go public."

"Ma'am, are you all right?" a casino employee asks me, and I pat the carpet with one hand, breaking out in a sweat.

"Lost a contact, it's fine!" I hiss, waving him off. And fortunately he shrugs and carries on his way.

"You remember that deal I told you about?" Erickson says. It's so dark and noisy in here, with so many overlapping voices, they must not have noticed me. "The first time we met?"

"Of course—the Cactus deal," Mark Winterson says. "I idolized you as a kid. Hung on your every word back then."

The jackpot sound from the slot machine rings in my ears. *First deal Erickson ever told you about!*

"Real smart, that one," Erickson says. "Enron did it up and we invested. Beautiful deal. Legal, aboveboard, but same logic as a lot of what they did later. Learned a lot from those boys. Their name is a dirty word now, but my point is: It's a fake line, legal and not legal. There's only what you can get away with."

Oh God, I need to go. I need to get out of here.

Crouched low, I sprint away from the sportsbook and plop down in front of a slot machine to gather myself. It's one of the older kind, with the actual mechanical arm.

I glance back over my shoulder, and Mark Winterson is leaving the sportsbook now, alone. So I feed the machine in front of me a twenty, head spinning, heart pounding. *Exnihilo-cactus2013!*

I flip the veil down to cover my face, like maybe that will hide me. I am too hungover for this shit.

Then Mark Winterson appears beside the machine.

"Hey," he says. "You look amazing in that. Wow." He flips the veil up to look at me, and his smile is weirdly melancholy and faraway.

He looks at his watch. "We still have time to kill before we have to leave for the chapel. I'll sit with you? While you get robbed by the one-armed bandit."

He takes the stool for the slot machine to my left, settling in to read on his phone.

So what can I do? I select all five lines and watch the reels spin, cherries and diamonds and bars of gold.

"You know unions are corrupt," Mark Winterson says out of the blue. My scalp prickles, and the little hairs on my nape stand on end.

Why is he bringing that up out of nowhere?

"And they're in decline, historically. Look at this—" He turns his phone screen toward me, and I peer at a Bloomberg article with some charts. "Ten percent of U.S. workers are unionized—*only ten*! Because they're a relic of Fordism—of a bygone era. They don't make sense anymore. Stagflation in the seventies ended that whole thing."

Over the weeks I've been his girlfriend, he's talked quite a lot about increasing profits, endless growth, doing more with less. And for me and everyone like me, that means running faster, like someone is chasing you, just to stay in the same place. Always feeling like you're on the brink of being laid off, falling behind, losing everything.

The invisible hand squeezing and squeezing, choking you

out—it would be nice to have some human hands to push back. Slap it on the wrist, get it to ease up.

But I need to play dumb. Make this into a joke.

"Well, I'm no economist, but . . ."

"Exactly! So you should relax." He fixes me with a penetrating stare. "Stay in your lane."

A chill runs down my spine. "Mark, what exactly are we talking about right now?"

He searches for something on his phone. "Erickson just gave me some . . . troubling news. But I'm sure there's an explanation, right?"

He turns his screen my way again, and there's a photo of me and Greg hugging on the balcony outside the conference center. It looks like someone must have taken it from the parking lot below.

"He's an old friend!" I exclaim, but Mark Winterson's eyes narrow.

"We know this guy is trying to organize a union at work. It's stupid—we don't need one. If it's bad for business, it's bad for everyone. But it's been a pain in my ass, running around trying to take care of that." His jaw moves, like he's grinding his teeth. "Are you aware of that? Are you part of it?"

In the shiny side of a nearby slot machine, I can see my reflection, and I look like I've seen a ghost.

My poker face has never been very good—it's a wonder I've made it this far. Mom tried to teach me how to play once, and she'd dissolve into fits of laughter at my facial expressions. *This really isn't your game, Roobs!*

"Wow," Mark Winterson says with a bitter chuckle. "You knew, didn't you? Un-fucking-believable. Have you been talking to them about me? You know what that means, given the contract you signed?"

Shit, shit, fuck! I'm found out! I'm had!

"Anyway, it doesn't matter," he says lightly, giving me a pitying smile. "The union's not going to be a problem anymore. Your whole team's getting let go on Monday. And Accounting's getting cut in half. But *you're* getting promoted. You'll be a manager—incidentally not qualified for the union, if they do find some way to make it happen."

There's the promotion I was striving for, dangling in front of me. But then, flashing before my eyes, I see Sarah laughing with me in the dark, Morgan coming to my defense, Al saying he'd have to give Mark Winterson a talking-to. Carol offering me some gruff advice, Adam fist-bumping me in the hall. Greg staring at me on the playground, saying he didn't want me to do this. The moment in the diner, when the people I spend so many of my waking hours with raised their hands, one by one, to say, *Yes, we trust you.*

Over the house speakers, above the din of the casino, I can make out a song Mom liked: Kenny Rogers crooning about an old gambler giving him some advice.

Mark Winterson leans back, looking less hurt now and more like a cat who caught a mouse.

"Maybe it's crazy, but I'm in love with you, Ruby." His tongue darts out to moisten his dry lips. "And I know everyone makes mistakes. I'll make this easy, all right? You can come clean, we can start over, and I can protect you. You'll be rich. You'll be with me. I'll take care of everything."

Someone to take care of me. It's more or less what Mom always wanted.

I'm trembling, still clutching the bouquet he got for me so tightly, I think the stems might snap.

"So, tell me—do you want to be on the losing team?" Mark Winterson leans close to whisper in my ear. "Haven't you already lost enough?"

I close my eyes and pull the handle of the slot machine, and a new thought sprouts in my mind, a weed struggling through the cracks: When you're raised with a controlling kind of love, however well-meaning, it can set a pattern. Maybe it gets comfortable wedging yourself into tight spaces, when you grow up doing it. They make you feel safe.

As the reels spin, everyone's faces flip through my mind—Greg, Sarah, Al, Morgan, Carol, Adam, the whole group in the diner, Greg again.

The spinning stops, no matches. My last $1.25 disappears into the void, balance $0.00. *Maybe I'll lose and keep losing—maybe I'll be a failure, but at least I'll be in good company.*

Over the speakers, Kenny Rogers gets to the part about knowing when to run.

"Let me remind you," Mark Winterson says, voice gone cold. "If you violate the NDA you signed, I won't hesitate to sue. I have an impressive legal team."

I lean close to whisper in his ear. "Good for you, having one impressive thing."

And I take off running.

CHAPTER 52

Dress hiked up and bunched in one hand, I sprint away from the casino floor, the *chngh chngh chngh* of someone cashing out ringing in my ears, and book it up the escalator, through the food court.

I shove past people standing in line—there's a smattering of *Hey!* and *Watch it!*—and speed toward the carpeted passageway that connects to the neighboring casinos. I check over my shoulder, thinking maybe I lost him, and—shit!—there's Mark Winterson, coming after me at a light jog, jacket thrown over his shoulder. So I pick up the pace, heading for the Bellagio.

Groups of tourists are clustered in the hall, some of them staring and pointing.

I realize that I'm still clutching the bouquet, and I raise it above my head. Ahead of me, people gasp and shout, pressing closer and raising their hands to catch it, so I lob it as hard as I can toward them as I run past, and there's some commotion as they scuffle to get it. Behind me, someone cheers.

"Ruby!" Mark Winterson calls after me. "Hey!"

I twist around to confirm that, yes, he is actually still running after me, red-faced and furious in the suit he was planning to get married in. "Come back!" he yells. "Stop! Don't make this harder than it has to be!"

I wrench off the ring and toss it at him, and he yelps and goes scrambling after it. Maybe trying to recoup his investment will slow him down long enough for me to get away.

I rush through the winding hallways and down another escalator, weaving more deftly between groups of people than Mark Winterson on the freeway, and wrench the veil off my head and toss that too.

A burst of floral scent overtakes me as I jog past the conservatory, with its fountains and unreal displays of plants. I nearly lose my balance on the smooth marble floor as I risk a glance behind me again—and sure enough, there, far down the hall, is Mark Winterson. He's slowed to a brisk power-walk—maybe because he hates making a scene—but he's still tailing me without hurrying, which is somehow even more sinister.

I scramble up and race through the lobby, beneath the Dale Chihuly glass blooming from the ceiling, and slip into the revolving door, panic rising as they force me to slow my pace, thinking, *Can this thing go any faster?*

Then the summer Vegas heat envelops me like a cozy oven, and I take off running down the drive alongside the iconic fountain. *There's no way he'll follow me outside. Too sweaty.*

Across Las Vegas Boulevard, a giant poster of Martha Stewart beams at me from the fake Arc de Triomphe. Something tells me to run toward it, and the lights are on my side—I barely catch the tail end of a Walk signal as I sprint across the twelve-lane street, sweating profusely into this (surely expensive) gown.

I don't see Mark Winterson behind me anymore. There's a busy street between us, but I don't know how much time that will buy me, so I scramble inside Paris and duck behind one leg of the fake Eiffel Tower, fumbling my phone out of my purse.

And my first instinct is to call Greg.

Multiple giant television screens on the wall in front of me show the same racehorse sprinting from different angles. *Relatable,* I think as the phone rings and rings. *Run, girl, run!*

"Ruby? Are you all right?" Greg answers. "Where are you?"

"P-paris! Paris!"

"You're not in Vegas?" He sounds as panicked as I feel. "You left the country?"

"No! No, I am! I didn't!" I can barely breathe. "Paris in Vegas! I followed Martha Stewart here!"

"What?" Greg yells.

"Paris the hotel and casino in Las Vegas, Nevada!" I yell.

"Stay there, I'm coming!"

"No! No, Greg, I—" He sounds so ready to spring into action, it makes me tear up. Wherever I need him, that's where he wants to be, even if it's a ridiculous distance away. "I'm touched, really, I am, but I can't wait here for, like, five hours, I—I called you because—" A strained laugh bursts out of me. "Because I'm on the run and you're the first person I'd call in an emergency."

"Ruby, I'm nearby. Stay there."

He hangs up, and my head is spinning, a mighty *What the fuck?* reverberating in my head.

But then there's Mark Winterson again, walking calmly through the front door.

I dive behind a cluster of video poker machines and scuttle sideways underneath the uncanny painted sky, inserting myself into a big Asian extended family moving together down the floor. I hop to a group of women who seem to be here for a bachelorette party, clustered around the bride, who's wearing a sash and, for some reason, rabbit ears and a cotton tail. "Oh my

God, I love your dress!" one of them exclaims, and I give her a strained smile as I duck behind a slot machine, low electronic rumbling sounds rattling my nerves. I realize with a sinking feeling that I have no idea now if Mark Winterson is in front of me or behind me. A motion in my peripheral vision startles me—but it's just some giant craps dice, bouncing inside a plastic capsule on top of another machine.

Someone touches my shoulder, and I shriek and spring to my feet.

"Shh, shh—it's okay, it's okay!" There's Greg's astonished face, and I fling my arms around him, on the brink of a sob.

Then, across the room, I actually *do* see Mark Winterson—and we lock eyes for a second as Greg tugs my hand and we sprint down the fake-cobblestone street to the parking garage.

My stomach drops, seeing the line for the pay machine, but Greg powers past it. "I already paid!" he exclaims, and my heart swells with pride. *Greg is so practical! Good in a crisis!* We hop into his car, and as we peel out, I see Mark Winterson behind us in the rearview mirror, tossing his jacket to the ground.

For a while, as the aging Acura speeds down the I-15 out of Las Vegas, we can't stop laughing. Every time we start losing steam and the car gets quiet, we look at each other and burst out laughing again.

"Can't believe you followed me," I say, grinning like an idiot.

"Couldn't let you be stranded with that guy," Greg says as his car strains uphill through brown hills dotted with Joshua trees and cacti. "Don't think I slept the whole time you were at that wedding."

Another mock business card flashes in my mind:

Greg De Leon

Childhood Crush and Hot Accountant
Doesn't Dream of Labor but Organized a Union
Actually the Most Reliable Man I Have Ever Known

For a while, we sit in silence—both shell-shocked, maybe, giddy from tearing out of a hilarious location, basking in the glow of speeding off into the desert as fast as this twenty-year-old car will take us.

But slowly it feels like the warmth drains out of this small bubble we're in together (even though I'm sweating, and the AC is weak).

Greg's eyes dart between my outfit and the road. "You're dressed up?" he says finally.

My hands twist in my lap. How am I going to explain any of this? "He asked me to marry him."

"Oh," Greg says, looking at me sideways again. "So did you . . . do that?"

"No!" I shout, too loud, all my nervous energy spilling out. "Because I don't love him! And he's kind of terrible! By all the metrics that matter, and some of the ones that don't too!"

Greg laughs at my outburst. "Okay?"

Some tears of frustration spring to my eyes, and I wipe them away while the words tumble out. "He just sprang it on me! And I thought, what if this is the thing that gets Mom out of Slack, finally? What if it is, and I never tried it? So I . . . I said yes, and . . . I got dressed up, but . . . I couldn't go through with it."

For an agonizing moment, the only sounds are the wind whistling outside the car and the rumbling of the engine. Greg sighs, wrestling with his own thoughts. Up ahead, the mountains look like streaks of muddy watercolor on the horizon, shades of brown fading to deep purple, the color of a bruise.

Greg checks his mirrors, like he's trying to see if a black Mercedes might be following us. And when he's satisfied with the empty highway behind us, he pulls over at a rest stop—a diner and a gas station, surrounded by desert scrub—and parks in front of the pump.

He kills the engine and turns to me. "You've had quite a day, huh?"

That makes me burst out laughing, but it quickly turns into sobbing. I almost wish I still had that veil to hide me.

Greg takes my face gently in his hands, wiping at my tears with his thumbs. "Shh, shh. I've got you. You're okay."

Everything around us goes into soft focus. I'm sticky and sore and so thoroughly exhausted, but I'm so filled with affection for him and the absurd way he just came through for me.

I lean closer to kiss him, but Greg gently presses me back, hands on my shoulders.

"Ruby, hey," he says, voice low, eyes roaming around my face. "I think maybe, by now, you know how long I've wanted this, but . . . you're all dressed up to marry someone else. Can't help feeling like a rebound?" A bitter little chuckle shakes his chest, and he glances away, out the window. "Maybe let's cool off for a minute. See how you feel after sleeping on it." He runs a hand over his face and sighs again. "Not wanting him . . . doesn't mean you actually want me."

I let myself fall back against the passenger seat, arms crossed. "Do you even realize how long I've wanted you? It's humiliating! It's completely ridiculous."

Greg scoffs, but still doesn't look back my way. "Maybe you should tell me."

"For ten years, basically." I glare at him. "Do you know how exhausting it is to be in love with someone for a fucking decade?"

He lets out a short breath, like he's trying not to laugh. "Okay, well, if that's true . . . then what's another day or two?"

Oh shit. Another day or two.

Monday! The layoffs!

I grab Greg's arm, gripping it for dear life. "I have his password!" I exclaim. "Did you bring your laptop?"

We move into the diner next to the gas station, using Greg's phone as a Wi-Fi hotspot.

I sign in to my Slack account, download the spreadsheet Mom found, enter the password, and—oh my God, everything is here, all laid out. Every clandestine payment made from TKCORP to one of the GERBO LLCs to Mark Winterson and then on to what seems to be Erickson's offshore bank account, in an amount just shy of $10,000.

There are routing numbers in the spreadsheet, too, apparently for Mark Winterson's own reference.

He was even using one tab as a to-do list.

> WIND DOWN SPECIAL PURPOSE ENTITIES
> ENSURE SOX COMPLIANCE
> PREPARE FOR IPO

So Erickson has been stealing from TKCORP—ever since he started, probably. And now that they want to take the company public, he brought in Mark Winterson to cover it up before they have to make more disclosures about the company's finances.

Greg peers over my shoulder from behind and whistles.

"Um, yeah, I think we have enough to make a stink," he says in a low voice. "Do you . . . know anyone in the media?"

I remember Anna from the reunion, telling me about her struggles in journalism. Maybe now she won't have to sell her eggs.

I write everything up in an email, attach all the evidence, and send it.

And then I text her: Hey Anna! I know it's the weekend, but I've got a huge scoop for you. Call me!

After I finish talking to Anna, we get back on the road, sandy earth and big sky stretching out around us while we sit in exhausted silence. An email notification pops onto my screen—a message from DocuSign. *Update to: Relationship Contract.* And in a text block in the body, it says:

> Contract terminated in person (fleeing). Clauses one, four, and five still binding, as per agreement.
> —MW

I can't help it—I start laughing, desperately, unstoppably, gasping for air, clutching my sides.

"What's funny?" Greg asks.

"I'm such an idiot."

My adrenaline peaked long ago, and now I'm crashing, my aching, hungover limbs so heavy, thoughts slowing and growing thick. My eyelids close and I drift off to sleep.

CHAPTER 53

"Ruby. Hey," Greg says, nudging my shoulder. "We're here."

I straighten up in the passenger seat and rub my sleep-swollen eyes. Outside it's the golden hour, and we're parked in front of my house. Jacaranda petals litter the sidewalk, shocking violet against the gray concrete.

"I really passed out there," I say, flipping down the visor mirror and checking my wild hair. I shook it out of its bun sometime before we crossed back into California.

"Yeah," Greg says. "Your snoring was cute."

Everything that happened today rushes back—especially how Greg stopped me when I tried to kiss him.

We're so close now, in this small space, and he's looking at me in a way that's hard to read. There's affection there, maybe? I'm so full of nervous energy, I'm practically vibrating. And I'm suddenly very aware of how gross I am in this rumpled dress, after so much running and sweating and the long car ride in the desert heat.

"I'll help you with your bags," he says finally.

"What bags?" I have to laugh. RIP to my favorite sundress and expensive Korean night cream.

"Oh!" A smile spreads over his face. "Uh."

"Do you want to just . . . come in?"

A terrifying few seconds pass while he considers it. But he shakes his head like he's judging himself, opens the door, and gets out.

"After you," he says, extending one arm toward the front door. I fumble with my keys in the lock and step inside, toes flexing with relief once I slip off my sneakers.

He follows me in, and then we're standing there staring at each other, air thick with all the memories living in this house—the confidences and false starts and old versions of both of us that we shed as the years went by.

I don't quite know where we stand. If I lost his trust in a way I can't get back. But here he is, anyway.

Greg gathers me up in a tight hug, and tears quiver at the edge of my vision again.

"I'm glad you're okay," he says into my shoulder. "I was scared there for a minute."

I give him a squeeze. "Could you . . . stay and sit with me for a bit?" I croak out.

"Okay!" He sounds relieved. "Twist my arm."

"I'm disgusting." I take a step back, out of his hug. "I should get cleaned up. Want to watch TV?"

"Yeah." Greg gives me a tired smile. "Sure."

I hurry to the bathroom, ridiculous train of this gown trailing after me, and turn on the shower as hot as I can. While the steam builds, I wrench off this cursed dress and toss it in the hamper.

It's a relief, getting under the hot water. Somehow even after that deep sleep in the car, the sensation of running lingers in my body. The anguish before it, and the adrenaline during, and the crash after—it's like I felt the whole range of human emotions today.

I dry off and put on a big T-shirt and shorts, the ones I usually sleep in, and tie my hair up in a loose scrunchie. And I pad my way back to the living room, stopping short at the end of the hall, where I have a view of Greg in profile—sitting on the couch, wearing jeans and a T-shirt, chain out today. He's got one leg pulled up underneath him, at home here, a socked foot peeking out.

Maybe I was testing him—giving him an opening to change his mind and walk out the door without direct confrontation.

But there he is, still waiting. He notices me hovering, glances over.

And there's something complicated in the way he's looking at me, in my new change of clothes. Like he has a lot going on under the surface, but he's trying his best to be restrained.

"Hey," he says.

"Hey." I sit on the couch next to him, tucking my feet up under me. "Thanks for staying."

It still feels like a barrier is raised between us. All those years of fighting how we felt, bad timing, missing each other. All that time we wasted, disciplining ourselves not to think about it, mutually misunderstanding.

A pang of longing hits me, but I'm scared to move—especially since I already tried to kiss him once today.

The corner of Greg's mouth tilts up. "Why are you staring at me like that?"

"I'm just glad to see you."

I close my eyes, breathe in and out. *I already did some scary things today. Might as well keep up my streak.*

I lower my head onto his shoulder, tense all over, wondering how he'll respond.

At first it seems like Greg is holding his breath. And then he relaxes into it, shifts his weight on the couch to give me a more comfortable resting place, and throws an arm over my shoulders.

For a long moment, we stay like that, pretending to watch TV.

"What'll you do with that dress?" he asks after a while.

"Burn it, probably."

He laughs, jostling my head.

"I just couldn't stop thinking about how I was failing," I say, staring at the ad playing on the screen. "And then suddenly there was something I could do to fix it."

"Mm." Greg's finger traces the ridge of my ear, and somehow this touch reverberates through my entire body.

"But I was wrong. I totally lost my bearings. And . . ." I nestle against his side. "I couldn't do it."

"Why's that?" His voice is taut, but he keeps tracing the shape of my ear.

"My heart's been somewhere else." I put a hand on his chest and feel his own heart beating, fast and forceful. "So I slept on it, like you said. You heard me snoring."

I'm still not looking at him, but I can feel him swallow. "And?"

"Greg . . . I never would have cracked the door open for him to begin with, if I'd known how you felt. But you seemed unavailable. And uninterested. And my undying crush on you had gone well past the point of being sad, like, several years ago already. I felt like I was delusional, clinging to that."

A strained laugh escapes from him, so breathy it sounds like a wheeze. "I can relate. The delusional, undying crush part."

My chest warms at those words, and I cross my arms, tucking myself into his side. "We should form a support group."

He caresses my ear. "When you came back, I thought you hated me."

"Oh, I do hate you. You ruined me for kissing."

"Oh yeah?"

"It probably sounds stupid, but . . ." There's a prickling in my gut, the sensation of crossing a threshold by admitting this. "Every time I kiss someone new, I still compare it to our first one."

We're quiet again, just the low sounds of the TV filling the room. And after a while, I take the remote out of his hand and turn it off.

I tilt my head up toward him, and he's already staring at me. A rush of déjà vu hits me. The memory I pushed down, that surged up when I didn't call for it, that I couldn't escape—now it's like we're living it a second time.

Greg's head lowers and his lips touch mine, a gentle brush that makes all my nerves pay attention, blows out my center of gravity, stomach weightless. My eyes close, and all my muscles relax with that full-body sigh: *This is what you've been missing.*

His tongue slips into my mouth, and I breathe in lemon zest softened by the scent of him underneath, sun-warmed skin and a hint of salt. All the years I avoided him tumble through my mind—the uncomfortable conversations I was scared to have, the times I thought I could grit down and plow through it. And now I'm here with Greg, not running from myself anymore, coming home after years of aimless wandering. It's such a relief, I want to cry—oh no, I *am* crying—and he pulls back and catches the tears with his fingers.

"That bad?" He cracks a smile, even though his eyes are concerned. "My technique's gone downhill over the past decade?"

It makes me laugh, like he wanted.

"I'm sad for all the years we weren't doing that," I manage to get out. "All that lost time."

He gazes at me protectively, like he's been feeling the same way but wants to cheer me up. "When you lose something . . . don't they say to retrace your steps?"

Greg cups my face in his hands—the way he did the second

time we kissed, sitting on this same couch—and presses his lips to mine. Without breaking the kiss, I shift so I'm straddling him, and he laughs into my mouth.

"Oh hi," Greg murmurs, blinking up at me. "Am I dreaming right now?"

I pinch his earlobe. "I don't think so."

Greg kisses me again, deeper this time, and I can feel him getting hard beneath me. Suddenly I've never been so turned on in my life.

He reaches up and undoes my bun, and my damp hair tumbles down over my shoulders as his fingers rake my scalp. It feels so good, I let out a soft moan, and his other hand drifts down to my neck, my pulse pushing into his palm, meeting it like it's saying, *Hi, I've been waiting for you.*

"It's my fault," he says between kisses. "I should have talked to you. Back then. Instead of assuming."

"Shh," I murmur as Greg's hands slide up the back of my shirt and his weightlifting calluses scratch my bare skin. "It's okay now. I forgive you."

"This is all I could think about," he says breathlessly. "The whole drive back."

I let out a shaky laugh and lean back, his hands cradling my waist.

He smiles softly. "What's funny?"

"I just . . . spent so long believing you didn't think about me like that."

"Ruby." He scoffs like I'm ridiculous and kisses me under my jaw, tilting my head and arching my back while his hands keep me in place. "I think about you so much it hurts."

I tug my shirt off, and he brushes his lips over the tops of my breasts. We're straying off script now, hurtling away from where we started, forward in time together. Then he takes a nipple into his mouth and sucks, and the feeling is so intense, I have to grip the back of the couch.

Greg glances up at me. "Too much?"

"No." I run my fingers through his hair, messing up the top. "This is perfect."

I push my hands up the front of his shirt, palms soaking in his warmth, and he pulls it off too. And damn, it is quite a sight—the lunchtime gym trips are working for him.

"Show-off," I say, and my hand strays down his stomach, dipping into his jeans, but he tugs it back upward and kisses my wrist.

"You've been through it today," he says. "You first."

Greg shifts me off him and presses me backward into the cushions as he kisses his way down my torso. His fingers hook beneath both of my waistbands, and his eyebrows lift, a question. When I nod, he slides off my shorts and underwear together, and I'm completely naked, prone before him. It's a little terrifying, after so many years of hiding from each other—but his lips part, overcome at the sight of me as he settles between my legs, hands on my hips.

Outside the sun is setting, and the light slanting through the blinds catches the flecks of gold in Greg's irises that I'd memorized long ago. And seeing him there—face framed by my thighs, and the lips I've thought so much about, hovering by the most sensitive part of me—is almost enough to send me over the edge on its own.

"Tell me if you like this," he says, peering at me like he's trying to read my expression, "and I'll keep going."

His eyes lock with mine as he plants a kiss on the spot that aches for him the most. It's whisper-light but it feels so overwhelming, and my head flops back against the pillows as I moan *yes.*

He drops more kisses there, teasing, ratcheting my want higher. It's a touch like a question, the opening of a conversation. And in reply, the pulse between my legs gets more insistent, and I whisper, *Yes, I like this.*

Greg traces the contours of that pulse with his tongue, and for a long, luxurious moment, all I am is that point of contact, the whole of me engulfed in warm velvet. My thighs tighten, and he gradually speeds up, going at it so fervently, like he's trying to make up for all the years he wasn't lavishing me with attention.

I've never felt like this before—never experienced such an adoring, methodical undoing of all my defenses. He builds me up, nudging me higher and higher while I'm panting, falling apart, hands in his hair, whispering *yes, yes yes Greg yes,* until the feeling crests and I'm crying out, hips jerking. Relief courses through me, and he laps at me gently while I drift back down.

I open my eyes and see him resting his head against my raised knee, gaze full of affection—like he knows me so well, all my failings included, and still wants the whole thing.

"I love seeing you like this," he says.

I have to laugh. "Like what?"

"Losing it like that." He kisses my knee absentmindedly. "You're always wound so tight, trying to keep it together."

I hit the couch cushion with my open palm and throw my head back for the drama. "Well, you sure unwound me there, fuck!"

That gets a real belly laugh out of him, shaking the couch. It's contagious. And laughing together like this, I don't feel like I've been washed out to sea, or like I forgot my own name. I feel like exactly who I am, exactly where I'm supposed to be.

Then he stands and scoops me up, one arm under my knees, and I cling to him, squealing, legs kicking, as he carries me to my bed.

It's surprising how forceful he can be, after years of being so tentative. The shock of it fizzes through me as he flips me over and fills me up and relentlessly, energetically undoes the rest of that knot inside me while I scream into my pillow.

Afterward, we're lying together, my head on his chest, his

hand running through my hair, tucked into my grown-up bed in my childhood bedroom. Our feet touch under the covers, his warm toes against my cold ones, and it feels like a small miracle.

And as waves of intense calm wash over me, a small voice inside adds: *This must be the famous "following your heart" I've heard so much about.*

CHAPTER 54

It's so surreal, waking up next to Greg on Sunday morning. For a few seconds, pressing closer to him, his arms around me, I feel weightless, like nothing in the world could be wrong.

It's just a few seconds, though. Because then I remember.

I'll be sued I'll be penniless I'll lose the house!

What if Anna doesn't have enough for the story!

What if I lose my job and then!

I lose access to Slack!

I scramble out of bed, and Greg startles awake. "What? What's happening?"

"Mom is still trapped," I say, throwing open drawers, pulling on clothes. "I need to get her out of there, before I lose access to the company systems and can't talk to her anymore."

I turn and lean against my dresser. "I'm going to try your plan. Of being honest with her. Really, really honest."

"Okay." He nods. "How can I help?"

"Can you call your mom?"

*

Tita Wendy sets up her orb in the kitchen, smoothing out the navy blue cloth she brought from her shop over the table. She straightens her spine and swirls her hands around the crystal ball, humming low in her throat, and it starts to glow again. My phone is open in front of her, connected to Slack. Tita Wendy's head bobs, and her eyes fly open again. "Try now," she says.

Whenever I tried to voice call Mom over Slack, aside from that last time in Tita Wendy's shop, all I heard was a horrible screeching noise. But this time the call connects, and Mom's voice comes through, on speakerphone.

"Ruby? Are you all right? How was the wedding? I didn't hear from you!"

Tita Wendy arches a brow at that, but she stays quiet.

"Mom!" I'm already blinking back tears at the sound of her voice. "Mom, I called because . . . I have to be honest with you about some things."

"All right, fine! No need to be dramatic!" Mom shouts, the sound of swirling wind in the background. "What is it?"

"I didn't get married!" I'm trembling, and Greg gives my right hand a quick squeeze. "I couldn't go through with it."

"Why not?" But Mom sounds more surprised than upset.

It feels like there's not much time, so I have to explain it the simplest way I can: "I didn't love him."

"Then good, I'm glad you didn't go through with it! That would have been awful! Life is hard enough."

I want to laugh and cry at the same time, but I steady myself and push past the tightness in my chest. "Mom, I'm not sure if you remember, but you died four months ago, and you've been haunting the TKCORP Slack, and I've been trying to find a way to free you. I tried a bunch of things to narrow down what it could be. I tried fixing the things that might be making you stay here—because you were disappointed in me, maybe. But I couldn't figure it out."

"I wasn't—" Mom protests.

"I know you were, Mom! It's okay! Let me finish. I keep thinking about that last conversation we had and wondering if—if maybe you're holding on because you feel like things aren't resolved between us, somehow. Because you're worried about me. And—" *Deep breath in, deep breath out.* I glance at Tita Wendy, and she nods at me to keep going. "And I wanted to tell you I'm grateful. For how hard you worked to raise me. For everything you sacrificed. And—"

"Ruby," Mom says sadly, over the increasing background noise.

"And I have a lot of good memories of you!" I need to keep going or I'll lose my nerve. "Maybe you don't know that, but—especially right after Dad left, and how we'd do everything together. Watching movies, eating ice cream, staying up late. And how we'd relive that as I got older, every time we had a movie night, and we'd pop popcorn and you'd ask me for all the gossip about the boys at school. Even though . . . I wasn't really honest then, and there was only one boy on my mind."

I squeeze Greg's hand a couple times, a quick pulse. Tita Wendy stares up at the ceiling, like she's trying not to notice, but I think I catch a little smirk.

Mom's quiet, and there's just some crackling on the other end of the line.

"I still think about those times we spent together, constantly," I press on. "And—and even though I've been struggling—you taught me a lot of good things. The grit I learned from you—I'll figure out how to use it for something good one day. You gave me all the tools, and—what's going on right now is my own issue, and—" I'm choking up, struggling against the lump in my throat. "I'm sorry I didn't talk to you more. In the months near the end."

There's an agonizing silence, filled with faint hissing.

"So you want to get rid of me, I see how it is!" Mom's voice comes through suddenly, crystal clear. She makes an annoyed sound. "You're saying I was a good example? I worked myself to death!"

She's laughing now, a sound I missed. And I remember that about her, the way she could laugh at the darkest things when she was alive, turn everything into a joke.

I'm laughing too. Oh God, what is happening?

"Mom—" My voice breaks, dropping to a raspy whisper. "I don't want you to be trapped at work forever. No one deserves that."

"Ruby, listen to me," she says. "I have regrets too. I think maybe I should have listened more. To how you felt."

My hands are shaking, my chest is shaking. A tear rolls down my cheek.

"And I'm sorry I overreacted about Greg. He has a good heart, I can see that now."

Greg is examining the ceiling like he's found a particularly fascinating stain up there. But Tita Wendy is smiling.

"I made a mistake," Mom goes on. "I wasn't seeing him clearly before. I thought I was saving you some heartache. Anticipating my life replaying before my eyes, instead of seeing a totally different life—yours—unfolding in front of me."

"Then . . . Mom, what is keeping you from moving on?" My voice quavers, and the sound of wind picks up in the background.

"If anything . . ." Mom sighs, exasperated, and clicks her tongue. "Ruby, my big regret is working too hard for a company that didn't know me from a can of paint. And being so tired and driven by fear—so focused on this idea of success. But it turned out to be a mirage that I would never reach. I regret . . ." More static now, the sound of her voice breaking up. "I regret that it made me miss some things. I regret being so critical, so controlling. I regret that it kept me from really *seeing* you. I'm glad we had this chance. To connect without all that."

I'm a mess of tears, and Tita Wendy reaches over and rubs my back.

"Not having to work," Mom adds, "has certainly given me time to think."

"So when—" I choke back a sob. "When will you be able to let go, Mom?"

"Soon, probably." The static on the line grows, almost swallowing her voice completely. "When I know you're okay."

The call drops. Tita Wendy rubs her forehead, exhausted. The stillness hangs over the three of us as we sit around the wooden kitchen table, afternoon light streaming in through the windows.

And then the doorbell rings. With a sinking feeling, I push out of my chair and stand.

"No, what if it's—" Greg puts a hand on my shoulder to keep me in my seat, but I shake my head.

"I don't think I can outrun it by pretending not to be home."

I open the door, blinking in the bright sun.

"Ruby Ocampo?" There's a man wearing a navy polo and jeans with a belt. Lawyer-off-duty, or so I imagine.

"Yes?"

"You're being served." He hands me a large manila envelope, and I take it with one shaking hand. "Breach of contract."

I've already pre-wallowed in despair enough by this point that my perennial anxiety about being polite kicks in. I give the guy a tight smile.

"Well! First time getting one of these. Do I tip you, or . . . ?"

He laughs and turns to leave. "You take care now."

CHAPTER 55

"Feels like a funeral in here," Al mumbles, coming back to his desk with a coffee from the kitchen. Everyone is staring stone-faced at their screens. It's so quiet, you can hear the buzzing of the overhead lights. I can practically feel Erica's aesthetic plants drooping from the harsh vibe.

Everyone who was involved in the union effort has received a calendar event with an ominous, generic title.

Morgan:
they're definitely laying us off
god, my husband's been out of work—what are we going to do?

Sarah:
i'll probably have to move back in with my mom

Al:
no, you're going to have a new job in two seconds
you'll be just fine

Morgan:
Ruby, what's taking so long with your big plan?

My leg is jiggling under my desk, because I'm wondering the same thing.

Ruby:
Anna needed to verify some things

Steve:
ugh, we're fucked

Carol:
we filed for the election

Steve:
do we even have enough support?
we'll lose

Greg:
it's a hail mary for sure
but if we wait, who knows who'll be left to start over

A few hours later, Sarah gets called into the conference room with Erica and someone from HR for her mysterious meeting, and fifteen minutes later she comes out crying.

But then a message appears in all of our inboxes.

From: TKCORP Union
To: All staff
Subject: Announcing the TKCORP Union

As some of you may know, we're forming a union at TKCORP, and we'll need everyone's help. We've submitted the paperwork to hold a union election, and we have reason to believe that today's layoffs are illegal retaliation. We're demanding they be halted immediately, or we will file an unfair labor practice charge with the NLRB.

A lot of you have worked here for a long time and care about this company and what happens to it—and, importantly, what happens to the people in it. If you're concerned about the way things are going around here lately, please come talk to us. We look forward to speaking with everyone about how unionizing can protect all of us and change TKCORP for the better.

Sincerely,
Greg, Sarah, Carol, and the rest of the union organizing committee

Sarah sniffs, sitting at her cubicle. "We went back and forth over the text of that email for like five hours."

Morgan gasps. "You guys, look!"

We get up from our desks and gather around her screen, which is opened to the front page of *The New York Times.* The top headline slot reads:

AT TKCORP, A TRAIL OF QUESTIONABLE TRANSACTIONS LEADS BACK TO NEW CEO

Just a few years after taking the helm of the ailing megacorporation amid much fanfare, CEO Winfield Erickson and his underlings have been implicated in a brazen fraud scheme.

9 MIN READ

The lead image is of Erickson emerging from TKCORP headquarters, and Mark Winterson standing in front of him—arms spread wide as if to protect him, mouth open like he's shouting at the person behind the camera. Eyes wild like he hasn't slept in days.

CHAPTER 56

It's lunchtime now, and I go out to get some fresh air. There are lots of people sitting on the benches and on the grass, talking about everything that's happened.

So there's a real audience when Mark Winterson comes out and stumbles across the street—there's something distinctly off about him, like he's sleepwalking. Someone gasps as a car stops short, inches from hitting him—*Watch it, asshole!*—and honks the horn, but he waves it off and keeps going.

"Is he drunk?" Carol says.

But my eyes are glued to Mark Winterson as he shuffles over to the pool—the one I worked at as a lifeguard—and falls in.

He's going to surface any second, limbs thrashing, water droplets flying. I know it.

But there's nothing. The water is still.

Before I have time to think about it, I'm running across the street. I kick off my shoes, toss the life preserver into the water, and jump in after it. Maybe if you ask me later, I won't be able to tell you why exactly I did this. But the only thought reverberating in my mind right now is, *How fucking dare you?*

I swim to the bottom where Mark Winterson is resting—somehow he sank straight down. When I try to haul him up, he's weirdly heavy. *Did he put something in his jacket?*

I'm struggling to get him out of it, wrenching the sleeves off his arms. I have to come up for air once, dive down again. His mouth is open, no more bubbles coming out. *Fuck fuck fuck.*

Finally I get the jacket off him and pull him to the surface, gasping, and get him into the life preserver, pushing him to the edge. Some people have run over to this side of the street, and a few of them help me haul him up.

I'm pumping the water out of his chest, the way I learned to. He sputters and coughs and a stream of liquid pours out of his mouth, onto the poolside tile.

"No no no leave me there I don't want this," he mumbles, words slurred. His head rocks side to side against the tile. "I just wanted him to be proud of me."

Ugh, God, please tell me we're not that similar!

"Stop it! Grow up!" I'm not sure what comes over me, but I'm shaking him, hard. "You don't get to do that! You don't get to! You don't!"

My brain realizes on a delay how incoherent I sound, how beside myself. And then I notice that people around us have their phones out, filming, and for a second I get nervous about how this will look.

Mark Winterson turns over on his side and throws up on the concrete.

He rolls onto his back again and scoffs. "So you do care."

"What the fuck did you take?"

"Xanax, Ambien, NyQuil. Whatever I had in my desk."

I glance around again and lean in close, like I'm checking his vital signs.

"Mark Winterson. Listen to me very carefully. You see those people filming?" I pretend to take his pulse and turn his head so he can see. "*You're going to drop the lawsuit.* Or I will not rest until the main thing you're remembered for—the main thing for which you're *known*—is being the giant weenie who sued the girl who saved his life."

He starts laughing and coughs up some more water.

"You kill me, Ruby," he croaks out.

"Quite the opposite just now, actually."

"Fine! Fine. Just one thing." He's lying there, half drowned and washed out to dry, looking like hell, but somehow he musters a grin. "Come on, be honest. I'm at least an eight out of ten."

Wow, how did that get back to him? I guess Morgan really is a gossip.

"Goodbye, Mark," I say, and head back to work.

CHAPTER 57

Everything at the office is so up in the air, but one thing is certain: There's no way we're getting any more work done today. Apparently, even Erica recognizes it. She walks out of her office and claps in her signature energetic fashion. "All right, everybody stop gossiping in your DMs and get out of here," she says. "Take the afternoon, let's regroup tomorrow."

So I pack up my things, and Sarah flags me down on my way to the elevator. "Come with us to the bar! You look like you could use a drink."

A bunch of union people are waiting for us outside—including most of the accountants, but no Greg—and we walk in a big cluster through the corporate campus. The lawn is such an idyllic Technicolor green after the recent rains, and the sun feels so good on my skin. Along the street, the jacaranda blooms sway in the breeze, unreal purple against the blue sky. Some municipal workers are putting a covering over the pool; a sign on the fence says TEMPORARILY CLOSED.

I feel giddy, being outside and wandering at this hour. And

walking in a slow-moving group like this, everyone chatting, it does feel like we're on some kind of field trip.

"Can't believe you saved that guy's life," Sarah says as she and Grace come up alongside me, holding hands.

"You would've let him drown?"

She must not have expected that question, because she lets out a big honking laugh.

"Yeah, I don't know," I add. "Lifeguard training dies hard, I guess."

"I respect it," Grace says.

Steve is walking in front of us, and Al passes us to catch up with him, clapping a hand on his shoulder. "Steve, my man, I believe you lost our bet."

Steve grudgingly retrieves his wallet and hands him a few twenties.

"Thanks, bestie," Al says with a grin, plucking the cash out of his hand, and Sarah and I both crack up as Al picks up the pace to join Morgan and Carol.

"What was the bet?"

Grace shakes her head. "Steve didn't think you could pull it off."

"Neither did I, to be honest," I say, laughing. But the knowledge that Al *did* sits warm in my gut for the rest of the walk.

We get to the bar and one of the accountants holds the door open for me while another gives me a fist bump.

"What are you having?" Sarah asks, nodding toward the bar. "I've got this, you earned it."

Then Greg runs in behind us and shouts, "Check your email!"

Morgan yelps from across the bar. "It's recognized!" she exclaims. "They voluntarily recognized! Erickson's been removed by the board, and they're pausing the layoffs!"

Sarah shrieks and runs over to hug Greg, who spins her

around, and when he lets her go, she jumps into Grace's arms. Greg pumps both fists into the air, and I can see, with a twinge in my chest, that he's still wearing my scrunchie around one wrist.

"Ruby!" Greg calls, waving me over. I work my way through the crowd, and he tugs me toward him and kisses me. And aside from Steve, who groans, *Get a room!*, everyone actually cheers.

It feels like sunlight on my face after too long not going outside. I'm blinking in it, disoriented, wondering what to do with it.

Greg drifts away from me, moving through the room to talk to different clusters of people, checking in on how they're doing after the tumult of the day. And I perch on a stool at one of the high tables and text Trisha.

Ruby:
maybe your affirmations worked

Trisha:
told you

I wiggle my thumbs, wondering what to say next. how's school? I ask and add an ogre emoji, so at least she knows I'm being an old person at her on purpose.

Trisha:
LOL it's a grind!
mom and dad are having another family party next weekend, you should come
and stay for karaoke this time
you didn't even introduce me to your boyfriend

I almost correct her, but then I realize there's no reason to. She was ahead of the curve all along.

Greg eases onto a stool next to me, and I squeeze his arm. "You in the mood for Tita Rina's lumpia next weekend?"

He kisses me on the cheek. "Always."

The party moves where Greg does, and everyone is clustered around us now. Sarah and Al are arguing about something to do with time signatures, and Steve and Grace and Ahmed are talking about the best birding spots in the area, and some of the accountants are shooting the shit behind us about a movie I haven't seen.

I raise my phone to take a selfie—everyone crammed in behind us, Greg with his arm around me—and out of habit, I send it into the DM with Mom.

sampaguita72:
Ruby you look so happy!
I'm so proud of you
I know you're going to be okay

It's like being splashed with a bucket of cold water. *She said she'd be able to move on once she knows I'm going to be okay.*

ruby.ocampo:
Mom! Mom wait

I'm typing frantically with my thumbs as a chant of "Chug! Chug! Chug!" goes up around me—over to the right, Steve and Carol are racing to be the first to drain their beers.

sampaguita72:
I was always proud of you, I hope you see that.
I learned too late, you shouldn't give too much of yourself
to this shitty job.

I know exactly what's happening right now, and my thoughts are crowding on top of one another, a chaotic and childish mess. *I'm still so flawed and broken—I'm still so disappointing! Don't go yet! I'll create more problems! I'll show you! Don't leave!*

ruby.ocampo:

Mom!

Mom, stop! I'm not ready!

sampaguita72:

I think it's time now, Ruby.

I know you're going to be fine.

I'm all out of words to say—except, I guess, for the obvious ones. The ones we had a hard time saying, in life.

ruby.ocampo:

I love you, Mom

sampaguita72:

I love you, Ruby

"Ruby, is that *Slack*?" Sarah exclaims. "How can you be working right now?"

I twist around for a second, waving her off and blinking back tears.

And when I look back, the light next to Mom's name has gone out.

sampaguita72 has left the chat.

ACKNOWLEDGMENTS

I started drafting *Unfinished Business* in earnest at a time when I thought I was sinking. This story made me feel buoyant again, and I have so many people to thank for helping keep me afloat.

Thank you so much to my stellar agent, Amy Bishop-Wycisk, for being excited about the idea for this book from the very first rambling phone pitch, and for your invaluable notes, dedication, and care (and for talking me down when I was losing my mind a few times!).

Thank you to my editor, Jenny Chen, for seeing the true heart of this story, for your impeccable instincts, expert guidance, and empathy, and for always being so on top of everything. Thank you so much as well to Jean Slaughter for all of your support, diligence, and kindness.

And I'm so grateful to the rest of the excellent team at Ballantine Bantam Dell: Managing Editor Saige Francis, Production Editor Cindy Berman, Production Manager Chanler Harris, Interior Designer Elizabeth Eno, Copy Manager Talia Fredette, Copy Editor Amy J. Schneider, Art Director Jeanne

Reina, Cover Designer Sarah Horgan, and Emily Siegmund from Marketing.

Thank you as well to the team at Trellis Literary for all your support, particularly to Allison Malecha and Tori Clayton.

They say writing is a solitary activity, but much of this book was written sitting next to friends. Thank you to Emily Charlotte, Trinity Nguyen, and Gayle Gaviola for that writing retreat where I got to the midpoint, and for all the writing dates before and after. Thank you to Emily for being the earliest reader and giving me the confidence to finish; to Trinity for literally sitting next to me as I started drafting the first chapter and for giving me the idea for the Microsoft Teams joke; and to Gayle for reading early and giving me my favorite compliment on this book: that you couldn't stop reading on your flight even when a girl accidentally whacked you in the face with her bag.

Thank you so much to S. Z. Ahmed for your early notes, for listening to me ramble about this story literally years before I started drafting it, and for talking to me about embezzlement. Thank you to Carolyn Huynh for reading an early draft and for all your support and advice.

My deepest thanks to Matt Pearce and Laura Nelson for talking to me about union organizing, and for your friendship and support along the way.

Thank you to Elaine Hsieh Chou and to everyone in her June 2022 Catapult class, where I workshopped the short story that contained the earliest seed of this novel.

Thank you to Sophie Wan for talking me down during revisions, and to Shannon C. F. Rogers for going above and beyond as a debut launch wingwoman and taking charge at KBBQ.

Thank you to Natalie Sue for being a workplace-book-writing inspiration, and for encouraging me when I said I wanted to write one too.

Thank you to P. H. Low and Alyssa Villaire for reading that other ghost book, and for cheering me on with this one too.

Thank you to the writers who lent a sympathetic ear, shared advice and a meal, or wrote with me in coffee shops as I was drafting and revising this book, especially: Alex Brown, Justine Pucella Winans, Anna Mercier, Lyssa Mia Smith, Hannah V. Sawyerr, Amanda Khong, Lilly Lu, Viviann Do, Trang Thanh Tran, Wen-Yi Lee, Mackenzie Reed, Rachel Moore, Kat Korpi, Jill Tew, Danica Nava, Ream Shukairy, Sara Hashem, Jade Adia, Racquel Marie, C. L. Montblanc, Angela Montoya, Melanie Schubert, Jessica Parra, Ashley Granillo, Alexa Donne, Gretchen Schreiber, Veronica Bane, Trish Lundy, Eva Des Lauriers, Diana Biller, Emily Doyle, Ryoko Hirose, Julie Tieu, Mae Coyiuto, Sonali Kohli, Pamela Delupio, Tracy Badua, Christine L. Arnold, Megan Davidhizar, Tauri Cox, Crystal Seitz, S. Hati, Channelle Desamours, Page Powars, Anahita Karthik, Birukti Tsige, Skyla Arndt, and everyone in the FilAm Writers' Kubo Discord.

Thank you to the booksellers and librarians and reviewers—your work is so essential, and your support means the world.

This book is ridiculous, but it was written with admiration for the people who do the vital work of union organizing. If you want to read a serious book about unions, might I recommend *The Hammer* by Hamilton Nolan and *Fight Like Hell* by Kim Kelly.

I'd also like to thank the authors of some other nonfiction books I read that loomed large in my mind as I was drafting this book: David Gelles, for writing *The Man Who Broke Capitalism,* and Bethany McLean and Peter Elkind, for writing *The Smartest Guys in the Room.*

Thank you to my co-workers, past and present. You're not in this book! It's fiction.

Thank you to Lauren, Brenda, Minhee, Sergio, Priya, Luz, Luis, Maddy, Raillan, and Will, for your years of friendship, for keeping me sane, and for reminding me I'm a person outside of being an author.

Thank you to my family, and especially to my cousins Tita, Alexa, and Michele for making sure my debut launch sold out—I'm so grateful for you!—and to my cousin Andi for always rooting for me from afar.

Thank you to Dana and Joe for all your love and support, and for being excited about the prospect of a haunted office book.

Thank you to Nick for so many things, but especially for taking me to Vegas for research (driving very responsibly the whole way) and making sure no one crashed into me as I walked the route Ruby runs through the casinos while taking notes on my phone.

And thank you to my mom, for doing the hard work of raising me alone, and for giving me my grit.

PHOTO: © TRINITY NGUYEN

Clare Osongco is a mixed Filipino American author living in Los Angeles who likes to write about falling in love, messy family relationships, and ghosts (real or figurative, sometimes both). Her debut young adult novel is *Midnights with You.*

clareosongco.com
Instagram: @clareosongco
TikTok: @clareosongco